Even Heroes Sometimes Sink

Ron Hertz

HELLGATE PRESS   ASHLAND, OR

©2022 Ron Hertz. All rights reserved. No part of this publication may be reproduced or used in any form or by any means, graphic, electronic or mechanical, including photocopying,recording, taping, or information and retrieval systems without written permission of the publisher. This is a work of fiction. Names, characters, businesses, places, events and incidents are either the products of the author's imagination or used in a fictitious manner. Any resemblance to actual persons, living or dead, or actual events is purely coincidental.

Published by:
Hellgate Press (an imprint of L&R Publishing, LLC)
PO Box 3531
Ashland, OR 97520
hellgatepress.com
email: sales@hellgatepress.com
Interior design: Sasha Kincaid
Cover design: L. Redding

ISBN: 978-1-954163-37-9
Printed and bound in the United States of America
First edition 10 9 8 7 6 5 4 3 2 1

For Joe

Author's Note

Although this story is based on actual people and events, it's a novel, not a biography or a precisely accurate memoir. I've been inspired, but not limited, by what really happened.

Tolling for the aching ones whose wounds cannot be nursed...

—Bob Dylan, "Chimes of Freedom"

One

"Not till we are lost, in other words, not till we have lost the world, do we begin to find ourselves, and realize where we are and the infinite extent of our relations."

—Henry David Thoreau, *Walden*

HE COMES TO ME IN DREAMS...ENTRANCED *by the sound of softly pounding waves, I don't know exactly where I am, but I can see Simon's face. It changes before me from young to old, the curly full hair now dark brown and long, now shorter and silvery grey—the beard appearing and disappearing, also changing from dark to light. He is sixteen or he's sixty, but I almost always see him smiling—his electric, exuberant smile. How did I not see beyond that gleam? How did I fail to perceive the subtle sorrow in his eyes—his concealed solitude, his unspoken loneliness? Sometimes, he stretches his arms wide as if to embrace me—or forgive me—or answer some enigmatic question of great significance. And then, inevitably, he fades away. Like a foggy mist disappearing into nothingness, he vanishes from my sight—and I feel guilty for not having held him closer, for not understanding more, for being too afraid...*

I've been agonizing over whether I should try to tell this story, or whether I'm even capable of telling it. Like most guys, it's a lot easier for me to talk about cars, sports, or politics than to discuss anything involving my deeper, more personal feelings, so certain things, which maybe shouldn't, generally get avoided. Don't most of us, men and women, get agitated and uncomfortable dealing with subjects which provoke our strongest, uncensored emotions? But then there's always the looming mirror and the fear of feeling like a wimp, who slips away from what ought to be confronted. After all, I'm supposed to have passed beyond childish things by now—I'm in my sixties. To face myself with any decent self-respect, I need to at least try to understand the truth about the most puzzling relationship of my life.

I want to tell the story of how I formed what I thought was my closest friendship, and how, without knowing it, I let that relationship slip away. In many ways, this might ring out like an anguished confession because it deals with the shortcomings of two men who were too unconsciously macho to be completely honest with each other. Intentional or not, we guys manage to evade each other at critical moments, to scoot around the heart of the wound—even guys who think they're best friends. And I've been as dense as they come, blinded, like most people, by my own self-centeredness.

Simon... Simon Isaac Lieberman and I thought of ourselves as extremely liberal and progressive, part of a new age of men and women who would transform the world. Like most people, however, we drastically underestimated the clinging power of old, instinctive values and habits that ran counter to our desires for emancipation and change. Despite growing up in the Age of Aquarius, flaunting our long hair and beards and feeling irrepressibly free, in many basic ways, Simon and I remained confused, hung-up males, trapped in the sad, patriarchal tradition of stifling some of our most profound and disturbing feelings.

There was no repression of feelings, however, when I heard the shocking news about my friend a few days after Christmas, several years ago, back in 2010. My wife, Danielle, came running from outside into our kitchen, cell phone in hand, her voice shaking with horror, her face streaked with tears, as she blurted out: "Simon's dead! He is gone! Simon's dead!" With her slight French accent, she repeated the last words as I stood there frozen in disbelief and bewilderment.

No, no—this is impossible. I struggled to comprehend the agonizing syllables I had just heard. Completely overwhelmed, I shook my head and crumbled into tears, whispering, "It can't be—it can't be true."

"I'm afraid it is, Cheri...I'm so terribly sorry..." She grasped my arms and held me as I stared at her blankly. "What a horrible shock and tragedy for Simon's family...It's Reuben on the phone. Perhaps he can explain." She handed me the phone.

Reuben was Simon's oldest son, whom I had known since he was an infant. Nearly forty and single, he worked for Simon's Los Angeles-based parking lot company, a firm that had doubled in size to five thousand employees since Simon became CEO about twenty years ago. It was a family firm, he was quite proud to say. His father and uncles had started it, and all three of Simon's sons worked for the highly profitable enterprise. Of course, the three young men made excellent money, but Simon had shared his doubts with me several times about whether his sons and the company were a good fit. Reuben was his biggest worry since he was the most determined and effective in hiding his emotions.

Although I could hear obvious grief in his voice, Reuben sounded almost matter-of-fact as he described what he knew of his father's death. "He drowned in a river in Buenos Aires, a few blocks from his hotel. He and my mother were there, trying to reconcile."

"Trying to reconcile? Had something happened to them?" My eyes widened with this second shocking revelation.

"So you didn't know? I guess he didn't tell anyone." Reuben continued his incredible story, describing how Simon, my supposed dearest friend, had separated from his wife, Rachel, two months earlier, after getting busted for a long-time affair with his secretary. The estranged couple had gone to counseling and then, on the counselor's suggestion, to Buenos Aires, to try to heal their broken marriage. Pathetically, I knew nothing about any of this.

Reuben explained more. Apparently, Simon had drowned in the Buenos Aires river, Rio de la Plata, in the early dark hours of Christmas morning after he and Rachel had spent Christmas Eve dining in a nightclub. He had been drinking heavily that night and later went walking alone by the river. Reuben's brother, David, had flown down to the Argentine capital to comfort their mother and to work with the police in identifying and releasing Simon's body. His excellent Spanish would help in dealing with the Argentine authorities.

"He drowned in a river?" I asked incredulously. Simon and I had become best friends taking classes and surfing together at UC Santa Barbara. It was hard to imagine my old surfing companion, a veteran of countless waves and wipeouts, drowning in a placid, big-city river.

Reuben offered a likely possibility: "It was Christmas Eve and he was under a lot of stress with my mother. He probably drank way too much—maybe enough to pass out and fall into the river... Or maybe he stumbled onto the wrong street and got assaulted by someone, who dumped him into the water... But I have to tell you something else... The authorities in Argentina are at least considering the possibility of suicide."

"That's got to be just a legal formality. Simon would never kill himself. You don't think he could have killed himself, do you?" I paused after this mention of what seemed preposterously impossible, but Reuben didn't say anything. "What about this affair you mentioned?"

"I thought you knew," Reuben replied.

"I didn't know a thing. Your father used to tell me that your mother was the perfect wife for him."

"Perfect, because she was perfectly blind. My father had been having an affair with his secretary for seven years. I found out about it six years ago when I saw the two of them walking on the beach."

"Six years ago! What did you say to him—or to them?"

"I told him, privately, that I think I understood his situation and that I could keep a secret."

I paused in reflection. "You were willing to hide his affair from your mother for six years?"

Reuben also hesitated a moment before continuing. "I think I understood his situation. Of course, I was surprised—and sad for my mother—but I guess I realized that something was probably missing from their relationship—for whatever reasons...and that he was trying to take care of things...in his own private way. I was okay with that...I could go along with that, and everything was fine...until..."

"Until what?"

"Until my brother David saw the same scene I saw—Dad walking hand-in-hand with Heather, his lovely secretary, in a skimpy sundress, right on the same Venice beach where I saw them six years earlier."

"How did David react?"

"David doesn't see things the same way I do. He's married, you know, to a very strong, educated woman, with strong opinions. And he tells Susanna everything—poor fool! The two of them got pretty upset. David and his wife demanded—they insisted—that Dad had to own up to everything in front of everybody—the whole family."

"In front of the whole family?"

"David and Susanna made Dad confess everything at a family meeting—in front of our mother, all three of his sons, his daughter-in-law, his brother and even our grandmother—his own mother. I think my brother just wanted to end the hypocrisy."

Reuben described how, according to David, the middle son, Simon's seemingly pious life was a total sham. His pretense of being an observant Jew, his self-righteous presiding over a large family and giant company—all this was a complete farce in the light of his years of adultery. "David's pretty religious himself these days," Reuben added, "at least compared to me. Not that he goes to synagogue that much...just in the way that he sees things more black or white."

Reuben explained what happened after Simon's forced confession. He and Rachel separated for a few weeks. Then they tried getting back together with the help of a counselor she thought would be good for them. Again, I knew nothing about any of this, not having spoken to my friend since the end of the summer. Usually we talked on the phone every few months, but these months, the most critical of his life, we hadn't spoken at all.

Reuben let me know the funeral would be in three days, on Friday. He hoped I would speak at the memorial service. He wanted me, as Simon's longest and closest friend, to be there for his memorial, but he understood if I wouldn't be able to make the 700-mile trip from Ashland, Oregon to Los Angeles. Of course, I would come, I assured him. We arranged to meet at Simon's house on Thursday afternoon. The whole family would be there. He asked me to bring my guitar.

Stunned with all that Simon's eldest son had just told me, I shared with my wife the bizarre details I had just learned that defied comprehension. Besides the agonizing reality that my cherished friend was gone, there was the fact that he had somehow drowned in a river in Argentina, the discovery that he had been cheating on his wife for seven years, and the curiosity that his two oldest sons had taken opposite positions on whether his affair could remain a secret.

"And which son do you think did the right thing?" Danielle asked, while she seemed to ponder the question for herself. "Which son was the most wise?"

"I don't know," I said blankly.

"I don't know either," she responded. "I like the son who asked for complete honesty, but maybe complete honesty was too much for Simon. And to ask him to confess in front of the whole family—to endure all that humiliation...that could make anyone want to die."

"Are you saying you think maybe Simon committed suicide? Reuben didn't say that! It's just a legal formality the authorities have to consider." I was revolted at even contemplating the possibility that Simon's death could have been intentional. "It had to have been an accident—or possibly a murder...Maybe someone was trying to rob him."

"I don't know anything" Danielle replied. I guess when we go down to Los Angeles, we'll know more. What do you want to do right now?" She stared at me patiently.

What I needed and wanted was a sauna. It would give me time, probably alone, to clear my head and think about Simon and the amazing revelations his son had just shared with me. After that, I wanted to see my daughters. Because of the holidays, my beloved girls, now grown women, were both nearby, staying with my ex-wife at her farm on the edge of town. They'd arrived in Ashland with their spouses and kids just a few days earlier. For my own solace, I wished to see my daughters, but I wanted them to come over without their kids, who were just toddlers then. To me, it didn't seem right for the little ones to see me like this—for them to have to witness, or for me to try to hide, so much grief. Danielle said she'd telephone the girls and tell them the tragic news about Simon. I headed for our health club and my old friend, the sauna, a comforting ritual Simon and I had enjoyed many times together over the years.

Sitting alone in my familiar wooden box, I contemplated all that I had just learned. I poured water on the rocks, and they hissed, producing swirling puffs of steam. The sweat pouring out of me seemed fitting. I wanted cleansing, deep cleansing. I longed to rid myself of something—to purge myself of the blindness and stupidity that had somehow allowed a cherished friendship to grow so thin. How had I permitted a best friend to become nearly a stranger?

I faced my own guilt in sweaty nakedness: Why hadn't I called in the past three months? But then again, why hadn't Simon called? If his marriage of thirty-seven years was on the verge of busting up, why wouldn't he call his closest friend? Admittedly, since my first marriage had lasted only half as long and I had a series of short-lived relationships between marriages, I'm certainly no expert on the subject. But Simon and I had pondered the mysteries of the opposite sex together since we were teens. Why, with his secret affair revealed and his marriage on the brink—why would he not confide in his closest friend?

The words of Simon's repeated phrase to me about his marriage, on the rare occasions that I would ask him about it, now echoed through my head: "Rachel is the perfect wife for me—she's every woman to me." He would say these words, half-laughing with his twinkling eyes and broad, handsome grin. Hearing this refrain, I would sometimes wonder if he might be alluding to his wife being content in her own sphere, running their home, while allowing him an unusual amount of freedom. I knew that as an extremely wealthy man who travelled a lot, he had ample opportunity for brief sexual encounters with women he might meet at business gatherings or bars, maybe even hookers. But these relationships, if they existed, would mean little or nothing to Simon emotionally, I assumed. And surely, he wouldn't want me to ask about such salacious things, right? Doesn't the transgression of cheating deepen, heaping more shame on the cheater and his deceived spouse, if we discuss steamy details with our closest friends? And if he tells me his secret, how do I not tell my wife? The dilemma deepens. So I was discreet. I didn't ask probing, potentially embarrassing questions.

Sure Simon…Rachel's perfect for you…

But having two significant relationships at the same time can kill you if you've got a conscience—and Simon had a big-time conscience. To have a seven-year relationship with another woman while he was married did not seem in my mind like something my deeply ethical friend would do. Had I lost touch with the person he had become? I struggled to accept that for years my best buddy had been living a double life: The pious, seemingly conservative Jew whose devoted wife lit the Sabbath candles and cooked delicious kosher meals for extended family gatherings every Friday night, the man who went to an Orthodox synagogue each Saturday morning, immersing himself in a Hebrew God's moralistic admonitions—this same man was a total hypocrite, living a completely separate life, frolicking with his secretary on the beach, or in a hidden bedroom somewhere in Venice.

I recalled an odd story Simon had told me involving his secretary. Simon's younger brother, a solitary, emotionally locked-up guy, probably a victim of Asperger Syndrome, had resigned from the family company, from his position as chief accountant, because of a secretary. Years ago, Simon had told me about the incident, about his brother demanding that he fire this secretary. Simon didn't want to fire the woman, and his brother quit over it immediately. The nearly silent, lonely man retreated to his Santa Monica condo where he plays video games endlessly in utter isolation. End of story, or so I thought. When Simon told me about the conflict and its resolution, I thought the point concerned his brother, his mathematically gifted, socially inept brother. I didn't think about the secretary. Simon hadn't even bothered to mention her name.

The sweat poured out of me as I faced a difficult truth: I realized I hadn't reflected on or asked enough questions about the secretary. I hadn't pressed Simon to explain why his brother was so intent on her being fired. My friend had offered me a hint, a possible doorway into what was really going on in his life, but I had missed the subtle opening. How many other invitations into his heart had I been too blind to see?

Two

"Let me admonish you first of all to go alone; to refuse the good models, even those which are sacred in the imagination of men, and to dare to love God without mediator or veil."

—Ralph Waldo Emerson, "Address to the Divinity Class"

When I got back to my house, my two grown daughters were there, to offer whatever comfort they could to their grieving dad. We all gathered on my bed—Danielle, my daughters, and I—and we cried for the loss of a beautiful man. We cuddled and held each other and cried. Our two mini-Aussies sat on the edge of the bed and stared at us, disturbed in their own way by our profound emotions.

My girls, who were then in their mid-thirties, had known Simon practically their entire lives. They'd swum in his gorgeous Brentwood pool. They'd enjoyed champagne at his elegant backyard parties. They'd been to his sons' lavish Bar Mitzvahs, just as Simon and Rachel had attended my daughters' weddings. They'd witnessed Simon's immense intelligence, the way he could catch you at just the right moment, riveting you with his dark eyes, to ask the perfect, penetrating question. They'd seen his kindness, his wild laughter, his unabashed joy for life. They understood the depth of my grief.

During these moments of profound sorrow, as I was compassionately cradled by my three closest women, I sensed how fortunate I was to be enveloped by so much love. They held me on our bed and comforted me for several minutes until eventually, my sobbing and shaking subsided. My daughters had almost never seen me cry, and never like that. Finally, I calmed down and with a shaky voice, talked about the deep connection I always felt with Simon, my pain in not knowing or asking about his marital troubles, my fears that I had let an intimate friendship dissipate on cruise control, and eventually, I got to some pragmatic details about upcoming traveling plans. Danielle and I would be driving to L.A. Wednesday, the following morning. The memorial would be on Friday, and the burial on Sunday, New Year's Day. We expected to return to Ashland in five days and could still, hopefully, spend a few days with my daughters and their kids. At least, that was our plan.

About a half-hour later, the four of us walked toward the front door and hugged intimately. As she and her sister were leaving, Joelle, my older daughter, inquired about my wife's son Albert, her rather new stepbrother, who lives in Southern France. She asked about his health, remembering that he had recently been struggling with dysentery, something he'd picked up on a trip to Senegal.

"That's so kind of you to ask," Danielle responded. "He is much better now. The dysentery, we think, is finished, and he is back in Aix. My son and his crazy voyages. Thank you for thinking of him." Danielle worries a lot about her son, my adventurous step-son.

After my daughters left, Danielle and I packed that night. Our two mini-Aussies, Luna and Biko, sat on our bed and stared nervously once they saw us stuffing our suitcases. They could read the signs of their impending abandonment, and they whined. To appease them, we repeated, "We'll be back soon." We all tell our own little lies.

I had to look hard in my closet to find any clothes that would be dressy enough for an urban funeral. In his life as an L.A. business executive, Simon was used to wearing suits and ties, but as a retired teacher living in laid-back Ashland, Oregon, it had been years since I wore a tie, and I still don't own a suit.

Danielle and I left early the next morning for the long trek to Los Angeles. Even though we were in the last days of December, we didn't worry much about hitting snow on the mountain pass just south of Ashland or the other highly elevated parts of the journey because recently, it had been unseasonably warm. After checking the weather reports, we were so confident about road conditions, we didn't think we needed to take our all-wheel drive SUV. We assumed our front-wheel drive Mazda, which got better mileage, would be good enough for what we expected to be an eleven-hour trip.

During our first hour, we were pretty quiet, lost in our own contemplations. Having so much to think about, we didn't listen to any music, preferring silence. After about an hour of driving, however, as we approached magnificent Mount Shasta, whose snowy peaks melted magically into the clouds, I pulled out a CD of the Beatles, *Abbey Road*. Simon and I had adored that epic album during our senior year at UCSB.

As we listened to the opening song, "Come Together," Danielle and I began to sing along softly with the chorus. Gently smiling, she turned toward me and said, "And now since we have such a long drive ahead of us—and especially now because of this tragedy, I want you to tell me again how you and Simon first came together, how you came to be the best of friends. Tell me, so I can understand better how you came to love this man so much."

"You know some of the stories already."

"I wish to know them better—and some new ones. Besides, maybe remembering the old stories with me will help you to think of what you might like to say when you speak at his funeral." She squeezed my thigh for emphasis.

"Maybe the stories will just make me more depressed than I already am."

"Cheri, how much more depressed can you get? Maybe if you talk about the best times you and Simon shared together, it will make you less sad."

"YOU make me less sad," I said, squeezing her hand still on my thigh.

"So now tell me again how you and Simon met. It was in high school, wasn't it?"

"No, it was in junior high. We had a bunch of classes together, and we were both going through the whole Bar Mitzvah training process at about the same time. Besides that, we were both relatively short. That was another connection between us, and Simon joked that our Hebrew ancestors must have drunk way too much wine when they chose the measly age of thirteen as the right time for entering manhood. After he says this, when the two of us were halfway alone in our school hallway, he opens his locker, suddenly pulls out a *Playboy* magazine, unfolds it and points to the juicy centerfold, the full-length naked beauty, and then with a huge grin, he says, 'I think before we can really enter manhood, we need to enter something like this.'"

"So being small didn't stop him from thinking big about the girls, yes?" my wife observed.

"Exactly. Simon was always interested in the girls, even when he was less than five feet tall." Intuitively, I could surmise what Danielle was going to bring up next.

"So you and Simon—you both lost your virginity with the same girl—am I right?"

"Yeah, we both lost our virginity with the same girl."

"Yes, and at the same time?"

"The same girl at the same time. In fact, I think we did it in the same way. You know this story embarrasses me."

"But I love it anyway. So tell me again, why did you choose this particular girl—to make love with her at the same time—for your first time?"

"I didn't choose her—Simon did." And so I began to recount with my wife the odd tale of how Simon and I managed to lose our virginity together with a stranger.

"We'd just graduated from our high school, and both of us were on the edge of losing our virginity with our girlfriends. We were mostly ignorant about the act itself in those pre-pornography days, and we were both pretty nervous about our upcoming performances, so Simon came up with the idea of a test-run. He suggested that we'd be more successful and hopefully more 'awesome' lovers with our girlfriends, if we had some 'mentoring experience.'"

"And then he met this girl to give you the mentoring experience?"

"Yes. You love this story, don't you?"

"Yes, I do. And this beautiful girl, this *jeune fille*—what was her name again?"

"I didn't say she was that beautiful, and her name was Dolly Johnson."

"Dolly Johnson—I love that name—not exactly a Jewish name. She was not a girl your Jewish mothers would have loved."

"She was not a girl our Jewish girlfriends would have loved. She was brown-skinned and pretty, a mixed-race girl Simon had met near one of his father's parking lots in downtown Los Angeles. She liked vodka and 7-UP. We were all barely eighteen. At least she told us she was eighteen. Anyway, we were just old enough to rent a motel room."

"So, who rented the motel room?"

"I did." I reminded Danielle that by the summer we lost our virginity together with Dolly Johnson, I had grown to five-foot nine, but Simon, with his late-growth genes, was still about five-foot four.

"So, the two of you cheat on your girlfriends, and then you have to live the lie of silence, all because you think this experience with Dolly Johnson will help you become fabulous lovers and then you can impress your girlfriends more. You poor boys! And did it work?"

"Of course not. But the weird experience did make us partners in crime. We eternally shared this half-kinky secret. Actually, that senior year in high school, we'd already been partners in plenty of crimes, sharing lots of secrets. We'd ditched school several times, jetting up the coast to go surfing in Ventura, sometimes getting away with it, but also getting busted three different times by the school authorities, who would inform our outraged parents."

Danielle smiled, "You and Simon must have loved that time. Two nice Jewish boys discovering the joy of rebellion."

As Danielle and I drove through the Siskiyou Mountains early that morning, I shared some old memories about Simon and me. Our friendship really took off when we were sixteen, and we discovered the University of California at Santa Barbara. Simon and I got to go there on a special program the summer before our high school senior year. That's when we became best friends. We thought we'd found heaven--living in the dormitory together, taking college courses on the gorgeous, ocean-hugging campus, learning to make music together, and wildly enjoying our first surfing adventures on the soft, user-friendly waves.

I described how Simon and I began each day that summer with a run on the beach. I'd been on our high school track and cross-country teams, and Simon, who had been on the gymnastics team, wanted to help me train for the coming season. We'd leave our dorm in the soft colors of dawn and run along the crescent-shaped beach to the Goleta Pier and back. It was about a mile each way, and although Simon, who was really strong in his upper body, would try his best, he wasn't that fast, so to keep us more even, I would wrap about twenty pounds of weights around my ankles and wrists, and we would accelerate together in bliss toward our imagined finish line.

Those mornings were heavenly, and we'd end our runs, diving into the ocean, completely exhilarated. Marveling at the distant, yet sharply focused contours of the mountains on Santa Cruz Island, deeply inhaling our fragrant new freedom by the sea, we asked ourselves how in the world would we ever be able to endure returning to our little high school, with its petty rules and drudgery, imprisoned again amidst the smoggy hills of West Los Angeles?

It was during that summer that Simon and I became good friends with Sally and Cindy, two girls from Ventura, who were also students in the special university program. With these two girls—the four of us were sixteen—Simon and I discovered the pleasure of making simple music together. No, we didn't sing "Kumbaya" by a campfire on the beach, I assured my wife, but we did sing "Blowing in the Wind" and "Mr. Tambourine Man," and we learned how to do harmonies. Sally and I played guitar, three of us sang, and Simon played harmonica. He and Cindy ended up getting involved more than musically.

We loved our classes that life-changing summer, especially a philosophy class taught by an enthusiastic fellow from Columbia University. He loved Nietzsche and his quest for unvarnished truth. To our profound delight, he made us love Nietzsche and our own quest for truth. This instructor—Danto was his name—would get all excited about proving God's existence with words. He called these verbal proofs of God's reality "ontological" arguments, and one day he came to class super-hyped because he'd come up with a new one himself. We called it the "Dantological" argument. To Simon and me, however, the short, bald professor's verbal proof, his enumerated logical argument aimed at verifying God's existence, although intriguing, failed to be any more spiritually significant than the archaic Hebrew we had to recite about God in the synagogues our parents had forced us to attend.

Our most meaningful and personal encounters with the divine, I reminded Danielle, came later that summer when Simon and I backpacked in the Sierras together, trekking through Kings Canyon, and, as she put it, we "lost our virginity with God." While we drove, I elaborated on a story my wife enjoyed about Simon and me, our exodus from our lives as observant Jews. A somewhat-bruised survivor of a rather strict Catholic childhood, Danielle loves to hear others speak of their own journeys toward spiritual emancipation. One day, in an enlightened age, she believes this forcing of one's religion upon an innocent, defenseless child, who knows little or nothing of any alternatives, will be recognized as a form of child abuse. And as for those of us who have managed to escape from and move beyond what we were indoctrinated with as children, naturally, we pray that day of spiritual freedom comes soon.

As for Simon and myself, we'd both endured years of Hebrew School, the arduous preparations for Bar Mitzvah, forced synagogue attendance on Saturday mornings, plus weekly obligations in Sunday School and Confirmation classes. Yet after that first experience of camping in Kings Canyon blew our minds, spiritually speaking, both of us resolved that we were finished with going to synagogue. We felt as if we had met God face to face—eye to eye—in the stars. Neither of us city boys had ever seen what the night sky actually looks like—not like that. You could say we discovered our own "original relation to the universe," as Emerson memorably put it.

"Don't you feel like you're finally feeling God!" That's how Simon expressed it, smiling exuberantly and stretching his arms out wide to the glory of the sparkling cosmos. The endless hours learning Hebrew, the weekday afternoons and weekend mornings spent confined under a synagogue ceiling—all these efforts seemed so misdirected and futile, when the divine could be felt so powerfully and personally, spending one open-eyed night in the mountains under the infinite, starry sky.

Danielle wondered how our parents accepted our decision to no longer go to synagogue. I explained that it was a lot harder for Simon's parents than for mine because both of his parents had barely survived the Holocaust, and they were more religious, more orthodox. After Simon told his folks about his spiritual experience on the mountaintop, his father exploded with, "No son of mine is going to become an atheist!"

"But on the mountain, Simon found God—he did not lose him," Danielle erupted with incredulity. "His father could not understand anything beyond his own way of thinking."

"Isn't that true for most everybody?" I countered.

As for Simon's father, he was a severely authoritarian guy, accustomed to giving orders to minimum wage employees in his parking lots. Often, as he barked commands, it seemed he treated his family as if they were his lowly paid workers. His dad was a difficult man to challenge, and to him, God lived in the Torah, in the Hebrew Scriptures, in Israel and on Mount Sinai, not on a California mountaintop. It was as simple as that. Therefore, from his father's vantage point, by refusing to go to synagogue any longer, Simon had become an atheist. "When things got bad with his parents after that," I explained in summation, "they blamed everything on the idea that he had lost God."

"Even though in reality he had found God," Danielle replied, amused at the irony.

"But he lost the Hebrew God," I added, "the one his parents still believed in, the angry guy in the Torah, who gives commandments and allows genocides. He came to a philosophical conclusion about that God."

Simon had become convinced that this omnipotent, supposedly benevolent, Hebrew God that his parents still worshipped dutifully, could not possibly exist because if God were all-powerful and all-good, how could He have permitted the Holocaust or any of the other horrible things that happen to innocent people? That was the unanswerable question Simon, like many perplexed souls, pondered, and the infuriating paradox definitely alienated him from his parents' religion.

Understandably, their son's new-found belief, the notion of the Hebrew God being dead, irrelevant, or non-existent, deeply upset Simon's parents. Quite aware of their disappointment and anger, I imagined they partially blamed me for his changed outlook since his departure from the old ways occurred after our summer at UCSB and our backpacking trip, weeks later, in the Sierras.

In spite of the Nazi nightmare which they had miraculously survived, Simon's, parents somehow never lost their faith, their belief in the religious traditions that had led so many to the gas chambers. After Simon left his inherited faith, influenced by the freedom-preaching Nietzsche we had read in our philosophy class and especially by our personal spiritual encounter in the star-filled mountains, his parents grieved over what they perceived to be his spiritual confusion. I tried not to feel guilty when I would see them, despite my sense that they believed Simon's friendship with me was fundamentally connected with his becoming the so-called atheist.

His mother once cornered me in her kitchen and barked with a heavy accent, "You used to be such a good boy, Ronnie, a wonderful student like Simon. But I can't understand why the two of you stopped going to *shul*. You know you'll always be Jewish, no matter what you do or don't do. Even if you marry a *shiksa* and live among the *Goyim*."

Many years later when, to my surprise, Simon found comfort in attending synagogue again, his parents were overjoyed. Their wayward son had somehow found his way back to his religious roots.

Listening to my story, Danielle expressed amusement at Simon's eventual return to religion. "God works in mysterious ways," she said, with a slightly mocking grin.

"He certainly does. Like when He managed to bring us together," I added with a smile.

Danielle laughed, but she corrected me on my paternalistic assumptions about the Creator. "Yes, She certainly loves the great Mystery. She's all about Mystery. Absolutely. But I myself would prefer a little less Mystery right now. Could you please slow down a little on these mountain curves?"

I eased off on the accelerator as we gazed down on tranquil Shasta Lake, encircled by snow-frosted mountains and forests of emerald-green fir. Glancing at the placid, dark blue water, my mind drifted to images of Simon sinking lifelessly in a far-away river in Buenos Ares. Somehow, he had jumped or fallen into the water, descended to the river's muddy bottom, and drowned. I cringed at what I envisioned, slowing down a little more for the sharper curves, as the road brought us dramatically closer to the gleaming water.

Three

"And I dreamed I saw the bombers
Riding shotgun in the sky
Turning into butterflies
Above our nation"

—Joni Mitchell, *Woodstock*

WE PULLED INTO REDDING ABOUT NINE that morning to stop for gas. Danielle wanted to call her best friend Mireille, who lives in France, in Aix-en-Provence. Actually, she wanted to know more about her son, Albert, and his recovery from dysentery. Of course, she could have called while we were driving, but I think she felt a little embarrassed, openly worrying in front of me about her son while I was so grief-stricken over Simon. It would have been fine. Anyway, while I pumped gas and got some coffee, Danielle walked off toward some trees to talk to her cherished friend. They usually talked once a week.

When Danielle returned to the car, she had gotten off the phone but looked concerned. I asked rather directly, "Was there some bad news about Albert? You look upset."

"It's nothing so very bad. The dysentery is finished. I hope he never goes back to that village again."

Danielle was referring to a tiny hamlet in Senegal, an obscure settlement with which her son had fallen in love. He had discovered the impoverished community in his early twenties, and in the ensuing decade, he'd returned there several times—teaching, building, digging ditches—doing whatever he could to make the villagers' lives a little better. My wife has been deeply proud of her son's idealism, but she's also intensely fearful for his health and safety. She's seen and shown me photos of her son's beloved village, with its clumps of raw sewage lying in puddles in the unpaved streets.

Genetically, but not culturally, Danielle's only child is half Algerian. She and Albert's father met in Paris at the Sorbonne. After several years of living together, they eventually married, much to the chagrin of both their families. Just as Simon's parents lamented the "loss" of their son when he declared he would no longer go to synagogue, my wife's relationship with an Algerian nearly severed her relationship with her Church-going parents. Her first husband Kareem was a scholar, not at all religious, yet because he grew up in Algeria in a Muslim family, and because he was NOT a Catholic, he was, according to her parents, completely unacceptable as a partner for Danielle. Kareem's family was only slightly less hostile to the "foreigner" he had chosen to be his wife. Understandably, the couple felt a little like Romeo and Juliet. The wedding was very small.

Separated by geography, culture, and religion, the two families—one in a small Algerian town, one in a village in Southern France—never accepted the love their children had found. There weren't many phone calls and almost no visits, just a few empty and repeated excuses, though nobody would admit to being cold or unkind because of any cultural or theological prejudice. We moderns pretend to be such progressive, enlightened thinkers in so many ways, but underneath, it seems most of us are still xenophobic, tribal animals, too blind and timid to go beyond our unfounded fears and assumptions about outsiders. With poisonous stereotypes and symmetrical, unconscious cruelty, the French parents of my wife and her first husband's Algerian parents passively rejected and isolated the young couple, who had dared to find love beyond their clan.

The marriage lasted twelve years. As Albert was turning ten, Kareem, influenced by the great changes taking place in the Middle East, began turning more religious. Sensing he would never be more than a second-class citizen in France, he grew a beard, immersed himself in the Koran, and became noticeably more paternalistic and self-righteous with his wife and son, who naturally didn't respond very well to his changes. He gave up drinking wine with dinner and chastised his wife for not joining him in his abstinence, mocking her for "taking pleasure in the poison of the infidels." He scowled at her if she put ham and cheese on a baguette, their son's favorite sandwich. The estranged man prayed more and more and took classes at a local mosque. Finally, he ended up abruptly leaving Aix, including his job as a university lecturer, to return to Algeria. Rejecting all aspects of his former "Crusader culture," at least, he cooperated enough to sign the divorce papers, much to my wife's relief.

Neither Albert nor Danielle has heard from him in years. Danielle jokes that he probably has three wives by now. I can only imagine his anger and humiliation, if and when he ever found out his former wife had married a Jew, who was now the stepfather of his son. But to be honest, Danielle still aches deeply over Kareem's abandonment of their child. No matter how many times she tells her son the problem rests with his father, not with something lacking in himself, Albert takes his father's disappearance from his life very personally. Like so many other children of divorce, somehow, in his unrepressed thoughts, he's blamed himself for his father's decision to leave and forsake all connection.

What her friend Mireille told her on the phone about Albert had definitely upset Danielle, but it had nothing to do with his health. It concerned politics, something he did not want to discuss directly with his mother. Mireille informed my wife that Albert planned to attend and photograph a dramatic protest-march in Marseille that weekend. The *"manifestation"* was expected to be huge and could quite possibly turn violent. The purpose of the march was to demonstrate opposition to new laws forbidding girls from wearing the Hijab, the Muslim headscarf, or any large religious symbols in their public schools.

Although he was not religious in any way, Albert passionately believed in the right of French Muslim girls to wear this sacred symbol of their modesty. He and his mother had argued about the issue quite vehemently. Danielle agreed with the new prohibitions and the idea that religious differences among students should be minimized by reasonable restrictions. Albert, however, felt the new restrictions were an unfair, insensitive, and unwarranted form of cultural imperialism. Throughout France, the issue had become quite contentious and divisive. I agreed more with Danielle's point of view, but in a way, I could sympathize with both sides.

Anyway, Danielle worried that in his quest for the perfect photograph, Albert might get his head bashed in at the upcoming demonstration. Surely, there would be counter-protesters at the march, the French nationalists, people who supported Le Pen and believed their darkening country desperately needed to be saved from the invasion of decrepit, parasitic Muslim foreigners. Besides fearing for his safety, in her deepest bouts of paranoia, Danielle worried that her son's compassion for the plight of harassed Muslims might one day lead him to convert to the religion, just as his father had unexpectedly taken up the faith.

Albert was certainly becoming quite sympathetic to anti-Zionist opinions popular in the Muslim world. From my perspective, considering our brief visits and occasional phone calls, his views about the Palestinian-Israeli conflict were becoming pretty radical, and they were definitely affecting Danielle's opinions on the subject. He seriously believed Israel should return to its 1967 borders, even relinquishing Jerusalem. I thought this was asking way too much of the tiny nation. Despite our intentions to be open-minded, even Danielle and I found it increasingly difficult to discuss the polarizing topic without contentiousness and finger-pointing. We want so much for our opinions to be reasonable and objective, but can anyone be truly objective when one's family and religious background are involved? Can we "emancipate ourselves from mental slavery," as Bob Marley put it, and enable ourselves to escape the omnipresent bias of our blood and culture? Simon would laugh and call such hope an exercise in self-delusion.

Certainly, he and I had argued heatedly about Israel and its neighbors over the years. My friend, who like myself had loathed the war in Vietnam, eventually became quite an ardent Zionist and a defender of Israel's expanding militarism. We argued passionately about Israel.

As we cruised through the billboard-splattered plateau nearing Red Bluff, several high-flying jets, reminders of America's globe-patrolling military, streaked the sky with parallel lines of white vapor, the so-called "chem-trails" that provoke strange conspiracy theories and fear among our more paranoid citizens. Danielle had more earthly worries. When she expressed her anxiety about her son's ardent political views and the possibility of his getting hurt at the upcoming demonstration, she laughed at the irony of the situation. "Now I'm in the position of my mother. She thought I was out of my mind, totally crazy, when I decided to enroll at the Sorbonne right after things had gone wild there in '68. And I thought I was entering Heaven! *Plus ça change, plus c'est la même chose.*"

Yes, some things never change, including our predilection for imitating our parents, despite our intentions. *"Vive la jeunesse!"* I chimed, knowing how my wife enjoyed my attempts at using some of her native tongue.

"Yes, long live youth," she replied, pausing as she refined her thought. "Long live youth, as long as they strive together for substantial, progressive change."

"You mean if they're conservative, they might as well die?" I liked to provoke her.

"You know what I mean," she said with a smile. "And I know that you and Simon, when you were young—you were both very idealistic too. I know you were, just like we were in France. We wanted to change the world. It was in the air...it was in the music."

"Are you saying I'm not idealistic now?" I asked.

"Of course, you are, Cheri, or else I would leave you."

"What?"

"Just kidding. But tell me more about those idealistic days with you and Simon at the university. You burned your draft cards, and you helped burn down the big bank, right?"

"We burned our draft cards, but we did not burn down the big bank. We were eye-witnesses, not arsonists. We got to see that big, fat Bank of America get completely devoured by flames and turn into a heap of ashes. Like a lot of others that night, we stood outside and watched the amazing scene, and somehow the fate of the bank seemed right. The square, corporate monolith definitely symbolized the huge money and gross profiteering that supported the war we despised...But a few months later, on another night of rioting, Simon and I did light up an old car to contribute to the chaos." I watched a look of shock come over my wife's face as I confessed this unknown little detail from my past.

"You and Simon burned a car! *Mon Dieu*, I never knew my husband was a terrorist! And only now you tell me! But why would you do such a thing?"

"The car was really ancient, an old green Ford. It didn't run, and we felt pretty sure the owner wouldn't mind too much."

"You were like anarchists...two totally crazy guys!"

"It was a time when craziness seemed to make sense. The streets were on fire. We were sick of the war and Nixon's lies, sick of the helmeted police, their tear gas and clubs, sick of the curfews and the arrests. We were extremely lucky we didn't get arrested. A thousand students, one-tenth of our university, got arrested our senior year. That's got to be an all-American record."

"You must have been very lucky indeed. And if you had been arrested, would they have still hired you at this high school in Thousand Oaks where we met?"

"No, I don't think they would have hired me. Just coming from UCSB placed me under suspicion. An arrest, even with the case dismissed, as they all were, would have been too much. The war was still going on. Nixon was about to be re-elected by a landslide. The community was even more conservative than years later, when you arrived—nothing but white-flight Republicans escaping L.A., its forced school busing and terrifying racial riots. The last thing the school administrators wanted was to have some out-of-control young teachers, with long hair and 'radical' ideas, leading students to protest and demonstrate against a war that was tearing our country apart. If I had been arrested, I never would have been hired in Thousand Oaks."

"Then I'm really happy you didn't get arrested."

"Me too."

Simon and I did nearly get arrested a couple of times, I admitted. First, there was the time after we lit the car on fire. We had to run and hide under a big bush while two police cars raced down the street, and a helicopter looked for us with its searchlight. We were definitely scared, making sure we didn't move a leaf as we lay face-down, with our hearts pounding in the dirt.

Our other close call was the night three hundred and sixty students were arrested for protesting the war and the curfew. I explained how we escaped getting locked up on that crazy evening after the infamous Jerry Rubin, earlier in the afternoon, had riled up a crowd of thousands in the campus stadium with a speech that bordered on calling for revolution.

"That afternoon, Simon says to me, 'Aren't you sick of this bullshit? Vietnam, Cambodia, Kent State, these stupid curfews, these dump trucks filled with National Guard, these asshole cops everywhere with their riot gear?' I asked him what solution he proposed. He suggested that we get out of Isla Vista, drive over the Santa Barbara mountains, hike to our favorite swimming hole, and see if we could catch some fish for dinner. To me, his plan sounded perfect."

Danielle laughed softly. "So, your political commitment was not really so strong. In the middle of the struggle, the moment of greatest crisis and confrontation, you abandon your fellow students and protesters to go fishing! Well, I hope at least you caught some fish."

"Yeah. It was pretty wonderful." I provided a few details. "After we drove over the mountain pass, we hiked about two miles to reach our enchanted spot, a place called Red Rock. In perfect solitude and silence, we swam in this long, oval natural pool. In our Garden of Eden, we enjoyed the clear water and late-afternoon sun. And when it was time for dinner, we grabbed our poles and within minutes, we each caught a plump, eighteen-incher. Soon, we made a fire and savored our perfect dinner in complete tranquility. A little wine, and a joint, all amidst the comforting company of a thousand glittering stars, reminding us of our jaw-dropping nights a few years earlier in Kings Canyon. But that night, while we relaxed in delight at Red Rock, back in Isla Vista, three hundred and sixty students got arrested."

Besides Nixon expanding the war into Cambodia and the shooting deaths of four students at Kent State, the more local issue that enraged people, in addition to the curfews, was the indictment of nineteen students for supposedly torching the Bank of America. To Simon and me and a lot of other eyewitnesses, it looked like there were at least fifty young people inside the bank on the night it burned. The authorities chose to blame the nineteen most prominent student leaders—the heads of the campus newspaper and radio, the leaders of the student Black and Hispanic groups, among others. Rather than seeking accuracy or justice, the indictments and mass arrests were meant to intimidate students: Don't attempt to organize, and above all, stay away from organized protests. The idyllic campus by the sea had become a cauldron of rebellion, and the authorities were determined to restore order.

What a senior year! This contrast between pastoral tranquility and the chaos of campus protests was a recurring theme for Simon and me throughout that epic year. After all, we were living with our *shiksa*-girlfriends in a two-bedroom, one-story apartment in Isla Vista on Sabado Tarde, one block from the cliffs and the beach. Across the street on an empty lot, we grew a vegetable garden, filled with tomatoes, cucumbers, and zucchini. There were countless peaceful pastel sunsets on the cliffs together, sometimes with our girlfriends, sometimes it would be just Simon and myself, maybe with a guitar and a harmonica.

Adding to the serenity, I had a work-study job that year with the UCSB Recreation Department. The organization owned and kept about twenty horses one mile up the beach from the main campus, at Devereaux Point. So during the wildest, most politically tumultuous year of riots, bank burning, and mass arrests, I would begin my school days riding my bike out to the Devereaux cliffs in the early morning hours, feeding and taking care of these beautiful horses in a lovely meadow, so close to the ocean that you could hear the waves. And the best part of the job involved Tom, this genial, portly African-American man who was in charge of the horses and lived in a little cabin near their meadow. The kind soul would let me take out a horse—two, if I had a friend with good balance—and I was blessed with the profound privilege, without paying a dollar, of getting to ride bareback on a long, open stretch of beach.

I smiled in describing to Danielle the amazing late-afternoon scene. Several times Simon went with me, and we'd savor the perfect joy of softly cantering on sand—no saddle, just feeling the back of the animal moving in gentle rhythm to the music of the waves—all while the sun slipped slowly down, dissolving into a sea of gorgeous colors. The memory seemed like an enchanted dream.

I recalled how it was mainly the horses that made me apply to be a camp counselor for the Recreation Department that summer, a decision that changed my life. If I could get the camp job, I could keep this incredible benefit of getting to ride bareback on the beach. The Recreation Department did indeed hire me for their day camp, and after spending several fifty-hour weeks as a counselor, I realized that I absolutely loved working with kids. Inspired by this epiphany, before long, I would be applying for UCSB's teaching credential program, specializing in high school English. Fortunately, the program advisor, a wildly enthusiastic Milton scholar who looked a lot like Woody Allen, had strongly encouraged me.

Discovering what I wanted to do for a career meant a lot to me that summer of 1970, especially because my mother had become very ill and was dying of cancer. My college years had been torturous for her. She agonized over my *shiksa*-girlfriend, my non-attendance at synagogue, my pot-smoking and experimentation with psychedelics. She had opened mail that she shouldn't have and suffered miserably because of her intrusion. I suffered in the belief that my actions and words had caused the stress that somehow led to her cancer. In my tormented brain, I realized our emotions obviously must critically affect our health. Therefore, with shame and guilt, I came to believe that I must have contributed to my mother's DIS-EASE and death. Thinking of oneself as an accomplice to matricide is no easy cross to bear, and I tortured myself for years wondering how I might have somehow asserted my independence without causing her so much pain and grief.

After my horse-assisted epiphany about my future, discovering the joy I got from working with kids at the summer camp, at least

I was able to tell my mom that I had found my destined vocation. Leaving at dawn, I was driving the 100-mile journey from UCSB to my parents' home in L.A. every Sunday that summer to spend time with her. From her bed where in her last weeks, she rested more and more, mostly just listening to music, she looked pleased when I told her of my career decision. Grasping my hand and focusing her warm, brown eyes on mine, she smiled, nodding and assuring me that she always knew teaching might be a good profession for me. Her voice was soft, yet confident. "Being a good teacher is important, meaningful work, just right for your creative temperament. And you can do what your father and I brought you into this world to do: You can help make this world a better place." Hearing her say these words, I felt pleasantly relieved. Maybe the ways I disappointed her were less devastating than I imagined—my painful, bewildering actions thankfully never completely extinguishing her hopes and her ultimate faith in me.

Things hadn't been much easier between Simon and his mother. She was a lush-haired, distinctly attractive woman with a great smile and a heavy accent from her native Czech village. Most of the time she seemed extremely cheerful, an odd fact that seemed radically contradictory to all that she must have experienced during the Nazi horror. Somehow, she had survived family upheaval, grueling endless death-marches, and near starvation. She had endured everything and created an entirely new, enviable and privileged life for herself. But her wonderful golden son, the bronzed, straight-A Adonis she adored—her magnificent son had somehow become a torment to her. Mostly, she had become furious with Simon over the way things had deteriorated between him and his father. She claimed that for some diabolical, inexplicable reason, in brazenly asserting his own independence, by abandoning his religion and expressing himself, supposedly with such ungratefulness and defiance, Simon was willing, if not actually trying, to give his father a heart attack. In truth, the tensions between father and son had escalated dramatically, and Simon's dad did, in fact, suffer from some serious coronary issues. Combined with his explosive temper, his father's heart problems definitely made their conflicts seem more threatening.

Right after our graduation from UCSB, Simon and his father really got into it over his five years of supposed atheism. Provoked by his brothers' judgments and determined to uphold his family's pious reputation, his father couldn't take it anymore and demanded that, in order to show at least a token of respect for their traditions, Simon had to promise to attend synagogue services during the next High Holy days, Rosh Hashanah and Yom Kippur, which were a few months away. I laughed a little as I recalled the story to Danielle.

A year earlier, during our junior year, Simon and I both had been trying something different. I was studying at Edinburgh University and Simon was trying his luck at UCLA—mainly because his father had enticed him back to Los Angeles with a brand new, gleaming blue Fiat 124 convertible. When we returned to UCSB for our senior year, we enjoyed wonderful trips together up and down the coast in that sweet-humming blue roadster. Then, right after our UCSB graduation, Simon's father was confident he knew how to regain control over his wayward son. Always an advocate for demonstrating strength, decisiveness, and leverage, the imperious, bald business executive offered Simon a clear choice: He could keep the gorgeous blue convertible, if he could keep God, the God of the Chosen People, and worship Him the way every good Jew should—in a synagogue, at least on the High Holy days. His other option was to remain an "atheist" and give back the car.

"So what did he do?" Danielle asked with a smile.

"He threw the car keys to his father, stuffed some clothes into a backpack, and began a three-month trip hitchhiking to Upstate New York and back."

"What was in Upstate New York?"

"Zach Sklar lives there, not far from Woodstock—and to us, Zach was an enlightened soul."

I elaborated on our friend's significance. Zach Sklar had been editor-in-chief of our high school newspaper. Decades later, in the early nineties, working with Oliver Stone, he wrote the movie *JFK*, certainly one of the most important political films of all time. Simon wanted to see Zach that summer in 1970, to thank him in a personal way for turning us on to what was really going on in Vietnam. After all, it was Zach who got Simon and me to co-write an editorial with him about the war a few months before we graduated in 1966, a small act of audacity that altered our lives.

Our high school newspaper staff had been exceptional our senior year. We'd won a lot of journalism contests and trophies, but Zach, our fearless leader, challenged us: Wasn't it time to write something meaningful about Vietnam, the enigmatic calamity that had grown so ominously since Kennedy's assassination? To be honest, Simon and I weren't knowledgeable or confident enough yet to condemn the war, but we were more than ready to question it.

Cognizant that high school students don't generally question their nation's wars, Zach, Simon and I took great care to write what we thought was a relatively restrained editorial. "We argued that we students needed to think for ourselves about the war—to think seriously and skeptically—rather than passively and childishly assume that our government was telling us the unbiased truth." I heard my voice rising with emotion.

"To think seriously about war? That's hardly a radical suggestion," quipped Danielle.

"That's not what our principal thought," I replied and offered more details. "Mr. James Tunney, the son of a famous boxer and brother of a future California senator, reacted strongly and immediately to our editorial. He stopped the printing presses on our campus, just as they were pumping out the finished copies. He charged into our journalism room, waving the offensive pages at us as if we'd committed an act of treason. Incredibly, he threatened us with expulsion and demanded that we get his signature on every future page before we printed another newspaper. And quite amazingly, this man, who obviously demonstrated tyrannical tendencies, would later become the top referee in the National Football League."

"Had your principal never heard of the First Amendment?" my irate wife inquired.

"I'm sure he'd heard of it. He just didn't think it applied to students."

"Was he right?"

"I don't think he was right. But he had the power to make his threats, and we capitulated. After that confrontation, we obediently got his signature before we went to press and we didn't try to organize a big campus protest."

"But I don't understand why you would not make a *manifestation*, a demonstration, after such injustice."

"Because it was 1966, not '68 or '70. Not enough people were against the war yet for us to provoke a major confrontation. People were too uninformed about what was going on in jungles on the opposite side of the world. They were wrapped up in their own personal lives, and besides, back then, there were student deferments. If you went to college, you didn't get drafted, and virtually everyone at virtually all-Jewish Fairfax High was going to college."

"You didn't think you could get enough of the students to support you—to stand with you against the principal for the right of free speech, the freedom to criticize the war?"

"Exactly. But Zach did us two great favors: First, he turned us on to a little black pamphlet about the Vietnam War. It was about fifty pages long, written by a journalist named Robert Scheer.

It was titled, 'How the United States Got Involved in Vietnam,' and it gave all the critical facts about the war, including the French colonial background and the Geneva treaty—all the facts our government was hiding that made you realize the war was completely hopeless and immoral. After reading this pamphlet, Simon and I both decided that when we registered for the draft in a few months, we would apply to be Conscientious Objectors."

"Sometimes what we read can change our lives. What's the other thing Zach did for you?"

"He let us know about the Los Angeles Inner City Tutorial Program."

Danielle recalled vaguely that I'd spoken to her about this program before. "That was the summer program...the one in which you and Simon taught some black kids in the poor section of L.A.—your little part in the Civil Rights movement—am I right?"

"Right. We each had one ten-year-old African American girl to tutor, and it was a really important, eye-opening experience for us because it got us out of our totally white L.A. neighborhood and introduced us to a completely different reality, the other America. We knew about the Watts riots that had exploded in our city a year earlier, but living in our tree-lined Jewish neighborhood, we'd been sheltered and insulated. Tutoring those two little girls helped snap us out of our protected womb. At least for a summer of Sunday afternoons, we got to see for ourselves some of the dire poverty, the dilapidated apartments with steel outer doors and jail-like bars covering their windows, the bleak, desperate world that had provoked riots and racial controversy. And again, for our widened perspective, we had Zach to thank."

"And so Simon hitchhiked across the entire country to see Zach right after you finished college?"

"He didn't go just to see Zach. He wanted to see, to experience for himself, the whole crazy country, from coast to coast."

"Kind of like Jack Kerouac?" Danielle glanced at me with an inquisitive look.

"Kind of like a lot of dreamers," I said, smiling.

The timing was perfect. It was 1970, just one year after Woodstock. The emancipated soul took just a few clothes, a couple of books, a journal and a harmonica. And thus, only a few days after the "atheist" ultimatum, even before his father managed to sell the blue Fiat roadster, Simon began his odyssey, with his backpack and thumb, his attempt to discover America. The country was in the midst of an amazing transition, and he didn't want to miss a thing.

Four

*"To see the world in a grain of sand
And heaven in a wild flower
Hold infinity in the palm of your hand
And eternity in an hour"*

—WILLIAM BLAKE, "AUGURIES OF INNOCENCE"

Danielle wanted to know more. She pictured Simon, fresh from UCSB graduation, his hair and beard getting longer, hitchhiking across the country the summer after Woodstock, but she wanted more of the inner story. She wanted to understand the mind and heart of the person who had stood up to his bullying father and set out with his thumb to discover America.

"Had he yet discovered himself?" she asked. "And had he yet discovered *l'amour?*"

"Isn't that what college years should be all about?" I replied, and continued telling her more details about our years at UCSB. I talked a little about some of the best classes Simon and I took together—literature, history, philosophy. In greater detail, I described some of the anguished scenes we'd witnessed during that critical time, while eating lunch on the lawn behind the university student center.

Below the grassy slope lies a U-shaped lagoon that leads out toward the ocean. On the other side of the Pacific, about ten thousand miles away, the war in Vietnam raged on, but it seemed very real and near as former soldiers would come back from the bloody massacre, tearfully and remorsefully confessing to atrocities in which they had taken part. While we sat there and ate our sandwiches, they spoke of shattered dreams, nightmarish carnage, and belated awakenings.

During one of those lunchtime dramas, sometime during our chaotic senior year, a repentant soldier spontaneously lit up a dollar bill in front of the crowd, condemning the financial motives behind the war and calling out for others to come forward and add their draft cards to the burning symbol. Simon and I and several dozen others gladly and immediately followed his advice, striding down the grassy hill, then using his flaming dollar bill to ignite and incinerate our hated military cards. As our small paper rectangles transformed into ashes in our raised hands, Simon and I stared at each other and our burning symbols. Like countless others of our generation, as our understanding of the war deepened, our hatred for the senseless slaughter intensified. For very good reasons, we were becoming radicalized. I tried to explain all this to Danielle, who had her own powerful memories of that time.

"You wanted to end the war. I think in France—at least at the Sorbonne—we wanted to end, or at least totally transform, the whole system of education and government. We felt that everyone—all the old petrified people—were trying to crush us, to smother our freedom. We were fed up, finished with having no power, no choice in our lives. Down with capitalism, conformity, religion, antiquated teaching—anything that restricted us and tried to make us into robots, just blindly repeating stupid mistakes of the past."

I couldn't dispute with her whose university years were most extreme. At UCSB, even during the notoriously "radical" years, the majority of students, including Simon and me, were preoccupied with our own more personal endeavors, not the war in Vietnam. Despite our angst over LBJ and Nixon, the pervasive lies and pointless deaths, we had arduous tests to take, demanding papers to write, thick books to read, as well as countless pleasures we hoped to pursue. Grade inflation, giving higher marks for lower achievement, had not yet arrived at the university, and therefore, hordes of undisciplined students, predominantly male, dropped below the 2.0 minimum and flunked out. These jolly fellows immediately became targets for the draft and Vietnam. In other words, those who partied too much at the campus by the sea didn't remain there too long, and some were soon dispatched to a very different world, in the perilous jungles of Southeast Asia.

The key was to find the right balance. We studied, we played, we loved. In addition to our classes and campus teach-ins and protests, Simon and I continued surfing together on occasional afternoons and listening to or playing a little music together in the evenings. Of course, we were also painfully bewildered in our romantic relationships, trying to deal with our girlfriends. Dazzled by new freedoms and mind-numbing sexuality, we were trying to figure out the subtler aspects of relationships, including when and how to end them. Naturally, these were years of sex, drugs and rock and roll, but how much should a guy really talk about such things with his wife?

It was easy to talk to Danielle about the music. Being at UCSB in the late sixties was magical. With Bob Dylan and the Beatles in the lead, music was transforming our culture and our lives. Neither Dylan nor the Beatles came to our campus, but practically everyone else did. Years before a much larger new concert and basketball facility would be built, amazing musicians enthralled audiences in cozy Robertson Gymnasium. With enormous gratitude and enthusiasm, Simon and I got to hear Peter, Paul, and Mary, Eric Clapton and Cream, The Band, the mesmerizing Janis Joplin, and most wonderfully, Jim Morrison and the Doors, the first concert in which hordes of students lit up joints in the gym, and the place exploded into a smoky wildness that annihilated previous rules and restraint. One Saturday evening Buffalo Springfield arrived at UCSB to play, and it wasn't even a concert—it was a school dance in the older and even smaller gymnasium. You can imagine the feelings we had when they played the song that begins, "There's something's happening here, what it is ain't exactly clear..." We sensed we were in the perfect place, at the perfect moment, experiencing a genuine cultural revolution.

Before this trip, I actually hadn't spoken that much to Danielle about my UCSB years, partly because I didn't want to arouse her jealousy. I think I underestimated her. She didn't seem at all jealous. She genuinely wanted to know more about some of the key experiences that connected Simon and me so intimately, with apparently no fear of what she might learn.

Trying to relax and be less self-censoring, I described our initial and enlightening encounter with marijuana. We were with another friend, Pablo, and all three of us had been influenced by the *Reefer Madness* mentality. Simon and I had actually seen the movie and laughed a lot at what seemed like ridiculous exaggerations—kids jumping out of windows or having uncontrollable sexual urges. In actuality, however, we knew nearly nothing about the subject. In fact, at our academically focused high school, only a few reckless or intrepid ones had dared to experience the evil weed.

As emboldened college freshmen, however, Simon, Pablo and I decided, with mild apprehension, that we were ready to step over the edge. With some green, seedy buds we scored from an older student, we would proceed with great caution. Since it was our first months at UCSB, November of 1966, and the three of us were taking a psychology class that emphasized lab experiments and empirical evidence, we decided our first pot experience should be done like a lab test. There would be one smoker, one person to write the smoker's words, and another person to write what he observed in watching. We wanted to be "scientific."

I volunteered to be the first smoker. Careful not to fill the hallway with any smoke, we opened a window and placed a damp towel under the door of Simon's dormitory room. With Simon and Pablo studiously observing and taking notes, I smoked about two and a half joints of the odorous stuff, but I wasn't sure whether I felt much of anything. After endlessly questioning myself out loud whether I was "stoned," I concluded that I must be somewhat affected, but the effect was far gentler than what I expected.

A day later, it was Pablo's turn, and the same thing happened to him. Pablo was a fine musician, a violinist. After smoking two and a half joints of the same stuff I had smoked, he too wondered incessantly whether the pot had really affected him. "It's subtle," he said, smiling, "really subtle." Then he picked up his violin and played an impromptu tune that wove the Beatles' "Please, Please Me" into Beethoven's "Ninth Symphony." "This is cool," he said, "really cool."

Two nights after I tried it and one night after Pablo's similarly mild experience, it was Simon's turn to be the smoker.

"And how did Simon do, in this 'scientific' experiment with the pot?" my amused wife inquired.

"He got totally loaded." I described the absurd scene in which, after smoking only half a joint, one-fifth as much of the same mild stuff Pablo and I had tried, Simon started hallucinating.

"I'm getting smaller and smaller," he cried out, sitting on the single bed. "The walls are closing in on me and I'm getting smaller and smaller...I think I'm turning into a caterpillar. I don't want to be a caterpillar—I want to be a butterfly!"

I grabbed him by the shirt. "You've got to be joking. You're fucking with our minds!"

"Please, please let go of me. I don't want to be a caterpillar—I want to be a butterfly!"

Pablo and I were dumbfounded. We realized from this experience, substantiated by numerous later attempts, that Simon was seriously sensitive to marijuana. "For him, it was almost like taking acid," I said. "He got used to it a little bit, but mostly he was better off with wine or whiskey."

"Maybe he smoked some strong pot with all those drinks he had on the night he fell into the river." Danielle offered what seemed like a plausible explanation for Simon's accident.

"Yeah, maybe that's what happened," I replied, though I wondered how easy it would or wouldn't have been for him to score some pot in Argentina. "Who knows what he might have taken, besides the drinks he had that night." I imagined Simon getting really wasted, wobbling down some cobblestone street, and banging his head on a rock as he fell by the river's edge and then into the water. The image seemed believable, certainly more believable than the notion that he might have intended to take his own life.

"Isn't it possible," Danielle asked, "that Simon could have taken something even stronger than the drinks and marijuana? Maybe he took something like Ecstasy or LSD, and that's what made him lose control and maybe fall into the river?" I nodded to acknowledge the possibility.

"Back when you were young, the two of you took LSD together, right?"

"LSD, mescaline, mushrooms, peyote. We were seekers, trying to find God."

"I thought you found Him—or Her—backpacking in the mountains, in the Kings Canyon."

"Don't you think we should meet the Divine again and again?"

"Without a doubt!" Danielle exclaimed. She smiled and gently stroked the inside of my hand with her thumb. But she wanted to know more. "So where did you take LSD for the first time? There is nothing like the first time, don't you think? A bit frightening—but what an awakening!"

"We took it on a beach in Isla Vista. It was perfect for Simon and me and our first experience."

"I agree a beach is perfect to try this kind of amazing reality-changing thing. But one does have to be so careful with it. One drop can be so incredibly powerful. For me, as I once told you, I had the most beautiful first LSD experience on a beach near Cassis with Mireille. We danced and sang and swam. We found our heaven. How lovely to think that at almost the same time, on a faraway beach, beside a different sea, on the other side of the world—you and Simon were trying the same thing. It was a time many of us were trying to expand our minds, isn't that true?"

"Turn on, tune in, drop out—wasn't that the phrase?" I asked, recalling my Timothy Leary.

"Yes, and did you and Simon tune into the beautiful truths and expand your minds in a beautiful way?"

"Of course, we did. We discovered the world in a grain of sand, just as William Blake said we could. We got to walk through the 'doors of perception' that Aldous Huxley wrote about. You know Huxley actually lived in Isla Vista and he died, they say, on LSD. Anyway, I think Simon and I felt the divine pretty deeply, wandering all over the Isla Vista beaches that day. We sensed this godly perfection in every grain of sand, in every leaf, every flower, each dog or cat, in every amazing face we met. It was spectacularly beautiful, feeling this profound spiritual connection with every living thing."

"And speaking of spectacular connections, did you and Simon ever take the LSD together with your girlfriends?"

I cringed a little at the thought. Okay, she's not jealous, I told myself, trying to relax and become less self-censoring. She seems to actually want to know the stuff I would never want to know about her. I decided to tell her about one memorable psychedelic Saturday during our senior year.

The day began normally enough, with Simon and me and our girlfriends, encouraged by the pleasing, peppy songs of *Sgt. Pepper*, cleaning house together on a bright, sunny Saturday morning. Pretty soon, however, it became clear that Simon was feeling a bit strange. He didn't want to clean house with us anymore, and with an odd grin, he retreated to his room. Then just when "Strawberry Fields Forever" was playing, he bursts out of the bedroom. Not only does he admit that he's on some great acid, he's sure that Herman Hesse, our favorite author, must have been on acid too. He thinks we all should drop acid. The whole world should drop acid. He starts raving about the magic theater in *Steppenwolf*, waving the book and passionately expounding about the conflicting personalities, the different selves, that exist and compete in our psyches. As I began to elaborate more on Simon's outburst about Hesse and his Jungian archetypes, Danielle reminded me of her original question and redirected me.

Trying to overcome my reticence, I told Danielle more details about that day and its pleasures. Yes, the three of us decided to join Simon for a memorable psychedelic adventure. Naturally, there was a lot of time on the beach, including ripping our clothes off and diving into the waves. This was after a bike ride out to Devereaux Point and running around and dancing like delighted children in a grove of pines called the Magic Forest. We each climbed our own separate tree—laughing, whistling and cooing to each other as if we were a quartet of birds, gleefully managing to communicate without words. The day ended with us all back at our place, coming down from the acid, taking long showers, making a salad and spaghetti dinner, drinking or smoking, singing, making music together and dancing some more. I recalled that when we had finally worn ourselves out with the music and the dancing, three of us lay down on the living room floor in a loving pile of entwined arms and legs—Simon, Kristi, and I—and Allison sat at her synthesizer and sang us into further bliss. We all loved her version of that Doors song "When the Music's Over."

I really didn't want to go further with this conversation. Yes, those were lusty, high-flying, wonderful days, but I didn't know or want to know everything about my wife's experiences during that time, or any other time for that matter. I guess I would rather know too little than too much. My imagination is too vivid, my caveman jealousies too strong. Yet my wife wanted to know more, so I told her more. She wanted to know more about Allison, the gifted musician, and Kristi, the free-spirited artist, the two alluring ladies we lived with that senior year. She wanted to know how we had met them and fallen in love.

Simon had met Allison at UCLA, where they'd taken a music class together and fallen for each other rather instantly. Simon wrote to me about it, with lots of sensuous imagery, that junior year while I was away at the University of Edinburgh. Meanwhile, I was writing to him about everything I was learning at that amazing, intellectually-demanding institution, and telling him, of course, as my best friend, how lovesick I was for Kristi.

I'd met Kristi and fallen for her immediately at UCSB during our sophomore year. Strawberry blonde, with a vibrant smile and a joyously liberated sexuality, Kristi had me smitten. Within weeks, I felt closer to this *shiksa* from a small desert town than I felt being with the Beverly Hills-raised, Jewish girlfriend I had dated for three years. Kristi and I probably wrote a hundred letters, mostly on those wispy blue aerograms, that lovesick year I was in Edinburgh. In June, she met me in Paris, and we hitchhiked all over Europe.

Meanwhile that summer, Allison and Simon were exploring the beauties of British Columbia in his Fiat roadster. We were all eager to try living together, all four of us, our senior year in Isla Vista, which is exactly what we did. But naturally, it didn't turn out quite as idyllically as we had dreamed.

Our romantic relationships got strained by so many things—the crazy times, our youth and innocence, our dreams, our wishes for perfect intimacy—so many things that made it seem wrong for Simon and me to continue our relationships by the time the school year was coming to its chaotic end. Yet arriving at the decision to break up was excruciating.

One day, as the colors of sunset slipped into darker shades of orange and violet, we were both feeling pretty tense and confused as we headed for a private place on the cliffs over-looking the salt-fragrant sea we loved. The women we adored were driving us crazy, and I'm sure the feeling was mutual. Simon brought a bottle of wine, and I had a joint. Creviced in our familiar hidden spot, we sat in silence a long while. Since the walls in our apartment were very thin, each of us had a pretty good idea of what the other guy was going through. We watched and listened to the waves.

Finally, Simon spoke. Staring at me quite directly, he shook his head and said, "This would be a whole lot easier if we were a whole lot stupider—if we just didn't think and feel so fucking much."

"I should have been a pair of ragged claws scuttling across the floors of silent seas," I mumbled, making good use of the T.S. Eliot we both knew. Should we break up with our girlfriends when we still loved them in many ways, even with all the confusion? How much love is enough, or better yet, what is the right kind of love, the kind that should make a couple fight through the inevitable struggles and pains? Simon and I had banged our heads probing these questions, alone and together. But that day on the cliffs, we mostly sat in silence. We watched the glistening rainbow of softening colors melting into the sea. We'd grown up in this place. So much had happened since we discovered this paradise and learned to surf here when we were sixteen. Now, nearly twenty-two, faced with serious decisions about serious relationships, we felt quite old. Simon brought up the wildly provocative movie we'd recently seen with our girlfriends.

With its open sexuality, including even some homosexual scenes, *Midnight Cowboy* was an exhilarating, boundary-breaking film. The four of us had seen it the first night it came out. The girls discussed it with us after we got back to our apartment, but after about ten minutes, they went off to their bedrooms. Simon and I stayed up for another two hours, reviewing the best scenes and underlying ideas that had stirred us most. As we sat on the cliffs and he recalled that evening when the two of us had been so absorbed talking about the film, he suddenly got to the heart of the matter and exclaimed, "I just want to be with a woman I can discuss a great film with for more than ten minutes." Seeing the gleam in his eyes as he made this outburst, I knew exactly what he meant.

Not long after that conversation on the cliffs, we each broke up with our girlfriends, though not very easily or peacefully. Shouldn't one be able to do so without shame or blame? Kristi and I were the first to fall. Allison and Simon collapsed a few weeks later and more tentatively, leaving open the possibility of trying again sometime in an indefinite future. I felt sad just telling Danielle about it. It's not as if the two young women Simon and I left behind had done anything wrong, it's just that...I looked at my wife and struggled for the right words.

She provided them. "It's just that with Simon and you, with your relationships with these women, there was just not enough magic, not enough—*je ne sais quoi*." She grinned at me and continued. "There is a mystery that connects two people if they are lucky enough to find it together. This magical, mysterious thing makes them want to never leave each other? There is gratitude and joy...and not so many questions. Don't you think so?" Again, she smiled as she gently tapped her fingers against her heart.

How do we manage to find the one who will become the great love of our life? The perplexing question amused me as I glimpsed at my beautiful wife and continued driving. Maybe Simon and I were just too young back in those college days, I thought to myself. Not just the wrong women, but bad timing. Without really admitting it, even fully to ourselves, we both had been pulled by a latent yearning for other relationships, not quite ready yet for the ultimate one. Ahead in the distance, I could see the faint shapes of tall buildings and the bridge leading to Sacramento, almost the halfway point in our journey. Danielle kissed me on the cheek.

Five

"I love the great despisers, because they are the great adorers, and arrows of longing for the other shore...I love him who lives in order to know..."

—Friedrich Nietzsche, *Thus Spoke Zarathustra*

While Danielle rested her eyes, we continued heading south, and my mind scrolled over several memorable scenes involving Simon. I remembered him, publicly and courageously exploding with rage the night we watched Nixon deliver one of his Vietnam troop-withdrawal speeches early in 1970, our senior year. We had ridden our bikes to campus and watched the President's oration with about fifty other students at the university Student Union, which had a large-screen projection television and comfortable chairs. In this lounge, packed with potential future soldiers, we observed our Machiavellian president proudly announce how few Americans were now in South Vietnam, thanks to his great policies, and how he had also drastically reduced the number of American deaths. Deceitfully utilizing and omitting certain key statistics, the cunning conman made it seem as if the war had practically ended. But everyone wasn't fooled.

Suddenly, with no apparent fear or embarrassment, Simon stood and shouted, "What about the number of HUMAN deaths, you fucking asshole? Or don't Asian deaths matter?"

Understandably, Simon's incendiary explosion ignited a heated response. "Would you rather have the communists attack us over here?" another student bellowed. He too arose from his seat and took a few steps toward Simon. He was wearing an ROTC uniform and looked big enough to be a college linebacker. Eyes widened and jaws dropped as everyone stared, expecting a physical fight might soon follow.

Simon didn't back down. "Why don't you run down to the beach with your binoculars and wait for the Viet Cong to arrive in their rice paddy boats? We're not defending ourselves—we're just murdering!" Though he could see this uniformed, muscular, crew-cut-topped defender of America looked ready to swing at him, Simon intrepidly added one more line. "What if the people we're bombing and slaughtering over there were your sisters and brothers, your own parents? How would you feel about that?"

For a few tense moments, Simon and the ROTC guy just coldly glared at each other. Simon was about five inches shorter and forty or fifty pounds lighter than the would-be soldier, but he was also a senior with confidence in his beliefs. His hair nearly touched his shoulders and with his unclenched hands below his waist, he looked ready and willing to receive the first punch. Did he want to get slugged, get his face bloodied, and become a victim, like the Vietnamese, of overblown American testosterone? Simon and his adversary were about three steps apart, and I didn't know what might happen, so I stepped between them. After a few precarious seconds, they each backed off, and Simon and I exchanged slight grins, both of us somewhat surprised at his growing audacity, shouting out among so many strangers, such brazen condemnations of the war, thoughts we had often shared safely and privately among friends.

My mind drifted to a scene that occurred a few weeks after that Nixon speech. Simon and I had gone to a pizza place in Isla Vista to watch our nation's second televised draft lottery. Who would get a lucky high number and win exemption from military service?

And who would get an unlucky low number and be asked to go to Vietnam? Although Simon and I had both applied to be Conscientious Objectors, our applications were on hold because of our student deferments, which would soon be expiring. In other words, we didn't know yet whether our impassioned essays about God and war would free us from the draft, so the lottery that evening certainly captured our attention. A nice high number, at least in the mid two-hundreds, would make our C.O. applications irrelevant. Of course, we had discussed what we would do if we received both an unlucky number in the lottery and a rejection of C.O. status. The choices would be Vietnam, prison, or Canada. Speculating on this worse-case scenario, we both had decided we would go for Canada. British Columbia would be cold, but much better than a prison cell or a rice paddy where we could be obliged--ruthlessly and pathetically pointlessly-- to murder innocent peasant farmers.

That night, we both got lucky numbers. Mine was 324; Simon's was even better, 360. We were hugely relieved and celebrated heartily, getting pretty drunk and wasted late into the night. From the pizza restaurant in "downtown" Isla Vista, with the full moon lighting our way, we rode our bikes along Del Playa and then along the cliffs to Devereaux Point. We sat on the bluffs and smoked and drank in the moonlight, laughing in relief at our good fortune, moaning with the guilty knowledge that mostly poor whites and darker-skinned Americans would continue to do most of the fighting and dying for our country. We anguished over war itself and why, despite all our intelligence and advancements, humans could still be manipulated into believing such mass slaughter is a noble endeavor. *"Dulce et decorum est..."* Yes, how sweet and noble it is to die for one's country...You might even end up with your name on some bronze plaque in your hometown.

Simon grinned at me with that knowing twinkle in his eye, suggesting he was beyond all common illusions and wishful overestimations of humanity. "People don't change, Ronnie. In our hearts, we're still primitive beasts, and even the murder of millions can still get rationalized."

I hated hearing Simon's rants about inevitable human stupidity and depravity. Like a life-raft, or the solace people seek in religion, I've held tightly to my hope and faith in some sort of moral evolution among people, that long arc of history that bends toward justice, as Dr. King put it. Simon liked to shatter my optimistic view with pointed references to historical delights like the Crusades, the Inquisition, Gallipoli, the Phoenix Program in Vietnam, or of course, the Holocaust, the ultimate of premeditated horrors. "Think of Dresden and Auschwitz, Hiroshima, Mi Lai, and napalm. Do you really think we're ethically improving?" There was little I could say to counter his entrenched cynicism.

As the full moon shimmered on the sea in front of us, we realized it was nearly four in the morning, yet we still weren't ready for sleep. Funny how a little life-and-death lottery can stir up one's adrenalin. We rode our bikes back into central Isla Vista, where our friend, Joe Cuellar, the baker, would be in the middle of his preparations for the new day. Besides making great donuts, this plump, balding Italian American with tufts of white hair over his ears, gleamed with a reassuringly confident outlook on life. While Simon and I struggled with anguish and confusion about our girlfriends, the war, and our future, Joe Cuellar was precise and clear about his purpose on Earth.

Like a priest offering communion, he gave us a few of his fresh warm, circular creations, puffy glazed delights that melted in our mouths. While we sat and ate slowly with great appreciation, he stood in the doorway and lit up a cigarette. As he watched us so obviously enjoying the product of his labor, with his raspy Italian accent and wearing his usual white, flour-splattered apron, he grinned and delivered his familiar refrain: "I dedicate my life to bake for the students." Simon and I exchanged smiles. Ah...if only someday we could reach such clarity.

While I drove and reflected on these memories, we passed beyond Sacramento and its suburbs, nearing Stockton, and soon Danielle, rested from her catnap, opened her eyes. I asked whether she was hungry yet, and we both decided we would rather wait a few more hours until we got to Harris Ranch, a place known for its steaks, provided rather freshly by a local herd. Yes, slaughter leads to luscious T-bones. Mentioning the steaks made me recall how when Simon hitchhiked across the United States the summer after Woodstock, he returned to California as a vegetarian, with a newly awakened compassion for all animals. He sent me a letter from Vermont in which he declared, "I'm not eating flesh anymore!"

"A vegetarian atheist," Danielle quipped. "That must have gone over really well with his super-Jewish parents. No more chicken soup."

"You think that's funny, but Simon's parents didn't think it was funny. It just distanced them further from their son. Those big Friday evening Sabbath dinners, that begin with all the Hebrew prayers—they were a pretty serious thing for Simon's parents. And the meals weren't vegetarian."

It was on one of those Sabbath evenings after his three months of hitchhiking that Simon arrived unexpectedly at his parents' home and announced to them his new dietary resolutions. What followed wasn't pretty. Since Simon's dad could hardly tolerate his son's wayward spiritual path, the young man's change in eating habits pushed the older man over the edge.

His father exploded about Simon's supposed complete disintegration as a worthy human, the embarrassment and disgrace he was willing to cause his family. His enraged face turned red, his eyes bulged, and he screamed, "No son of mine is going to be a vegetarian!" Meanwhile, Simon's mother gasped and sobbed about her poor husband's heart. The intended peaceful aura of the Sabbath was thoroughly spoiled, and Simon ended up leaving the scene abruptly, walking two miles to get to a place of refuge, my parents' home.

At about eight in the evening, Simon knocked on their front door. The home of my parents was considerably smaller and more modest than the two-story, Spanish-styled mansion Simon had fled. He arrived with his backpack and looked understandably stressed by what had happened in the brief, volatile encounter with his father and mother. There he stood in my parents' living room, with full beard and shoulder-length curly hair—the atheist, vegetarian refugee, somewhat disheveled and in need of a shower.

My parents and I were just finishing our Sabbath meal, and we were startled to see him. My mom and dad took pity on him, suggested he wash up in the bathroom, and offered him a glass of Sabbath wine, some bread, a baked potato and salad. Obviously, he wouldn't be interested in the chicken my mom had managed to bake. Her cancer was pretty bad by this time. She had only several weeks left to live, yet she and my dad felt sympathy for my distressed friend and were interested in his plight.

Simon told my parents and me more details about the short but tempestuous reunion he'd experienced with his parents. Graciously, my father volunteered to talk with Simon's dad the following morning, if he were willing. Simon thanked him for the offer, and my dad shuffled off to the kitchen and the telephone to find out whether the irate parking lot tycoon would meet with him.

The two fathers did get together the next morning. After their coffee shop rendezvous, my dad drove across the city to his jewelry shop in downtown L.A., while Simon's father went to his usual synagogue for Saturday morning Sabbath prayers.

Simon and I hung out together that day anxiously waiting for news from my dad. I remember we played some music, working on a pretty spirited rendition of "Nowhere Man," a favorite Beatles' masterpiece, whose lyrics intrigued and delighted us. *"Doesn't have a point of view/ Knows not where he's going to/ Isn't he a bit like you and me?"*

Anyway, I know Simon was taut and nervous that day. He asked me several times what I thought about our fathers' rendezvous and how much of an influence my dad might be able to exert on his dad. To me, it seemed at least fifty-fifty that my thoughtful, articulate father would be able to soften Simon's dad and help him deal with his son more tolerantly. Simon had actually hoped he could make enough peace with his father so that he could temporarily work for the parking lot firm, live at home and save a few bucks, at least for a few months, before journeying onward. At the moment, that plan seemed probably like wishful thinking. I was worried about my friend, but I was far more concerned about my mom.

That Saturday afternoon, we took my mother to one of her chemo sessions. While Simon waited in the outer room, I stood behind and held my mom as a nurse poked and probed and poked again repeatedly, trying to find a vein from which to draw blood. Like fearful beings with their own minds, my mother's veins were running away, hiding deeper in her arms and getting harder to locate. To this day, I can't stand seeing anybody getting injected with a needle, not even in a movie. My mother and I were both pretty shaken up by her chemo sessions that September. She called the treatment facility "the poison palace."

A few hours after we returned to my parents' home, my dad showed up. We sat down for an early Saturday evening dinner, which Simon and I had picked up at the local deli—lox and cream cheese, bagels and smoked white fish—a very Jewish Saturday evening meal. We were all eager to hear my father's report. Could his calm temperament, his irrepressible reasonableness, enable Simon's dad to calm down and become more accepting of his atheist-vegetarian son?

Apparently, my dad's well-meaning attempts to pacify the big boss had fallen flat. At our dinner table, in one blunt sentence, he summarized succinctly what he had learned from their morning get-together: "The only thing that man has going for him is the volume of his voice."

Danielle reacted strongly to this part of my story. "I know exactly this kind of man, like Simon's father. The exploding voice, the unquestioned authority. My father, especially after too much wine, could become that kind of man. My first husband became that kind of man—and he didn't need any wine. Unfortunately, these men are all over the earth—with all their force and intimidation... and they don't even know how ugly they are."

"So you can understand why Simon wanted out of L.A. at that point," I said. "There was no way he was going to work for his father or stay at home. They couldn't even get through a dinner together, yet he's totally broke. He knew he had to leave, but his options were pretty limited."

"For the sake of his freedom and integrity, he almost lost his family. That's exactly what happened to me, with my family, after I got together with Albert's father. Freedom can be expensive," she said with a mild grin. I nodded in agreement and offered more details about Simon's next moves.

Determined to pursue his personal liberty, he decided to take off and let his beard and hair grow even longer. He stuffed his backpack with a few necessities and hitchhiked up to Mendocino, a magical coastal village in redwood country, about a hundred miles north of San Francisco. He imagined it'd be a peaceful place to hang out for a while, somewhere he could read and write and contemplate, before moving on to who knows what. No car, no money--yet somehow, his desperation led to a stroke of luck. Incredibly, he managed to find an amazing place to live in Mendo, as the locals call it, a quaint little unpainted, redwood-planked house on the outer edge of town near the cliffs. When he discovered the beautifully situated dwelling, surrounded by tall weeds, he realized at once no one was living in it.

He had prowled the whole town for days, sleeping on the bluffs and asking a lot of questions. The economy was depressed. Jobs were scarce and housing scarcer. Finally, on a tip from a postman, he learned about the empty house beside the cliffs and the sad story of a Mrs. Moat. It seemed the old woman, after losing her husband, had lost her wits as well. Quite against her will, she was locked up in a mental hospital several miles away. If Simon were willing to look after the feeble, kind woman, the postman speculated, he could probably be assigned some sort of guardianship, earn a few dollars, and get to live with the "pretty normal" lady in her house by the sea.

The postman's suggestion ended up providing Simon with a roof over his head, a small salary, and a roommate. Mrs. Moat was extremely pleased to be liberated from the mental hospital and returned to her old home. Curiously, she spoke to and apparently visualized her deceased husband quite frequently. These conversations often took place in the middle of the night as she would wander through the house. Her relationship with Simon was less important to her and more confused. "Who are you again?" she would repeatedly ask, whenever he brought her a meal or helped her with some stairs.

Now that he had found such a beautiful home, he intended to fill it with warmer companionship. After all, not only did the living room offer a beautiful view of the sea, it also included a lovely old piano. It was time, Simon believed, to resume and attempt to improve his relationship with Allison—their passionate, tumultuous, unresolved relationship.

Their nearly two-year affair had gone through many trials. Each had left the other before. Both were fearful and wary, battered with bruises from some of their explosive verbal clashes. Yet they were also hopeful that in a new environment, outside of the craziness of Isla Vista and the small apartment, often filled with guests who stayed for too many days or weeks and rarely helped clean dishes or toilets--maybe things could get better. Like Simon, Allison was up for seeing whether they could take the next step in their relationship. She would come down from her parents' home in Seattle and join him and Mrs. Moat immediately. In addition, she had one thing Simon and his older roommate lacked: a functioning automobile, her less-than-beautiful, yet reliable, crème-colored VW bug.

"With Mrs. Moat, Allison and Simon made a threesome. After my mother passed away in early October, I joined them, and we made a foursome."

Danielle arched her eyebrows and smiled. "Not so fast, my love. Let's get back to the threesome. May I ask you a question?"

"Sure." I wasn't that surprised at what she asked next.

"Did you and Simon, since you were so close, and since you even lost your virginity together, did you ever consider doing a ...?"

"*Ménage-à-trois*? Sure, we talked about it. Simon liked to talk about sex more than I did."

"And what did you think of the *ménage-à-trois* idea?" she asked, pronouncing the words with a curious grin.

"I think we had different fantasies. I, of course, thought of being with two girls. Simon thought being with a girl and a guy might be cool."

"And what did you think of that?"

"I thought it was weird. I guess I was just surprised that he would feel that way. I didn't know what to say. I knew for sure I wouldn't be a part of any threesome he envisioned."

Although I stayed with Simon and Allison in Mendocino only a month, it was a profound month, the month right after my mother died. "And that's what I'm realizing about my whole relationship with Simon over the years," I explained. "It's not that we had that many years of close-contact relationship, it's just that the years in which our friendship formed, the years we were closest, happened to be the most important, character-shaping years of our lives. I guess that's why we thought our friendship could survive anything."

Those weeks with Simon in Mendocino were poignant and memorable. We read, we wrote, we made a little music together. Enclosed in a cold, grey fogginess almost every day, we spent introspective, quiet hours walking on the cliffs and beach. We took turns making meals for and feeding Mrs. Moat. It was a melancholy time for me. And Simon and Allison weren't doing so well either.

In fact, things were getting seriously tense between them. He questioned how much she valued his writing, the poems and short stories he'd composed and the ones he hoped to write. She questioned how much he valued her music, her complex jazz-pop compositions, and whether he considered her creative efforts to be an amusing hobby or something as valuable as his writing. They'd reached a painful impasse. But just like the time he came up with the idea of going fishing in the mountains to escape the Isla Vista riots, again Simon came up with a cool-off plan, a way to escape, at least temporarily, from an anxious situation. Simon's plan would allow us to get away for a few days, and it would also give him the time and space he needed to reflect on his predicament with Allison.

He had met three unusually interesting guys on ocean-fronting Main Street of Mendocino. They were living in virtual isolation back in the forested mountains a few miles outside of town. According to Simon, they seemed extremely smart and non-conforming, and we would be welcome to stay with them if we wished for a few days. Since Allison and Simon needed some time apart anyway, he and I decided we'd check out the little hideaway where these three refugees from modern life lived. It turned out to be a memorable visit.

Robert, Dan, and Orion lived in three tiny huts far enough from a dirt road to be well hidden by a forest. The huts were dome-shaped little dwellings, held up by thin, bent branches and covered with plastic tarps. Though not exactly beautiful, the humble domiciles kept out the rain. They stood in a triangle about thirty feet apart from each other, with one larger dome, the library-meeting room, in the center. There was a very bountiful vegetable garden on one side, and the young men had amassed a fine library of classic literature as well as more pragmatic books, mostly on topics like horticulture and herbal healing. In addition, they had several musical instruments, a few that looked hand made.

The miniature community achieved its isolation thanks to a thick forest of redwood and pine. There was no electricity, and the closest paved road was nearly a mile away. I don't know who, if anyone, owned the land. The guys used creek water for their basic needs and seemed to get along fine without a toilet. They were survivalists.

All probably in their late twenties or early thirties, the three bearded men believed civilization as we knew it, was heading toward a catastrophic tragedy, in all likelihood a nuclear one. When you consider the fact that our established Cold War "defense" policy at the time was MAD, Mutually Assured Destruction, which was just another way of saying globally apocalyptic nuclear war, the three men's apparent paranoia didn't seem so unjustified. Just a few years earlier, we had barely escaped all-out nuclear war during the Cuban missile crisis. Looking back on it now, our whole culture resembled Jonestown, the seemingly insane commune in Guyana where over nine hundred people drank lethal Kool-Aid, collectively committing suicide. Like the poor fools of Jonestown, our nation was poised for mass suicide, but Robert, Dan and Orion were determined not to drink the Kool-Aid.

Even if the potential nuclear holocaust were somehow averted, the three believed our society was so morally and intellectually corroded, that those who wished to remain uninfected needed to isolate themselves as much as possible. Usually, one or two of the guys would walk or hitchhike into town every two weeks to pick up a few supplies, mostly government surplus food like peanut butter, white bread, and cooking oil. Otherwise, they tried to live without any dependence on the outside world.

Simon and I arrived mid-afternoon and stayed for two nights. There were two things that especially captured our attention during our time there. First of all, we realized that the three men had designated, distinctly different, roles in the group, and they were not equal. Orion, a thin, sharp-eyed African American man, was clearly the leader, presiding over prayers and group-study sessions. Dan, the red-haired gardener, was also the carpenter, fix-it man and maker of musical instruments. On the bottom rung of the social ladder was Robert. Short, with long, stringy blond hair, he cooked meals, carried water up from the stream, and generally cleaned up after everyone, including always doing the dishes. He seemed like a maid for the other two, and that really bothered me.

Simon thought the division of labor worked quite well, and that Robert's seemingly servile role was just like that of an ordinary housewife, something that ought to be accepted. In the home in which he grew up, Simon's mom never complained about her husband's domineering demeanor or her role as the dutiful, kitchen-centered housewife. She accepted such paternalism as an inevitable reality, the sign of a strong, good husband, the dependable provider. Raised in such a family, Simon understandably accepted traditional gender roles much more than I. He gave lip service to feminism, but his heart wasn't in it.

When it came to gender roles, my family was nothing like Simon's clan. My mother worked part-time as a surgical stenographer in a hospital, and my father was too kind and sensitive to want to dominate anyone. In my family, standing up for the "right" of males to rule over women would be compared with the archaic right of whites to continue oppressing minorities, and it would be condemned just as emphatically.

Whenever we would argue about feminism, Simon would raise his favorite point—that people are generally incapable of substantially changing and that to believe otherwise, was a sugar-coated delusion. "People don't change their basic natures. Women can march and burn their bras, but we're never going to make the genders equal. We're just too different," he proclaimed. And Simon was certain that most housewives, including his mother and Orion's "housewife" Robert, were relatively content in their subservient, protected roles. Seeing no great need to "liberate" women, Simon was fine with Robert doing all of the dishes.

The other most remarkable part of our stay with the hut-dwellers in the forest was an informal class, a seminar Orion led on Herman Hesse's novel, *The Glass Bead Game*. Simon and I were big fans of Mr. Hesse, so we loved hearing a brilliant man read and comment on passages from the master's final novel. Seated on pillows, with only a single kerosene lamp for light, the five of us were gathered in the library hut. It was our second and last evening there. With all the wisdom and insight of the best professors we'd been lucky enough to hear at UCSB, this intense, dark-skinned scholar, whose apocalyptic views on our culture might have gotten him committed to the same mental hospital from which Mrs. Moat had been freed, brilliantly got to the novel's core message. His eyes glowed with enthusiasm as he read Hesse's words: "There is Truth, my boy, but the doctrine you desire—the absolute, perfect idea which alone provides absolute wisdom—that doctrine doesn't exist...Long for perfection in yourself. The divine is within you."

The divine within Joseph Knecht, the main character in Hesse's novel, called upon him to find a way to serve. Orion looked up at us and asked the big question: "So what greater purpose should each of us strive to serve?" With his face illuminated in the lantern's golden light, he gazed around the circle slowly, pausing to stare intensely at each of us individually.

The question of how we might be of good service both enthralled and perplexed Simon and me. We had talked about our dreamy goals, months and years before on the Isla Vista cliffs, and more recently on the bluffs of Mendocino. We both longed for something greater than ourselves, something beyond monetary rewards, some idea or noble purpose, to which we could dedicate our idealistic energies, our passions. Maybe we weren't ready to become refugees living in a forest, but we certainly didn't want our lives to become petty or mundane, rotting away in some office on the fourteenth floor. From the crucible of chaos—the war, the assassinations, the ghetto riots—a new world with new values was emerging, and both of us wanted to play a role in the forging of that transition.

In the morning, after thinking deeply during the night about Joseph Knecht and idealistic service, Simon and I returned to the Mendocino house on the cliffs, back to Allison and Mrs. Moat, with clarified visions of our future. Allison and he were finished, he concluded. Despite their hopes and efforts, their relationship, with all its inherent limitations, had reached its endpoint. And suddenly he had an exit plan: He would accept his uncle's recent offer of a plane ticket to Israel. The uncle had suffered a heart attack and possessed a transferable ticket to the Promised Land. Thus, rather impulsively, and maybe mainly as an excuse to break up with Allison, Simon made his decision. He called his uncle and said he'd take the ticket. In less than two weeks, he would leave for Israel. Though he didn't yet know it, soon he would become a passionate Zionist.

I headed for L.A., to be of some comfort for my father, and to take on a job as a teaching assistant. In a few months, I returned to UCSB and a better teaching assistant job. Soon I would be entering the UCSB credential program. I believed with increasing confidence that education would be the higher goal to which I could dedicate myself.

Allison retreated to Seattle to pursue further music studies. Hopefully, she found a partner better matched for her than Simon, who loved her musical gifts, her sensuality and laughter, but never felt quite comfortable with her feisty independence, her separate and powerful aspirations.

With no one to care for her, poor Mrs. Moat was forced to return to the mental hospital, where at least she would be able to continue her conversations with her deceased husband.

For some inexplicable reason, I wandered back to Mendocino the following summer. A "For Sale" sign stood on the brownish front lawn of the house by the cliffs, now empty again. My thoughts meandered and drifted to my dear friend who was now on an Israeli farm, getting absorbed in a new life and a new relationship. In the cool grey mist, with the ocean waves offering their ancient cadence, like a huge heartbeat echoing from the rock-strewn beach below, I listened to the calm, constant sound of the crashing. Slowly and deeply contemplative, I walked away from the greying-brown wooden house and closer to the edge of the cliffs. Staring out at the silver, fragrant sea, an image of Simon serenely smiling floated through my mind. Taking in slow, deep breaths of the salty air, I felt grateful for the few poignant weeks I had spent here a year before, a time of tenderness and transition, just after my mother had died.

Six

*"Wherever I went, a new life had begun,
Hidden in grass or waiting beyond trees.
There is a spirit abiding in everything."*

—William Stafford, "You Don't Know the End"

As our Mazda wagon cruised through Stockton, Danielle and I calculated that Harris Ranch and our anticipated steaks were about two hours away. We were starting to get hungry and eagerly envisioned those juicy T-bones that awaited us. I guess the lure of meat is pretty natural for most of us.

The carnivorous appetite returned to Simon not long after his arrival in Israel. On a cousin's advice, he had moved to a kibbutz, a commune where everyone ate in a dining hall, and many meals featured chicken or turkey, as well as delicious, non-vegetarian soups.

Not only was he eating meat again, he resumed his interest in Hebrew, the language he had abandoned after we found our starry God together in the Sierras. When he got to the kibbutz, a relatively small one not far from Jerusalem, he joined an *ulpan* program, a six-month arrangement which allowed him to work half a day and study Hebrew the other half.

I was back at UCSB, moving toward getting a teaching credential, and he was milking cows, learning Hebrew and falling in love with his Hebrew teacher. We were writing long letters to each other, trying to better understand the changes we were both experiencing. The letters helped.

In the fall of 1972, I began teaching at Newbury Park High School, a recently built campus just north of Los Angeles, with a predominately young faculty. At the same time, Simon and his new Israeli bride, his former Hebrew teacher, were moving to a new kibbutz, a place they thought would be better for raising their family. He had become a husband and a citizen of Israel.

Yes, my best friend had "tied the knot" with Rachel, an Israeli girl, a native kibbutznik. He'd written me all about her and even sent me a photo of the two of them. "I've found happiness," he wrote rapturously. "I've finally found a woman and a land that make me feel this is exactly where I belong." In the picture, she looked small and pale, with a lovely smile and long reddish-blonde hair. Beside her, Simon appeared tall and satisfied, with a big grin and a bushy beard. She was of Hungarian background, and like so many Israelis, her family was fortunate to have gotten out of Europe alive. Intelligent, kind, and highly educated, Rachel was also a master in the language Simon now was decidedly eager to learn more fluently.

Simon's parents travelled to Israel to witness and participate in his wedding. Even though, like most Jews who grow up on a kibbutz, Rachel was not religious, at least she was a Jew. After suffering through Simon's supposed atheism and his serious relationship with Allison, the *shiksa*, his parents were elated that he had married a Jew, even a non-religious one. And they liked her for more than just her Jewishness.

They could sense she was a strong, confident young woman and that their son was smitten. Rachel and the kibbutz had already led Simon back to eating meat. With a little time and perhaps a child or two, they hoped she could lead him back to their Jewish culture and maybe even their religious traditions. They had suffered too much, escaping the European death camps, for their son to continue rejecting their faith. They believed Rachel was just what he needed to rediscover his sense of being a Jew. And their hopes were eventually fulfilled, when gradually, after many years, Simon began praying in synagogue on Saturday mornings and observing more and more rituals of his faith.

On hearing this part of my story, Danielle laughed and commented that people often have tragic relapses with their "addictions." But she wanted to understand why Rachel and Simon moved to a new kibbutz. What would make them leave the kibbutz where they had met, the home where her sisters and parents still lived? I explained that Rachel and Simon moved because, unlike most Israeli communes back then, their new kibbutz was designed for children to stay with their parents in their own apartments, rather than sleeping separately in a children's house. And the kids came soon. Reuben arrived less than two years after they moved to the new kibbutz. In addition, as a young, new Israeli citizen, Simon was legally required to get his active military service out of the way.

The mere mention of the military startled my wife. Understandably, she questioned how a guy who had been protesting the Vietnam War for years could manage, in good conscience, to serve in the Israeli army. Simon and I had passionately discussed that issue in several of our letters. He thought Israel's near-constant fighting was nothing like our military adventure in Vietnam, and I reluctantly agreed. One was about legitimate defense, and the other was about imperialism and lust for power. Certainly, Vietnam wasn't going to invade the United States, but Egypt, Syria and Jordan definitely seemed poised to attack Israel.

"So Simon was really okay about joining the Israeli military?" Danielle asked quite bluntly.

"Yeah, the Vietnam protester started patrolling the West Bank," I admitted.

The issues were complicated, often making our letters quite long. I recalled his description of having to walk through an Arab village as a patrolling soldier. He struggled to maintain his faith in the cause, yet as the eyes of the local residents stared at him with wariness and contempt, watching his every step, he thought back to our time during the Isla Vista riots when we, like the Arabs, were the ones staring with hate in our eyes at our foreign invaders, the police and the National Guard.

Danielle questioned how an essentially liberal-spirited person like Simon could justify the continued occupation of land that had belonged to the Palestinians. "Simon's heart was so sensitive—I don't understand how he could fight for Israel and be a part of all that aggression. I didn't know him well enough or was not bold enough to ask him that question." I could feel Danielle's stare. I reminded her that although Simon would admit there was a major Palestinian problem, he would always emphasize the huge populations of hostile neighbors that surround Israel, and he would refer back to the Holocaust, the ultimate horror that at least somewhat justified what otherwise might be thought of as aggression or cruelty.

This discussion rekindled a tension between Danielle and me. She wanted to know whether I went along with this belief that the Holocaust justifies the kind of things Israel is doing these days— the continued occupation and all the settlements they've built on Palestinian lands. Like Simon, I feel somewhat defensive about the land of my blood relatives, and I responded with the rationalization that although some Israeli militarism is unquestionably aggressive, the country has faced an authentic existential threat, a justification that certainly doesn't apply to American military aggression. I could hear myself sounding like Simon, who was very intense and convincing in expressing this point. He grew irate with American "liberals" who would scream about tiny Israel's supposed imperialism while passively accepting American invasions, coups, and bombings.

Simon's military service was only a small part of his ten years in Israel. I described for my wife how he plowed and developed a vineyard. He even got to visit Southern France, probably not far from where she used to live, to learn some of their grape-growing and wine-making techniques. Simon loved becoming a farmer. The days of cruising the California coast in a blue Fiat roadster were long gone. On the kibbutz, he powered around on an old green tractor. By the end of 1975, not long after my father died, I was able to get to Israel and see him in his vineyard on that tractor.

"So first you lose your mother, and you voyage to Mendocino to see your best friend. Then five years later, you lose your father, and again you choose to see this friend," Danielle said, her voice filled with compassion. "But this time you have to go all the way to Israel. When you were most hurt and most vulnerable, you chose to spend time with Simon."

I explained how, following my father's death, I felt the urge to go to Europe, to see where he came from, and then travel to Israel to be with Simon. Leaving behind a serious relationship with a faculty colleague who had a small son, I took a leave of absence from teaching and then, just as Simon had done four years earlier, I hitchhiked across the United States.

After that amusing adventure, highlighted by an exciting few days with a tantalizing golden-haired siren from Tulsa, I flew to Amsterdam where I bought an old VW van. It provided me with a bed and a mini-kitchen. For about ten days, I drove through France, mostly checking out smaller towns and reviving my French, reading *The Stranger* again and trying to make sense of *Le Monde*.

I headed toward Luxembourg, my father's old home. He and his immediate family had managed to escape from Europe and the Nazi genocide, but four of his mother's sisters, my great-aunts, were murdered in Auschwitz. For me, as I travelled through places where swastikas once lined the streets, the aura of the war remained, even though it had ended thirty years earlier. I could see and feel it in the weary, wrinkled faces of older people I met on my walks, wondering to myself as I stared, which of them had probably loved the Third Reich.

Reaching Luxembourg, I visited one of my dad's surviving uncles, a kind, forgiving man who was able to return from the States to his native country after the war. Small and slightly plump, with gentle brown eyes, Uncle Jules lived without complaint among his neighbors, those who had complacently tolerated years of Nazi occupation and the "cleansing" of neighborhoods just a few decades earlier. Despite its Nazi legacy, Luxembourg, to my father's youngest uncle, represented culture and civilization. Living across the street from a beautiful park, he loved the fine local white wines and the delicious smoked ham, which he was sure Moses would have blessed as kosher, had he tasted it. His lack of orthodoxy and his ability to joke about it showed an independence of spirit I admired. He spoke lovingly of his deceased wife, whose pictures were everywhere, and I appreciated his old stories, his warmth and hospitality. I imagined my father's childhood was relatively happy in little Luxembourg—at least until the Nazi madness got too close.

After spending a week with Uncle Jules in Luxembourg, I headed south and east toward Italy. Michelangelo's David beckoned me. I longed to see the naked youth who launched a small stone that changed history. The city of Firenze, of course, is a place celebrated for its beauty and immortal art, but after standing under a glass dome and gazing with awe for many minutes at the gleaming white marble hero who stood so relaxed and completely at ease, I soon began to grow restless. The constant rain was getting to me. After only two days in Firenze, rather impulsively, I decided to leave the fabled city.

With women dilemmas and father issues pressing on me, I drove all night, my troubled mind buzzing. Why had my relationship with Bonnie, the dark-haired teacher I'd been dating in California, been so arduous? Why couldn't I simply allow myself to love her and her young son more fully? And how could I leave her, and so quickly and so easily jump in the sack with a stranger, an uneducated woman from Tulsa, who had picked me up hitchhiking and worked in a car dealership? And how had I failed to appreciate and manifest my love more consistently for my overworked, ever-humble father? Why had I complained so much about his shortcomings while Simon smiled tolerantly about his dad's far more blatant flaws? Driving all night, the prickly, haunting questions never stopped, until finally, my orange-and-white, shoebox-shaped home rolled into Rome, just as dawn's first light arrived.

After several days in the legendary imperial capital, anxious to see Simon, I sold the van and bought a plane ticket to Israel. There was a large, looming question I wanted to ask this closest friend whom I had not seen in years. Actually, I had two questions—one that I knew I would ask, and one that I wanted to ask, but didn't know whether I'd have the guts. The question I knew I would ask concerned Simon's father, something haunting my conscience for months, ever since my dad passed away so suddenly and unexpectedly. I simply couldn't understand how Simon had somehow managed to be far more sympathetic and understanding of his dad than I had been of mine.

My dad was a kind, sweet man whose life opportunities had been ruined by the rise of the Nazis. Living in Luxembourg, only fifteen miles from Germany, his father had realized Jews were increasingly being dismissed from professional jobs, so he persuaded my father and his younger brother to drop out of school when they were in their early teens. My uncle learned the craft of working with animal furs. My father, who already knew five languages, apprenticed in Brussels and Paris, learning the art of jewelry. But when the Nazis began their conquest of France, he escaped to Marseilles, caught a ship to Haiti, and made it to Cuba. His fluency in German, French and English helped him get admitted into the U.S. just before we got into the war. Of course, he immediately got drafted, but he managed to meet my mother in a most amazing way.

L.A.'s Union Station was a wild scene during the war. There were too many people who wanted to get on the trains, so priorities were established: soldiers got on first, close family of soldiers got on next, and finally, if there were any seats left, other civilians were allowed to board. Scanning the room full of uniformed young men, surely searching for a kind, Jewish face and hoping to improve her chances of getting on that train, my mother walked up to my father and asked, "Will you say you're my husband?" He gladly agreed. They sat together, hit it off instantly, and were married a few months later.

Their marriage lasted twenty-eight years, but my mother's death led my father to the uncomfortable world of dating. Women liked him; however, he hardly knew how to handle it. I watched him struggle with horrible guilt and tension because of his women problems. He'd been seeing and sharing intimacy with two ladies at the same time, not telling either about the other, and he suffered through his role in deceiving both of them. At least he could honestly tell me about his predicament, and I could see from his obvious anxiety that his lies of silence had caught up with him, and he definitely needed to resolve the situation. I told him so rather frankly. After much reflection, including a soul-searching trip back to Europe, he decided he wanted to try living with one of the two women. Painfully, he realized he would have to own up to the truth and tell the other woman their relationship was finished. This difficult meeting and his embarrassing, face-to-face confession caused him enough stress to land him in the hospital the morning immediately after the awkward rendezvous. Three days later, he died from a massive heart attack, but at least I was able to see him a few hours before he passed away.

Modern hospitals provide some sort of medicine that can keep a person alive for several hours even following what ends up being a fatal heart attack. When I arrived at the hospital, I found my father, half-reclining in his raised hospital bed, quite conscious and even able to talk, though the doctors were telling my sister and me that he had only a miniscule chance of surviving. I wondered how fully he understood that he probably had only hours to live. Certainly, I wasn't ready for him to pass. Unlike cancer, heart attacks don't give you much opportunity to reach closure with a loved one. There hadn't been enough time to fully express my love.

After my father died, I started thinking more about Simon and his dad. What I knew was that Simon never directly criticized his father. I knocked my dad plenty—in conversations with Simon and with others. Why wasn't my dad more assertive, more independent in expressing his beliefs, more willing to contradict my mother? For instance, he wasn't nearly as religious as my mom, but I didn't even discover this fact until after she died. He didn't really care whether my girlfriends were Jewish. So why then had he not defended me when my mom was screaming at me hysterically about my *shiksa*-girlfriend and the half-Jewish, identity-bewildered children we might have. Yes, I had lots of gripes against my gentle, reliably reasonable father, and I had shared them with Simon without self-censorship.

But here was Simon, who had a genuine ogre for a father. He was a domineering, callous bully, about whom I had never heard his son utter a word of harsh criticism. I knew of their clashes—about God and vegetarianism, among other things. I knew Simon laughed and raised his eyebrows in disbelief at times, but he never spewed hatefulness or anger about his irascible father, and I wanted to know why. That was the first question I wanted to ask him when we reconnected in Israel.

My wife knocked me lightly on the shoulder. "And what was the other question?"

The other question was a lot harder for me to talk about. I struggled to share with her something that had disturbed me for years about Simon, yet it was something I had never spoken to anyone about. My voice softened as I revealed my secret: "After he was on the kibbutz for a couple of years, and we were writing each other these long letters," I paused as I thought of how to phrase what I was trying to say. "After about two years, Simon writes me about an affair he's having—an affair he's having with a man."

That last short word riveted my wife's attention. "He had an affair with a man?"

"Yes, I was as surprised as you seem to be."

"You had no idea?"

"Exactly. I had no idea. So here we are, supposedly best friends. We'd lost our virginity together. We'd been discussing the opposite sex and all her mysteries for years. We'd lived together and struggled with our girlfriends together—and okay, he's mentioned sharing a girl with another guy in a threesome, yet still, I have absolutely no idea this whole other reality is going on inside him, and that besides his obvious intense interest in females, he's also lusting after men, or at least, he ends up lusting after one man."

"So what do you do?"

"Basically, I do nothing. I don't know what to say or ask, so mostly I ignore it. In my next letter I write something conspicuously vague like, 'I can tell you've been going through a lot of stress.' But I avoid addressing the topic head-on because, to tell you the truth, I'm half disgusted and definitely hung up just imagining Simon with a man in a sexual way, so I just move on to other less upsetting topics." I flashed Danielle an embarrassed half-smile. "You know it was many years before the term 'homophobia' entered our cultural vocabulary, but clearly, I was suffering from a hearty dose of it."

"And how did Simon react to your evasion of the subject?"

I shrugged. "He didn't mention the guy or the affair for the next two or three letters. Like me, he wrote about other things. And then a short time after Reuben was born, in this one letter, he's mostly writing about his new son, and then he briefly refers to breaking off his relationship with this guy—Alan was his name. He says their thing, whatever it was, is over. He says he doesn't want his son to have a 'queer' for a father."

"So when you meet up with him in Israel, what's the question about his affair that you want to ask him?"

"I didn't know exactly what I wanted to ask him, but because I'd said virtually nothing in my letters about the whole shocking episode, the thing was haunting me. I wanted to know more, but I was afraid."

"What happened when you got to Israel?"

"At first, nothing happened. I wasn't ready to ask any serious questions when I first got to the kibbutz. I was just trying to observe and understand this whole new world that Simon had entered."

I described to Danielle some of the most memorable aspects of Simon's life on the kibbutz. There were about five hundred people in the community, including about fifty who, like myself, were just visiting for a while. We temporaries worked five days a week; the regular members worked six days. There was virtually no money anyone was earning, yet all needs were provided for, which allowed people more free time than people who live in an ordinary capitalist, non-communal society. On the kibbutz, no one had to shop for food, cook, or clean up after meals. There were workers to do that. There were even workers who did the washing and drying of clothes for everyone and helped with your children if you had any. All one had to do was one's job.

My job was installing aluminum roofs on the new turkey houses. The metal edges were sharp, and it was easy to get cut if you weren't paying attention. We worked in pairs, and it was satisfying to see, so immediately and tangibly, the product of one's labor. In contrast, teaching English in a high school was nothing like that because your products, your students' improved skills, were not so immediately and obviously evident. It was nice to be able to look with satisfaction at those long rows of turkey houses with their shiny corrugated roofs.

Simon's job was in the vineyard. He drove his green tractor, plowing away at the brown earth he hoped would eventually lead to bottles of delicious red wine. Sometimes he'd let Reuben ride with him on the tractor, which for a giggling two-year-old must have seemed like heaven. Simon's life had grown as full as his beard. Just before I arrived near the end of November, he and Rachel had their second child, another boy, whom they named David.

The little fellow was just a few months old during the four weeks that I stayed with Simon and Rachel on the kibbutz. Their apartment was quite small, just one bedroom, with a tiny living room, which is where I slept. Rachel would come in during the middle of the night to nurse her new-born son. I would wake up and get to witness in a dreamy state this primordial image of serenity: the long-haired mom in her robe, nestled in a soft chair, offering her nectar to her babe. He would express his delight with little gurgling sounds. Observing this classic scene of utter maternal and infant bliss, I would lie there in the dark on the sofa and think about the relationship I'd left behind in California, the long-haired woman and child I'd thought a lot about recently, especially during my all-night drive from Firenze to Rome. I started to believe that, maybe like Simon, I too might be ready for this change in life, ready to settle down and start a family.

I would get to discuss such matters in depth with my best friend when we got away for a few days to the Red Sea about a week before I was due to leave. There were serious things to talk about, and surely these days camping under the stars by Sharm El Sheikh would provide the best opportunity. I wanted to ask him about his dad and why he put up with him so relatively complacently. Of course, I also wanted to ask him about his affair with Alan. Naturally, this would be much more sensitive and difficult.

As Simon and I sat in the public bus that carried us in about three hours from Israel's middle to her Southern border, with both anticipation and anxiety, I looked forward to our being able to spend uninterrupted time together. I would finally get a chance to ask him those questions that had been tormenting me. Mostly, I was elated at having this opportunity to be together alone, but I also sensed in myself a trace of fear.

Was it possible that my closest friend was now a transformed person sexually? Was it conceivable that he might try to make a move on me? The awkwardness I felt about this uneasy situation remained with me, even decades later, as I struggled to tell my wife about the days and nights I spent with Simon, camping by the Red Sea.

Seven

"Why do you frown on me, you puritans,
And condemn the honesty of my latest poems?
Be thankful for fine writing
That makes you laugh instead of weep.
What people do, an honest tongue can talk about."

—PETRONIUS, *Poems from the Greek Anthology*
 (Translated by Kenneth Rexroth)

SIMON AND I THOROUGHLY LOVED OUR time together by the Red Sea. My unspoken worry that he might want a change in our relationship—that thought disappeared by the time we were setting up our tent our first night there. Whatever change he went through, whatever allowed or motivated him to have a relationship with a man—none of that seemed to have any effect on our relationship. We were still Ronnie and Simon—two guys who had grown up together in L.A. and at UCSB, and who were now camping by the Red Sea, a treasured paradise with exquisite coral reefs.

I understand that Sharm El Sheikh today is very different from the way it was in 1975, when we camped there and experienced that perfect serenity. Today the town and beach are part of Egypt, not Israel. That change resulted from an historic peace agreement negotiated by Jimmy Carter and the leaders of Israel and Egypt, the Camp David Accords. Sadly, the courageous Egyptian leader, Anwar Sadat, was assassinated not long after signing that peace treaty with his nation's dreaded enemy.

Years after our time there together, Simon told me I wouldn't recognize Sharm El Sheikh anymore because so many hotels and restaurants had been built. More tragically, he told me that most of the coral reefs, which had enthralled us with their gorgeous shapes and colors, had been ruined, demolished by Egyptian fishermen using explosives to catch their prey. It was difficult and disgusting to imagine such oblivious desecration and destruction. Although I didn't question him at the time, I wondered to myself, then and afterward, whether Simon's version of this supposed ecological catastrophe might have been colored and exaggerated by his Zionist bias. He had definitely implied that the Egyptians didn't know how to take care of a sacred natural treasure as well as the Israelis.

Sharm El Sheikh in 1975 was a skin-diver's dream. I've been to a few places where the fish may have been equally or even more spectacular, but nothing I had ever seen could compare to the Alice-in-Wonderland-like splendor of those Red Sea coral reefs. Like the countless stars that blew our minds when we first backpacked in Kings Canyon, the extravagant, miraculous beauty of the reefs in all their captivating pastel shades struck us in profoundly spiritual ways. We felt again, through our enlightened eyes, Emerson's great invitation to experience "an original relation to the universe." As Simon and I glided through the warm, clear waters, wide-eyed with awe and gratitude, we both sensed that transcendent cosmic connection that so many great poets and prophets have sung about. This abundance of astonishing, jaw-dropping beauty was not conducive to atheism. Something pretty wonderful had created these incredible, curvaceous living miracles. Through his diving mask, Simon's face under water, revealed his irrepressible joy as he caught my gaze and spread his arms wide, embracing with ecstatic reverence the spectacular, multi-colored spectacle.

Our stay at the Red Sea certainly was conducive to great conversation. Simon and I now had the perfect setting and opportunity to take on the deepest, most meaningful subjects. Rather pathetically, I failed to bring up the subject of his affair with Alan, at least not directly. I had lots of rationalizations for avoiding the confrontation. That's what it felt like—a confrontation and judgment. Why would I want to spoil the comfort and intimacy of our time together by asking for potentially sordid details about his fling with this man I had never met. Simon never even pointed him out on the kibbutz. He never mentioned him. Of course, I never asked. But their thing was over. He didn't want his son to think of his father as a queer. He probably didn't want his best friend to think of him that way either. If I avoided the subject, I was protecting my friend from having to talk about an embarrassing episode that was in the past. At least that's how I tried to rationalize my not asking him about his affair with Alan.

"Cheri, you were simply protecting yourself from embarrassment." I could feel Danielle staring at me and smiling. "You were just a normal man of the time with the normal fearful reactions. I think of how when you first came to France with me, you would squirm a little and be not so comfortable when other men would give you the *bises*, that little kiss on both cheeks."

"I like it more when the *bises* come from a woman."

"Yes, of course, you do." She leaned over and gave me a soft kiss on each cheek. "You know you are a little more conservative than many people would think. So if you could not talk about his affair with this man, what did you and Simon talk about when you camped together?"

"We talked about things connected to our work, books we'd read, movies we'd seen, American politics, Israeli politics. We had no shortage of subjects."

"But what did you discuss that was more personal? Or did you just stay with the safe subjects—the intellectual ones?"

"Of course, we talked personally—at least a little."

"Probably very little. And what did you talk about that was personal?"

"There were two personal things I remember getting into with him. First, there was my relationship with Bonnie, which had definitely reached a critical crossroad, with marriage as a distinct possibility. So, we talked a lot about that. And then there was also that question about Simon's dad and why he never criticized him. I finally got to confront him with the paradox: Why, when his father acted like such an obvious bully, why had he never directly criticized or demeaned the man? And he responded by telling me a story about his father and what happened to him when he was thirteen."

I shared with my wife Simon's unforgettable tale. When Simon's dad was thirteen, it was the early 1930's, and he was living in a small Polish town, just as the most virulent anti-Semitism was flourishing. The young boy, his mother and younger siblings became concerned when their breadwinner, Simon's grandfather, didn't return home for dinner after a day of chopping wood in the forest. His labors provided firewood for local people and a small sum of money for his family. The worried, thirteen-year-old boy ventured into the forest to look for his father. Eventually, he found him, among the trees where he had labored, lying on his back on the ground, with an ax embedded deeply in his forehead and the word *"Jude"* scribbled in blood on his cheeks--a simple four-letter explanation for murder. As Simon related this horrid piece of family history, he looked at me plaintively. With his face shining in the glow of our campfire, he reached his pointed conclusion: "So all and all, what I'm saying is my father has always done, and continues to do, just about the best he can, considering where he came from and what he's experienced."

That story helped me understand Simon's genuinely compassionate acceptance of his dad. Naturally, the ghastly image of what Simon's father had witnessed as a young boy opened my heart and altered the way I looked at the family patriarch as well.

Years later, when Simon and his family were back in the U.S. and I went to their home for one of those big Friday evening Sabbath dinners, I stared at the old parking lot tycoon with far less judgment. Okay, he was still loud and bossy, but from my more sensitized perspective, he seemed far less tyrannical and more like a man who in his own way simply loved life passionately—his family, his fine food and wine. And he relished the odd fact that somehow, he had managed to survive the European genocide—changing his identity, hiding in forests, bartering cigarettes and booze. Yes, somehow miraculously, with God's implicit blessing, he had arrived in America and established a very privileged life. Why shouldn't he be proud and boisterously happy?

On this one particular Sabbath, we were sitting at Simon's dinner table and his dad was finishing his second or third glass of wine, when Simon brought up the recent news about Poland. It was the Eighties, and the Soviet Union was trying to deal with the labor union Solidarity and their powerful, organized strikes across the country. Remembering that Simon's father had grown up in Poland, I looked at him across the candle-lit table and said, "Isn't it amazing that the Russians have decided to invade the poor place with their tanks? They're taking these troubles in your old homeland pretty seriously, right?"

My somewhat casual remark ignited an unforgettable response from Simon's dad. Every trace of happiness the Sabbath gathering and fine wine had brought to his face immediately vanished. With unambiguous clarity and direct reference to his former Polish countrymen, he stared, first at me, then at Simon, and declared: "I hope the Russians go in there and kill them all. They would turn you in for a pound of sugar."

Simon's father's terrifying declaration stunned Danielle as she listened to me describing the scene. She looked at me with the saddest eyes, and her voice cracked with sorrow: "That poor man,

Simon's father...He was so completely broken...To wish for murder like that upon a whole group of people...That is such a sick thing to desire and yet...I suppose you can kind of understand why the poor, suffering man would say such a thing...considering what he had been through."

She redirected our conversation back to the Red Sea. She wanted to know what Simon and I had to say about love. I shared with her what I recalled.

Naturally, Simon had wanted to know about my relationship with Bonnie, the woman I had left in California, the woman I thought perhaps I might marry. Just as we had done years before on the cliffs of Isla Vista, we pondered with frustration how much love is enough, and what constitutes the right kind of love? Of course, Simon had never met Bonnie, and when I tried to describe our relationship, our intellectual and professional affinities as fellow high school English teachers, our parallel dedication to opening students' minds and helping to transform our culture, I realized I sounded a lot like Simon when he talked about Rachel. He would describe their kindred intellectual passions about Hebrew and Israel, the kibbutz and various Jewish writers. Our complements for our erudite ladies seemed to mirror each other.

But something was missing in our cerebrally centered descriptions. We danced around the heart of the matter, the mystery Danielle calls the *"je ne sais quoi,"* which literally means "I don't know what." She truly believes in that strange, inexplicable magic that can mystically unite a couple, a miracle that can mate them forever, or when it's missing, make them go searching elsewhere to fill that aching emptiness. Whether it was out of self-protection, a veiled desire to defend our women, or our own opaque ignorance, Simon and I didn't talk with each other about this most mysterious and crucial part of our relationships.

"You men miss out on the juiciest subjects, the most interesting and intimate things," Danielle chimed in with a smile. "You back away just when you should ask more."

And yet we're supposed to be the stronger sex, I thought to myself with a little embarrassment. Our fear of not knowing a definite answer and our wariness about triggering an unbridled emotional response too often persuade us to avoid the most provocative questions. Good buddies don't stir things up too much, right? Keep it cool and under control.

Simon and I spent three beauty-filled, tranquil days and nights by the Red Sea, but something was missing in our long discussions about love and relationships, something that had been too painful to verbalize. In Simon's case it had led to his affair with Alan and would lead him on to his affair with his secretary and who knows how many others. I did marry Bonnie, and years later, in my case, the missing element eventually led to the break-up of my family. How much love is enough? No, maybe that's not the most crucial question. Maybe it's about the way that other person makes you feel about yourself, the parts of you that your lover recognizes and loves, or fails to notice and cherish. As we sat together by our campfire, with the Red Sea behind us reflecting an abundance of twinkling stars, Simon and I presumed we were discussing the most critical aspects of our relationships, but we were fooling each other as well as ourselves.

Eight

*"Was he free? Was he happy? The question is absurd
Had anything been wrong, we should certainly have heard."*

—W.H. Auden, "The Unknown Citizen"

Our journey toward Los Angeles seemed to be going well enough until we shot past Santa Nella and its cluster of motels, gas stations, and restaurants. It was about two o'clock, the weather was fine, and we were about an hour away from our anticipated Harris Ranch T-bones. Van Morrison's "Into the Mystic" was playing, Danielle was almost sleeping and I was driving, half drifting into a reverie of Simon and me surfing together in Isla Vista, when unexpectedly, we received a call on Danielle's cell. It was Reuben, and the news wasn't good.

His brother David and their mother had returned from Buenos Aires with Simon's body. While Danielle and I listened anxiously on the speaker-phone, Reuben's voice cracked noticeably as he got to the point rather quickly: "It looks like my father did the unimaginable. He had a piece of concrete or steel tied to his body when they pulled him out of the river. The Argentine authorities have ruled that it was a 'probable suicide.' My brother David was able to negotiate that." He paused and I could hear him take a deep breath. "David was able to get them to leave things ambiguous, so we can still probably bury him in a decent part of a Jewish cemetery."

I pulled over to the side of the road, and Danielle and I stared at each other as we listened in disbelief, and Reuben continued. "He didn't leave any suicide note, but he left his wallet and watch and wedding ring on a dresser in their hotel room, and he tip-toed out of the hotel, holding his sandals. The hotel video camera caught that—at four in the morning. So it looks like a suicide, not an accident. I thought you should know. Of course, our whole family is devastated. Nobody imagined that he could do this."

Reuben went on to explain that the suicide issue had to be dealt with discreetly. First of all, there was the unfinished, delicate matter of getting permission for Simon to be buried in the honorable part of the Jewish cemetery, not in a shunned corner relegated for suicides and other disgraced people. Reuben and David would be meeting in a few hours with a rabbi representing the cemetery to make sure that the "probable suicide" declaration from the Argentine police would not exclude Simon from a respectable burial. I wondered whether a little cash under the table would be needed to facilitate things.

There was also the question of keeping up Simon's reputation. According to Reuben, the family expected a packed house for Simon's memorial service in two days. There would be hundreds of people in a Brentwood synagogue honoring Simon as an elite businessman, a generous philanthropist, and an observant Jew devoted to his family. They did not need to know embarrassing details about his marital difficulties or the fact that he killed himself. The general public could be told his death was an accident. Only the immediate family, Danielle and myself, and two other friends, Jerry and Rebecca, would know the truth. Jerry and Rebecca had known Simon and Rachel since their days together on the kibbutz, and the two couples had become very close after they moved to Los Angeles. We would all be obliged to keep Simon's secret to ourselves.

Most importantly, Simon's mother was not to be told the truth about her son's suicide. The family had decided that informing the aged woman with the agonizing facts about her son's death would be cruel and unnecessary. After all, Simon was her golden boy, the perfect son—handsome, immensely successful, and dependably devoted to her. Even believing her son's drowning was accidental, the Holocaust survivor, who was in her early eighties, was going to find it unbearably difficult to handle the loss of her most adored child.

Hearing Reuben's explanations and warnings, I realized immediately that I was being put into that awkward position of becoming an accomplice to a lie. Speaking in front of hundreds of people who knew Simon, I was to conveniently leave out certain prominent facts about his life and death. And interacting with his mother, whom I would see the next day, I was also expected to be part of a small conspiracy of deceit. These expectations and the fact that they were thrust upon me without any choice, made me somewhat uncomfortable. But I won't get too sanctimonious about my honesty because, unfortunately, our slippery lies of silence and convenience are far more common than we would like to admit, and I've certainly participated in my share of them.

The whole family would be gathering at Simon's home, and Reuben hoped we could get there by noon for lunch and a "family meeting." Immediately, I thought of the family meeting David and his wife had demanded, the public confession family meeting and the horrible shame Simon had to bear, maybe enough humiliation to lead him to the edge of the river. The whole confession scene, as I imagined it, reminded me of the ending in *The Scarlet Letter*, in which a revered man publicly confesses his adulterous acts, revealing his pent-up guilt and torment just before he dies in front of everyone. The phrase "family meeting," when Reuben spoke of it, did not sit peacefully with me.

The telephone conversation with Simon's eldest son was relatively brief and one-sided. Like his call the day before, Reuben's electrifying news made me gasp in grief, as I struggled to assimilate the stark new reality. How could such a joyful, successful, exuberant and brilliant person choose to kill himself? And how had I, a reasonably intelligent and sensitive person, managed to avoid seeing any signs, any hint that something so dreadful could happen?

"You had no idea, Cheri, that your friend could be this depressed?" Hearing my wife's question, I felt ashamed and guilty. Yes, how had I allowed myself to be so oblivious? Of course, I hadn't known about all that had happened in his marriage—Rachel's discovery of his affair and their existential crisis as a couple. But even the potential collapse of his marriage didn't necessarily explain his suicide.

In the first minutes after Reuben's horrific phone call, another possibility, like a suspect in an unsolved murder, crept into my mind. I shared my suspicions with Danielle. "Maybe Simon's suicide wasn't just about his marriage being shattered. I think Simon felt pretty crushed by other things, especially by all the anti-Zionism and anti-Semitism that's been on the rise. He spent so much time in the last years researching the Holocaust, immersing himself enough to write two books about the nightmare, and then he looks at all the hatred directed at Israel today, and he thinks about the millions of Israel's neighbors who'd like to see all the Jews drown in the sea...I know he was deeply depressed about that."

"I hope you're not including my son with those anti-Semitic fanatics," Danielle snapped, with an alarmed look.

"Absolutely not," I shot back. "Like me, Albert can be extremely passionate with his opinions, and we may disagree strongly about Israel and how the country should settle things with her neighbors, but your son has nothing in common with those who talk about obliterating Israel and the so-called Zionist cancer."

"I'm sorry if I sounded too defensive. You know how we mothers can be, how our claws can come out, when it comes to protecting our children."

"Relax, it's not that I think of Albert as some sort of crazed jihadist. But I know Simon was in deep pain over what's been going on in the Middle East. The Arabs and the Jews, still at each other's throats. And he thought it all came back to the Holocaust. People hadn't really grasped its lessons. That's what he had come to believe. That's the reason he labored through writing two books on the gruesome subject. And maybe that's also the reason he decided life wasn't worth living anymore."

"Maybe we'll never know the real reason, and maybe there were many reasons. Why someone chooses to die cannot always be understood—even if one chooses to die slowly, like my father, when he grew old and drank himself to the grave, hardly saying anything to anyone. I feel so bad for Simon's family, and for you." Danielle leaned over and kissed me on the cheek.

Shaken to the core by this latest news about Simon, I felt infinitely grateful for this woman sitting next to me, for her love and understanding. I thought about Simon and Rachel and all the pain inflicted by infidelity. I wondered about my friend's secretary—what she looked like, what sort of personality she possessed, and how much she might have known about Simon's depression. One thing seemed clear: Whatever love she and Simon shared during their seven-year relationship apparently was not enough to give him the will to live.

Danielle and I grew quiet as we continued our southward journey. I struggled to more fully accept and understand the horrid news Reuben had just thrust upon us. I scanned my memories, searching for some clue, some subtle hint that Simon had been experiencing the kind of deep depression that could possibly lead to suicide. As I thought of him and his huge smile, I envisioned him lifting a glass of wine and declaring *"le chaim,"* toasting life itself. When could he have lost that belief in the inherent goodness of life?

Of course, suicide might be considered a reasonable philosophic choice under certain circumstances, and Simon was certainly a philosophic person. When he and I were studying literature, the subject definitely came up a few times. I remembered a conversation we'd had about Ernest Hemingway's suicide. Simon had been much more sympathetic about the great author's end than I.

"Maybe he'd just had enough," I remembered him saying. "All the wars, all the drinking, all the love affairs gone sour. He wasn't writing well, and he was getting fat. Maybe he'd just had enough, so he chose to go out with a bang, not a whimper." What seemed pathetic and cowardly to me, Simon apparently admired, or at least could sympathetically understand.

I recalled another literary reference to suicide Simon and I had encountered together. For one of our UCSB classes, we'd read a Japanese novel called *The Sound of Waves*, by Yukio Mishima. Both the protagonist and the author ended up killing themselves. In both cases, the suicides were committed in accordance with the Japanese tradition of *hare kare*, a ghastly ritual which requires the participant to slice himself open through the stomach with a knife. This "honorable" death is supposed to compensate or atone for whatever wrong had been committed. Once again, like the Hemingway example, Simon was decidedly more sympathetic to the victims than I. Where he saw resolute courage, nobility and integrity, I saw utter foolishness, self-deception and futility. I remembered our disagreements being spirited, but never did I even remotely imagine at the time that my friend with the radiant smile might one day choose to end his own life.

Most memorably, Simon and I had both been fascinated by Albert Camus' masterpiece, *The Stranger*, the odd story in which the tragic hero faces death quite stoically. We'd read it in French, with our magnificent high school teacher, Madame Pusey, as well as in English, years later for a UCSB class. The hero, an ordinary fellow named Meursault, calmly awaits execution for a "murder" which was really self-defense. His passivity and the horrible injustice of his punishment enraged me when we read and discussed the book. In contrast, for Simon, Meursault's complacent acceptance of his undeserved fate demonstrated true heroism. Yes, one man's hero is another man's fool. While Simon smiled at the thought of innocent Meursault stoically going to the guillotine, I grimaced at a life thrown away in vain.

The image of Meursault allowing himself to be killed, making no move to save himself, made me think of Bobby Kennedy. Simon and I were both enthralled with our beloved JFK's heroic brother. I know, the young idealistic leader didn't literally commit suicide, yet when he decided to seek the presidency just a few years after John had been gunned down in Dallas, he certainly knew he was gravely risking his own life.

I recalled the time Simon and I got to see the charismatic senator when he spoke to a crowd of thousands crammed together on the lawn at the Santa Barbara Courthouse on a Thursday evening in June of 1968. Martin Luther King had been assassinated in Memphis only two months earlier, yet Bobby Kennedy was undeterred in passionately speaking out, like Dr. King, against the war, against pandemic racism and poverty, and in demanding a dramatically more just and humane society. Five days after we witnessed and raucously cheered his inspiring, extemporaneous speech, and just after he'd won the California primary and looked like he would win it all, he was fatally shot at the Ambassador Hotel in Los Angeles. Oddly, it was the same place where, six years earlier, I'd celebrated my Bar Mitzvah.

Like millions of others, Simon and I felt anguished by Robert Kennedy's assassination and its devastating implications. Our most inspiring and beloved leaders were all getting murdered. But deeply admiring Bobby Kennedy, or anyone who intrepidly risks his own life, is quite different from deliberately choosing to die. I struggled in vain trying to remember anything that hinted more directly at Simon's fatal decision.

Danielle and I smelled Harris Ranch before we reached it. The flat acres with the large cattle herds just north of the restaurant reeked of cow shit. Even with our windows closed tight, the stench from the vast amounts of excrement seeped into our car and began to sicken us. We'd already decided we weren't going to stop there. The latest news about Simon was not the sort of thing to stimulate one's appetite. Similar to my initial reaction to Simon's death, the desire for cleansing that led me to the sauna, I felt a need to purge myself, to deprive myself a bit and abstain from sensual culinary pleasures like steak and salad. Considering the latest news about my friend, what had seemed halfway alluring, now felt quite irrelevant, even slightly disgusting.

Besides, Danielle pointed out a practical benefit to our not stopping for a meal. The afternoon was getting late and it would be best to cross through the mountains known as the Grapevine before dusk. If we had any desire, we could grab something to eat in a few hours, when we expected to arrive at our motel in Santa Monica. "What do say, Cheri? Can you keep driving?"

"Sure, my love. Let's keep driving."

My soulful, beautiful friend had for some unknown reason, or reasons, chosen to end his life. The dark clouds in the distance definitely looked threatening. Although I was already exhausted from eight hours at the wheel, I was happy to delay or forsake dinner. If I could keep on driving, maybe things could make more sense. Anyway, at the moment, I couldn't stand the thought of sitting in a restaurant booth, hearing some cheerful waiter or waitress recite the choices for salad dressings or inform us of the daily special. The groan of the long road ahead, though arduous, seemed far less dreadful.

Nine

*"...To die, to sleep—
No more, and by a sleep to say we end
The heartache and the thousand natural shocks
That flesh is heir to—'tis a consummation
Devoutly to be wished."*

—William Shakespeare, *Hamlet*

As we approached the Grapevine, Danielle and I discussed some of the possibilities, the potential motivations that could have led our friend to the Buenos Aires river at four in the morning. Besides the obvious suspects, his affair being discovered and his obsessive concerns about the Holocaust and anti-Semitism, we thought of other potential catalysts. Maybe something really bad was happening to his company. With five thousand employees spread all across the country and with all the uncertainties and undulations in the capitalist world, Simon felt a burdensome responsibility. He knew his employees wanted raises and better benefits. Two workers from one of the inner-city parking lots had actually been murdered recently in a robbery. Of course, his workers wanted more money. Yet naturally, there were other pressures, needs to maximize profits. His thick curly hair had turned grey very quickly after he became CEO. Was his death possibly a declaration of guilt for some disastrous business deal?

Or perhaps Simon had discovered that he had some disease or deteriorating condition like Parkinson's. Even more than most people, he feared the infirmities that generally come with age. To put it simply, he was scared shitless about growing old. I remembered one oddly ancient guy we'd see occasionally in Isla Vista, where almost everyone is nineteen or in their early twenties. The odd old fellow would walk along the cliffs looking quite pitiful because his torso and head curved downward like the handle of a cane. He could barely elevate his head high enough to see where he was going. I remember Simon shaking his head back and forth at the pathos of the old man's spinal condition. Rather unforgettably, he said, "If I were that old man, I'd just walk off the cliff—before things get worse and he won't be able to see anything but his own smelly feet." Maybe Simon died because he couldn't bear the thought of becoming aged and infirm. His lower back was already in bad shape, and maybe he feared that other parts of his anatomy were also inevitably destined soon to deteriorate and cause increasing pain.

Trying to be positive, Danielle thought we should still hope for the possibility that Simon's death wasn't intentional. "Let's say he just wants to go for a swim—maybe to clear his head from all the drinking and the stress. He jumps in the river and on the bottom, there is this heavy thing with some ropes attached. His foot gets tangled up in the ropes, and he can't escape."

As much as I wanted to believe Danielle's hope-inspired theory, it didn't seem too plausible. I popped the bubble of optimism with a few pointed questions. "Would Simon really go swimming at four in the morning?" I asked. "And why would he be tiptoeing out of the hotel, holding his sandals, if his intentions were innocent?"

Danielle paused and reflected. "It's still a possibility."

"Sure, I guess it's a possibility," I admitted, wishing Danielle's theory were true. I also wished for some remote possibility other than suicide. Maybe Simon was assaulted by someone, a thief who made his death appear as a suicide. Or maybe he went swimming but got caught in some powerful current that entangled his foot in those ropes connected to that heavy thing. Maybe...maybe...I longed for some explanation besides the obvious, anguishing one. Denial is a deep and attractive river.

As we approached the Grapevine, the weather abruptly started to change. The ominous, billowing dark clouds we had seen in the distance rolled in, the wind picked up, and suddenly the sky unleashed massive torrents of rain. Knowing the implications of this development, Danielle and I became noticeably more anxious. We knew that with each minute as the storm intensified, the likelihood increased that the Grapevine would be closed. We knew we might have to take an alternate road if we wished to continue toward Los Angeles. That's exactly what happened.

By the time we reached the Grapevine, it was, in fact, closed due to snow, and all vehicles, even those with chains or four-wheel drive, were being redirected to another highway. Of course, we weren't exactly pleased with this development, but considering what had happened to Simon, the driving detour and delay seemed trivial. We backtracked several miles and made our way to the Mojave Highway in reasonably good spirits, having no conception of what we were about to encounter on our detour route.

At first it wasn't too bad, and we cruised moderately along the alternate route at about forty miles per hour in our little Mazda. But as the road rose into higher elevations, the rain turned into snow, the sky darkened, and we had to go slower and slower. The snow grew heavier and the road more treacherous. Forty miles per hour declined to twenty and then to ten. After about an hour of the heaviest snow, we were creeping along at five miles per hour. The big trucks weren't moving at all. They were all blocking the right lane, with their engines and lights still on, allowing only one lane for the rest of us to somehow keep going. A snowplow ahead helped clear the solitary, narrow path.

Honestly, it was the most difficult, harrowing road journey I've ever experienced, yet to whine about it seemed absurd. What could even a horrendous detour through the snow mean compared to the tragedy of Simon's suicide? Therefore, we accepted the terrible luck and timing of our journey without serious complaint. Had we left Ashland an hour earlier, at six in the morning rather than seven, we could have avoided the snow and made it over the Grapevine, arriving in Santa Monica around five or six in the evening. As it turned out, we wouldn't reach our destination until shortly after one in the morning.

And so, mostly without grumbling, we fought through the raging snow and horrible road conditions that night. We thought about Simon and the torment that led him to the Argentine river. Why hadn't I heard, why hadn't I sensed his pain, his overwhelming suffering? Watching the relentless snow cover every patch of visible land, I thought about Simon and how somehow, without my noticing it, his delight for life had been inexorably extinguished, frozen and smothered like the lush green landscape that had just transformed right in front of us into white emptiness.

During those hours of driving through the snowstorm, Danielle and I were mostly quiet. Our focus was on making it through the mountains in one piece, not getting stuck in the snow, avoiding the diesel-spewing trucks stopped a few feet away on our right. When things finally began to get a little easier, we did talk a bit more about Simon. One thing Danielle wanted to know was why he had chosen to leave the kibbutz. As an ardent socialist, Danielle thought Simon's life there, plowing his vineyard and participating in a vibrant community, sounded idyllic. I reminded her of the not-so-great aspects of kibbutz life that led Simon to move back to California.

Simon ran into two painful conflicts with the kibbutz that made him decide to leave the would-be Utopian community. They both occurred about the same time. First, there was the winery project. My friend had been successfully growing grapes for nearly a decade, and he was led to believe a winery would be built on the kibbutz. He'd travelled to France, read books and studied the techniques of master winemakers. For years, he'd plowed his fields, trimmed and fertilized his vines, anticipating that soon the kibbutz would be producing fine red wines for its members' own use and for profitable sale and export. Waiting for the kibbutz to give its assent to the winery project, however, turned out to be a little like waiting for Godot: What was expected and highly anticipated, never arrived.

At its heart, the kibbutz was an entirely democratic enterprise. Members met each week to vote and make practical decisions, like how many new clothes-washing machines should be bought, how many new turkey houses should be built, or whether they should begin construction of a new winery. Simon's prospective winery did not arouse the popular support that he had hoped for and envisioned. The project was rejected in a close vote. Most members thought the existing vineyard was working efficiently, yielding a small, yet dependable profit. They considered the winery a somewhat risky adventure that should be postponed until the kibbutz finances were on firmer ground. In other words, Simon was told to keep waiting for Godot. Understandably, this decision deeply disappointed and disillusioned him.

The other kibbutz decision that exasperated my friend involved his father. The family patriarch had suffered a moderate heart attack in the summer of 1980, and Simon wanted to fly to the U.S. to be with his parents. His desire to make this trip was not looked upon favorably by the kibbutz. A member was required to ask permission to make a journey like this, and other members could then vote on the proposal. Simon's request to see his dad was rejected by a democratic vote. Most other members regarded his prospective trip as a luxury they couldn't afford. Simon's family could have provided the money but using private funds for such private indulgences invited socialistic condemnation. Making matters worse, Simon and his family had visited their relatives in California just a year earlier. Furthermore, his father was not in critical condition, and most importantly, Simon's labors were needed in the vineyard, where his expertise was crucial.

Coming in close proximity, these two decisions by the kibbutz members triggered something in my friend. Perhaps the need for a major transition was already brewing and just needed a catalyst to make it explode. Essentially, he concluded that he had to leave the kibbutz because he could no longer subordinate his personal autonomy to the will of the community. He was sick of asking for permission. By the time the Seventies had turned into the Eighties, and Ronald Reagan was beginning his presidency, Simon moved with his wife and children to the United States. They would live in Los Angeles and Simon would join his family's parking lot company. Hopefully, his father's authority as one of the firm's top leaders would not feel as oppressive as the collective decisions of the kibbutz.

It was when we were in Mendocino together, just after we had graduated from UCSB and my mother had died, that Simon first told me he would be going to Israel. His uncle had offered him that gift of a plane ticket that would propel him into new experiences and also extricate him from his doomed relationship with Allison. He'd predicted to me that he expected to be in Israel six, maybe ten weeks. Ten weeks turned out to be ten years. He entered Israel as a bachelor and left with a wife and three sons.

When he returned to California, Simon's life was dramatically transformed. He left a kibbutz life where money was practically non-existent, and he entered a world of intense business deals involving millions of dollars. The parking lot company started by Simon's father and uncles was already hugely successful, but Simon's abilities contributed greatly to the company's fortunes. He rose quickly to the top echelons of power and made shrewd real estate deals that reaped large profits.

Instead of living in his six-hundred square foot, two-bedroom kibbutz apartment, Simon and his family moved to a modest section of Beverly Hills. Their home wasn't as large or luxurious as the one they would move to in Brentwood several years later, but it was several times larger than their kibbutz apartment. This transition from austerity to luxury, from a simple agrarian life to a mega-capitalist urban existence led me to playfully start calling Simon "Siddhartha." Like the hero of the Hesse novel we both adored, Simon's outer life had undergone complete transformation, but inwardly, he remained the same beautiful, truth-seeking soul. His clothes had become more formal and expensive, but we could still have our deep conversations and laugh together at whatever profound observations we might be sharing.

As Danielle and I continued plodding our way through the snow, which seemed to be lightening up a bit, I explained how my relationship with Simon, once he moved back to the U.S., was nothing like the friendship we shared when we were younger. We lived about sixty miles apart, and we both became immersed in our jobs and in raising our families. He was working in downtown Los Angeles making major business decisions. I was living in Ventura and teaching high school English to a hundred and sixty students a day. Simon was raising three sons. I was raising a stepson and two daughters.

And maybe a few things were coming between us that potentially bothered us and separated us a little, things that were touchy and difficult to talk about. I think each of us in our own way suffered guilt from implied judgments. I questioned how Simon could tolerate the suit and ties, the long hours and capitalist amorality of his big business world. I felt perplexed trying to comprehend why in the world he had begun to enjoy praying on Saturday mornings in an Orthodox synagogue, a choice that, considering some of our mutual spiritual experiences, seemed like getting jammed into a shoebox, after you've been jetting across the cosmos like a shooting star. And on the other side of our mostly repressed, shadowy criticisms, I think Simon was surprised that I still liked smoking my mood-enhancing herb every day, and perhaps my friend, who after all, climbed to become CEO of a huge company, questioned my relative complacency toward my career in education, my willingness to settle for being a high school English teacher, never even going for chairman of the department or a university job. Even though these subtle, latent judgments were probably mostly imagined, they still may have pushed us apart without our being fully conscious of it. Yet despite some widening differences in our lives and lifestyles, we still felt close and connected.

We'd see each other a few times a year. He might come up to Ventura and we'd walk on the beach, throw a Frisbee and catch up on our lives. Or I'd go down to have a Friday evening dinner with him and Rachel as part of a Los Angeles weekend, in which I could also visit my sister and her two boys. Sometimes, he'd treat me to a Lakers game, or we'd take in a concert, a play, or a film. Somehow, Simon and I never lost that sense of connection and intimacy when we got together, but our individual preoccupations, our responsibilities and our distractions, made us see each other less and less. We still felt like soulmates, uniquely connected, even as we allowed ourselves unintentionally and unnoticeably, to drift further away from each other.

As I described these years after Simon's return to California, Danielle pushed me a little more, wanting to better understand why Simon and I didn't make more of an effort to see each other or communicate more often. Like the snow that was still lightly falling all around us, making our passage through the mountains so difficult, my wife's questions about Simon and me were discomforting. She reminded me that even in the handful of years that she'd known us, I hadn't made that much effort to see or talk to Simon, and when we did get together, she knew we would inevitably get into some intense debate, usually about Israel or some other contentious issue, rather than speak about more personal things.

"So, you think of Simon and me as being argumentative?" I asked, somewhat defensively.

"That would be putting it mildly." She flashed me that look that let me know she was ready to say something she thought I needed to hear. Fine...I was tired of trying to describe my various memories and perceptions of Simon. It was time to hear my wife's thoughts about our lost friend.

Ten

"In later life this economical tendency to leave the old undisturbed, leads to what we know as 'old fogeyism'...Old fogeyism begins at a younger age than we think. I am almost afraid to say so, but I believe that in the majority of human beings, it begins at about twenty-five."

—WILLIAM JAMES, *Talks to Teachers*

ALTHOUGH DANIELLE HAD KNOWN SIMON ABOUT one tenth of the time that I'd known him, she had her own vivid images of him, her own sharp perceptions and opinions. It's difficult to admit, but in some ways, she seemed to see and understand his behavior better than I did. She prides herself on her ability to relate to people, to disarm them into being more open and revealing than they normally would. It's a talent she's developed and perfected, and I've seen her use it on lots of people. But Simon had become a Zen-master at evasion, and even Danielle had trouble penetrating his shield.

Danielle and I had been married only five years at the time of Simon's death. She had come to Newbury Park High School as a part of what was supposed to be a one-year teacher-exchange program. It was September of 2004, and I was in my last years of teaching, struggling to cope with the potential re-election of George W. Bush. My penchant for ridiculing the president had landed me in the principal's office and my doctor's examination room. Because of parent complaints and high blood pressure, I was being told by two different authority figures, a principal and a doctor, that I needed to calm down.

It was during my prep period, period three, that I first met Danielle. A few weeks earlier, she'd been briefly introduced, along with a few other new teachers, at a faculty meeting, but I hadn't met her personally until that morning in the faculty cafeteria. I was sitting at a table, grading through a pile of papers and sipping coffee when I noticed her across the nearly empty room, reading from her own thick stack of papers. With her cup of coffee, she was very slowly enjoying a piece of chocolate cake. She had short-cropped blonde hair, a long willowy neck, and thin, muscular arms that tapered down to a delicate wrist. But what particularly caught my attention was her slight smile and her look of utter relaxation. She seemed so beautifully content as she leisurely savored each bite of the freshly baked, dark brown delight. I decided to walk across the room and introduce myself.

For certain reasons, some more mysterious than others, we immediately connected. She loved the fact that I knew some French and could pronounce her name, Madame Rochette, the maiden name she had regained after her divorce. In addition to our French connection, I loved the fact that she laughed when right away, I confessed my major anxieties about teaching in a public school while a jingoistic President deceives us into fighting a completely unnecessary war. Clearly, she understood the duplicity involved in America's premeditated invasion, and yet she laughed. Intrigued by her nonchalance, I asked, "How can you seem so carefree and lighthearted when you know all this killing and destruction, this whole invasion of Iraq, is based on complete lies?"

"I laugh so that I can still enjoy life. I am not going to let little Monsieur Bush or any other crazy leader take away my *joie de vivre*. That would give him entirely too much power." I admired her apparent ability to rise above what was driving me crazy.

In that first half hour together, we broke through the usual superficialities that make most conversations so dull. I learned a bit about her childhood in Provence, her marriage and its demise, her motherly worries about her idealistic son, her dreamy ideas about California that had led her to Newbury Park High School. And before I realized what she was doing, she had disarmed me into revealing far more than I normally would about my marriage and its demise, my guilt about emotionally damaging my daughters, my tendency for relationships that lasted about two years, and the painful awareness that my present relationship had apparently reached its expiration date.

By the time the bell rang for us to go to our next class, I managed to get her phone number. Within weeks, we were dating. By Christmas vacation we were living together, and by the time the following school year began and Danielle had been rehired at NPHS, we got married.

Our wedding was at our favorite Ventura park, the one right beside the ocean and the marina. Danielle's dad, assisted by his gradual plunge into more frequent and bountiful glasses of wine, had died a few years earlier, but her mother managed to make the long journey from Provence to see her daughter marry a nice Jewish boy from California. Admittedly, in her mother's mind, a Jewish background wasn't as good as being Catholic, but it wasn't nearly as bad as coming from a Muslim family, like her previous son-in-law. Somewhat frail and unaccustomed to travelling, she definitely wanted to support her daughter and celebrate her marriage. She was intrigued by the idea of our getting married in a park rather than a church or synagogue, or a city hall, where most young people in France today exchange their vows.

Our reception was about a mile up the beach from the park where we married. It wasn't the Ritz or the Hilton, but our modest setting was comfortable, in the upstairs part of our tennis club, with the ocean right across the street. Danielle's mother, the other Madame Rochette, looked quite splendid in a silvery gown as the dancing began. We didn't hire a band, but our favorite music sounded great on a portable stereo—Linda Ronstadt, Michael McDonald, Annie Lennox, Francis Cabral. The slender, small French woman swayed with pleasure as she listened to the music. Inexplicably, Simon was drawn to her.

He was able to charm her with his elementary French and his ability to ask a few personal questions that made her feel important. His greatest gift to my mother-in-law, however, was in asking her to dance. It worked out perfectly since Simon's wife, Rachel, didn't really enjoy dancing. So one of the highlights of our wedding day, and we captured it all on video, was the sight of Simon and Madame Rochette gliding all over the dance floor together. Fast or slow, rock or love song, they moved so comfortably and smiled so brightly that some who were there and didn't know better, probably thought they were a couple.

Obviously, Danielle was delighted to see her mother so enchanted on our wedding day. That was the first thing she brought up when she began her recollections of Simon, as we continued our drive through the dark mountains. Fortunately, the snow was getting less threatening, and we were able to increase our speed a little and relax our nerves a bit.

"You know I came to love Simon very much on the day of our wedding. He was so handsome in his black suit and white shirt. He was so much more formal than everyone else, but the way he danced with my mother that day, the way he won her heart—I will never forget that. My mother thought he was the most charming American she had ever met."

"Maybe she thought you were marrying the wrong guy. But you know, even with all of his charm, he wasn't really American."

"What do you mean?" Danielle looked at me with a startled gaze.

"I mean he spent the first eight years of his life in a Displaced Persons Camp in Germany."

"Thanks for the technical detail, a rather important detail, you've never mentioned. But may I go on now?" She hesitated, then continued. "My point is simply that I could see on our wedding day that Simon was really an exceptionally kind man—so sensitive and intelligent. He could see and feel my mother's vulnerability that day. He could understand her worry and her shyness, and so with just a few French words and a few dances, for my mother, he turned what would have been an awkward, lonely evening into a wonderful celebration. And for me to see that happiness in my mother, it made our wedding day that much happier. So that is the first thing I think of when I think of Simon."

"What about your perceptions of Simon and me being so argumentative? I don't really see it that way."

"That's because you argue with everybody. To you, it's just talking."

"And what do you think we argued about so much?" I asked.

"You know the answer to that question."

"Okay, I know Israel became a pretty hot topic for us. But it's not as if we couldn't talk about it."

"No, you talked about it all the time. You would criticize Israel for some new settlements in the West Bank or some new attacks, and he would be on the defensive. I think you talked more about Israel and American imperialism than your own personal lives. Politics, literature, movies—all this was easier for you to discuss than more intimate things. That's how it was for Simon and you, isn't that so?"

Although it was painful, I had to acknowledge the truth in my wife's observations. Simon and I had been more comfortable and spent more time dissecting the ills of the world, rather than sharing details of our personal lives. He'd offer me his latest thoughts about the Middle East and Israel's pressing predicaments. I'd share my latest revelations about the CIA or the mysteries of 9/11. Unfortunately, we didn't spend enough time focusing on our own more personal mysteries.

Placing her hand on the back of my neck and squeezing some of the tension from it, Danielle softened her tone and tried to clarify. "Simon was not an easy person to understand. He could look you in the eyes and ask you very personal questions about your life. But if you returned the favor and turned the question around toward him, he could avoid it, like the way a matador steps away from the horns of the bull. Simon was a master at this. He preferred to be the one asking the questions. And when they would come back at him, the personal questions, he could be as vague and evasive as a good politician."

"Do you remember what he would say whenever the subject of his marriage came up?"

Danielle grinned at my question. "You mean that thing he used to say about Rachel being the perfect wife for him?"

"Yeah. What did you think when you heard him say that?"

She paused. "I thought he said the words like they were cute or endearing, but who knows what he meant. I thought perhaps he was admitting that he liked the way she took care of their home so well—that she did all the shopping and cooking and dishes. When he said she was the perfect wife, I thought he was admitting that he was an old-fashioned man in his heart. He liked having a smart, educated, artistic wife with whom he could discuss books and plays and movies. But he also liked having this wife taking care of everything at home in the traditional way. His perfect wife had brains but no real career of her own, so she could devote herself almost entirely to him and their children—the perfect wife!"

"Did you think he and Rachel shared a good marriage?" I asked with a slight smile.

"Cheri, that's a hard question. Of course, they seemed happy enough and respectful toward each other, but you remember, don't you, from *Le Petit Prince*, that most important line?"

"What line?" I searched for the phrase she might mean.

"That what is most important is invisible to the eye."

"That certainly applies to Simon's suicidal thoughts," I said, turning toward my wife.

"Maybe it also applies to his marriage," Danielle responded, grabbing my hand. "We think we see how two people act together, but perhaps it's just an act, an image they wish to project, and not the reality of their relationship."

"So what do you think was the reality behind Simon and Rachel's relationship?"

"I think that although he tried to hide it, Simon felt superior to Rachel and didn't fully respect her intelligence."

Her words to me seemed surprisingly accusatory. "What makes you believe that?" I asked.

"All the times he would respond to something she was saying by laughing at her and asking, 'So what's your point, Rachel?' Just because she would express things in her own way, not in the way that he would express himself, he would act as if she were somewhat thick in the head, rambling on with pointless words."

"So what's your point, Danielle?"

"Cheri, that is not so funny," she replied, poking me in the stomach for emphasis. "If you would talk to me in that same patronizing tone that Simon could sometimes use with Rachel, you would be a lonely guy again, looking for a new girlfriend."

"I think I get your point," I said, trying to avoid any hint of condescension. "Do you remember the last time we saw them?"

"Of course. The four of us had dinner in their backyard at the end of August. Simon barbecued some chicken. The two of you went swimming."

"What do you remember most about that afternoon or evening?"

"I remember his back was hurting him, and he complained about the pills he was taking. And I remember his talking about their recent trip to India and his struggle to deal emotionally with the horrible poverty he and Rachel had seen. I think it got to him more than he expected. I remember him asking, with such an intense look on his face, 'How is anyone supposed to enjoy the splendor and beauty of the Taj Mahal when it's surrounded by emaciated, begging children with desperate eyes?' What I remember most about that last day we saw him is something Simon said to me when we were alone. I never told you this, but I had confessed to him that sometimes I still worry about the two of us. I worry about your attraction to other women. I question whether you will get tired of me."

"Or whether you'll get tired of me," I interjected.

"That has not been my problem, and will you please stop interrupting me?"

"Absolutely."

"So your beloved friend takes me by the hand, he looks right into my eyes, and he says in the kindest, most reassuring voice: 'Listen to me, Danielle. I've known Ronnie practically my whole life. I've seen him with other women, and I've watched the boredom grow. He's not getting bored with you and he's not going anywhere.' That is what he said to me, and that's what I remember the most about our last visit with Simon."

On hearing this, I felt a great wave of gratitude for my lost friend. Here he was, calming my wife's fears about our relationship in the most loving way, even as his own marriage was about to explode a few weeks later when his affair would become known. While he reassured Danielle that she had nothing to fear about our future, it was his future that should have howled for our attention. After all, the lies of his double life were about to become unveiled and erupt into a chaos that would end up with him tiptoeing toward the Rio de la Plata in Buenos Aires. But of course, that last day we saw him, he acted as if everything with him, and everything with him and Rachel...everything was just fine.

The snow was no longer falling. We climbed out of our treacherous mountain detour and reconnected with Interstate 5. Finally, we were able to drive at a normal freeway speed again, but it was nearly midnight, and our nerves were shot. About an hour and a half later, nineteen hours after we began our unforgettable journey, we pulled into our Santa Monica motel, physically and emotionally drained.

Eleven

"Do I contradict myself?
I am vaster than I thought—
I contain multitudes."

—Walt Whitman, "Song of Myself"

After our grueling and emotionally exhausting journey, we slept later than usual, but during the night, I woke up several times, trying not to obsess on certain images. I envisioned Simon leaping into a dark river, drifting to its bottom, struggling in frantic futility to untie the ropes he himself had knotted. His eyes bulged with the terrifying realization of his fate. I could see his body in its final convulsions, until finally it was still, and bubbles emerged from his mouth. I tried, mostly in vain, to escape from these ghastly images, unable to find much calm or restful sleep, despite my exhaustion. But what's a tortured mind and a disturbed sleep compared to the absurd horror of self-inflicted death?

By eight the next morning, Danielle and I began walking toward the ocean, which was only about a half mile away. I wanted a chance to sit by the water's edge and put together some thoughts for Simon's memorial service the following day. Danielle wanted to get a good cup of coffee and read the newspaper. She had a recent issue of *Le Monde* in her purse. We parted ways, agreeing to meet two hours later at the beach. She found her way to a nearby Starbucks, while I, notebook and pen in hand, located a fine spot beneath the cliffs on the wide, white-sand Santa Monica beach.

Sitting on the sand and staring at the waves collapsing on the frothy shoreline, I thought about Simon as the words and music of Leonard Cohen's hypnotic "Suzanne" swirled through my mind. Simon and I both adored Leonard Cohen in general and that song in particular. I could picture Simon's face, entranced in listening, as I played guitar and sang the poetic images. The middle verse about Jesus seemed especially poignant at the moment: "*He sank beneath your wisdom like a stone.*" Yes, that's exactly what happened with Simon and me. For reasons I couldn't begin to fathom, my best friend had chosen to end everything and drown himself in a dark, foreign river.

Thinking of what to say for Simon's memorial service wasn't that easy. Of course, there were the obvious things that I knew needed to be avoided—his suicide, his teetering marriage, his seven-year affair with another woman. Some of my most memorable experiences with Simon, our adventures involving women or psychedelics or Isla Vista riots, would also, for the sake of propriety, best be avoided or at least mentioned only vaguely. After all, the audience would consist of several hundred Angelenos, most of them well-off, business-oriented, slightly conservative, Jewish and probably halfway religious. They might not appreciate stories about Simon and me setting a car on fire or diving naked into the ocean with our girlfriends on an LSD-enhanced afternoon. My mind wandered, searching for memories that might be more suitable for sharing.

I thought of when I first got to know Simon in junior high school. No, better stay away from that story about him pulling out a *Playboy* centerfold in the hallway. But that memory triggered other images that could be shared. I thought of our unforgettable ninth-grade English teacher, Mr. F.F. Doucette. He was also our homeroom teacher, so we got to appreciate his antics for all three of our vitally impressionable years at Bancroft Junior High.

A tall, elegant man with a most expressive face, horn-rimmed glasses, and a ringing baritone voice, F. F. Doucette became an inspirational figure in our lives because he was completely and blissfully liberated from any ordinary constraints of conformity. As an English teacher, he drilled us on grammar and infused us with enthusiasm for great literature and exquisite beauty. That included an appreciation for beautiful females. He would ask Bonnie Radford, a girl who looked like a potential future Playmate, to come to the front blackboard and write a few key words on the board. Then, placing his chin on his hand and smiling broadly like a connoisseur of fine art beholding a masterpiece, he'd ask her to point to a word, and as the slender, blonde, compliant girl followed his instructions, he would excitedly exclaim, "What superlative exquisiteness!" or "Oh my! What a veritable gem!" Once, he'd shook his head and declared, "With such magnificence among us, I foresee a transcendently glistening future...for our nation!"

Rather insensitive to how Miss Radford might feel, Simon and I and our classmates would laugh raucously at this routine, but our favorite of Doucette's many inspired rituals involved his checking of our homework. He would walk up and down the aisles to see that our homework was done, and if our efforts looked praiseworthy, he would smile widely, and addressing us as "Herr" Lieberman or "Herr" Hertz, he would offer a succinct complement for all to hear and then pound the back of our hand just above the wrist with a rubber stamp bearing his name, F.F. Doucette. Then came the part Simon and I loved best. For really great-looking homework, he would shout, "Oh my! The other hand cries out with shrieks of jealousy!" And excitedly, in his delighted madness, he'd pound the other hand of the deserving recipient with his rubber-stamped personal gift of honor. (Years later, to my delight, I realized this "jealousy" game could be played with other parts of the human anatomy. Thank you, Mr. Doucette.) Anyway, Simon and I were enraptured by the man, and on our graduation day we brought him a smuggled bottle of wine and a year's subscription to *Playboy*. Both gifts seemed to please him greatly. Needless to say, teachers like F.F. Doucette could never be tolerated in our public schools today.

I reflected on another teacher who, like Mr. Doucette, had shaped our thinking and writing skills and whose antics would today provoke condemnation. Mr. Ben Adelson was our high school journalism teacher. We called him the benevolent dictator. Publishing our campus newspaper every two weeks, he wanted it to be good, really good. No editorials were allowed about keeping our campus clean or our school spirit high—too trite, too self-evident, too meaningless. Mr. Adelson scowled, yelled and belittled. Caring little or nothing about our "self-esteem," a phrase we had yet to encounter, he believed our job as journalists was to say something important and say it well.

In his own way, he inspired Zach Sklar, Simon and me to write the Vietnam War editorial that enraged our principal, our act of evolving conscience that he felt compelled to suppress. During that dramatic confrontation in our journalism room, while our principal's eyes burned with fury as he issued his ultimatums, Simon and I both definitely detected on Mr. Adelson's face a faint trace of a smile, just restrained enough to save him from accusations of insubordination. To our immense satisfaction, we could see that we had clearly pleased our demanding master. He had prodded us relentlessly to write with significant intention—and we had answered the call.

At first, like most everyone else, Simon and I were both slightly intimidated by Mr. Adelson and his merciless criticisms. By our senior year, however, after we'd won numerous trophies in journalism contests and after that head-on collision with our principal over our Vietnam editorial, we felt a heightened appreciation for the exacting instructor, our benevolent dictator. With his devilish mustache and glaring eyes, he looked a little like horror film star, Vincent Price, but he had managed to make us recognize and honor what it means to be a good journalist. I think what Simon most admired about Mr. Adelson was his single-minded dedication and his relentless focus on that esteemed goal.

In my memorial speech about Simon, I hoped to convey the enthusiasm and intense thirst for knowledge that were at the core of who he was. Whether plowing through a difficult novel or poem, a volatile current political topic, or his most engrossing subject, the Holocaust, he wanted to get to the heart of the issue, the key truth that might be hidden from easy view.

And yet I knew that whatever I chose to say about my friend—he who so loved getting beyond the bullshit—I would be offering up my own share of shit by avoiding telling the truth about his death or the events leading up to it. I envisioned Simon, hiding somewhere in the synagogue, laughing bitterly at the façade and unspoken lies of my memorial speech—a little like Prince Hamlet mocking his cheery stepfather and mother, who have conveniently avoided admitting cruel truths about a king's mysterious death. Lies of silence fester into considerable anguish when we think about them too much. How could I be real in my talk about Simon, without exposing what was supposed to remain hidden?

By the time Danielle found me on the beach, I'd written enough anecdotes and thoughts about Simon to feel well enough prepared for his memorial service. The morning fog was thinning, and Danielle, and I decided to walk toward the water and then up the nearly empty beach.

I told her about some of the difficulties and anxieties of my trying to put together ideas for Simon's memorial. As she so often does, Danielle managed to ease my troubled head with some sound advice: "Talk about the good things, the idealistic, beautiful things that bound you together. Let the people who hear you be able to understand Simon's spirit, his passion for life. Leave the rest to their imagination."

Although Danielle's words about Simon's passion for living sounded perfectly reasonable, they also seemed perfectly ironic. How does a man with such a profound passion for life choose to drown himself in a river? Truly, Simon contradicted himself. He did, in fact, contain multitudes. Here I was, worrying that I would be hiding too much about the real Simon in my speech, and yet how many facets of himself had he hidden from me?

To know is to become responsible. Maybe Simon kept his affair and depression from me to free me from any responsibility. In contrast, I had not kept my most severe problems from him. When my first marriage had reached its breaking point and I agonized, conscience writhing, over half-abandoning my young daughters, Simon calmed me down and helped me see a path through the turmoil, a way that could liberate me without alienating me from my kids. "Ronnie, you can do this with love and honesty," he advised. "You can make this transition without losing your kids. They'll know your heart is still with them, that you'll always love them as deeply a father can."

Yet when Simon's marriage and life reached its crisis point, he chose to be isolated and stoic. Did he think there was nothing useful or supportive that I might have been able to offer him? As I continued walking along the shoreline with my wife, struggling to make sense out of what was essentially senseless, the waves in their eternally reassuring way, rose and crashed, making their soft music. A few looked pretty rideable, and I imagined Simon and me in our surfing days catching the curling, translucent beauties. Danielle snapped me out of my dreamy state with a somewhat jarring question: "Do you think Simon had affairs with other women besides his secretary or other men besides the guy on the kibbutz?"

"I have no idea," I replied. We continued walking, and I popped a question on her: "Did you ever suspect Simon might be having an affair?"

She paused and reflected before responding. "Only once. I don't like to be suspicious about other people—at least not about their love lives. You know we French don't have such a good reputation ourselves, with the way we seem to accept love affairs outside of the marriage contract. And of course, with Simon, looking at him, it seemed he loved Rachel and their children in the deepest way, and I wanted to believe in him, that he was a good man, because the two of you were so close."

"You mean if Simon were cheating on his wife and you knew it, you would be more suspicious of me, as his close friend?"

"Exactly."

"But that's not fair! That's guilt by association."

"Not guilt—suspicion. That's why one should be careful in choosing one's friends."

"So when did Simon arouse your suspicions?"

"During the summer three years ago when he and Rachel spent a week with us in Aix. We were renting that house, *La Maison Rose*, near my mother's place, but while Simon seemed to be having a great time in Southern France, he was on the phone way too much."

"You mean those business calls that he had to deal with?"

"I'd say it was a risky business he was dealing with, a naughty business. Some of those calls had nothing to do with his parking lots. I'm sure of it."

"What makes you think so?"

"The way he would always walk away from the house when he'd make or receive those so-called business calls. Why does the business of parking lots have to be so private? And more than once, I saw Rachel look worried or upset when he would have one of those long calls."

"Maybe she just wanted him to get off the phone. Do you think she was suspicious about those long conversations?"

"It certainly looked that way to me."

Her matter-of-fact declaration surprised me. "Why didn't you say anything to me at the time about your ideas concerning his supposed business calls?"

"Maybe I should have. But it was pretty early in our marriage, and I think that maybe I was too concerned that you would believe it was all in my head, or that I was thinking too much like a detective. And what man wants to be married to a cop?"

"I'd be happy to be married to you if you were a cop—just as long as you didn't arrest me or our friends for our innocent habits." I mimed smoking a joint.

"Since when were you ever innocent? Didn't you even smoke cigarettes when you were a little kid running down the boulevard on your way to Hebrew school, which sometimes you decided to skip, choosing instead to play ball in the park?" We both laughed at those absurd images from my past. Yes, as a kid, I was guilty of smoking cigarettes and occasionally ditching Hebrew school, and more recently, my transgressions included my continued enjoyment of a fragrant herb and a slight propensity for tardiness.

Danielle glanced at the time on her phone, raised her slender index finger, and pointed. We needed to turn around and head back down the beach toward our motel and car. It was time to go to Simon's house for lunch and the promised family meeting. Surely in the next few hours, we would learn more about our friend and his mysterious demise.

Twelve

"The achievement of the hero is one that he is ready for, and it's really a manifestation of his character. It's amusing the way in which the landscape and conditions of the environment match the readiness of the hero."

—Joseph Campbell, *The Power of Myth*

We arrived at Simon and Rachel's Brentwood home shortly before noon. Though not ostentatiously opulent, the neighborhood is extremely expensive, highlighted with lush landscaping including willowy palm trees, massive ferns, and tall sycamores. Their home, like most others in the area, had been significantly remodeled. What had once been an upper-middle class neighborhood had become an enclave of considerable wealth. Although Simon could have easily afforded a much flashier home, perhaps in Beverly Hills, he loved his cul-de-sac canyon location—a few houses from a park, a few miles from the beach, yet with easy access to the 405 freeway.

It felt unreal walking into his home that day, the lovely, orderly home with Rachel's avant-garde paintings and the family photographs everywhere, the comfortable familiar furniture, and several familiar faces—except one. No trace could be seen of the chaos that had shrouded the lives of this dwelling's occupants, yet of course, a tragic pallor filled the space. This home, which had always seemed to me to be filled with happiness, now felt like part of a crime scene.

Danielle and I were welcomed at the front door by Reuben, who offered courteous questions about our lengthy drive from Ashland.

We mentioned the snow on the Grapevine and the arduous detour without going into details. Obviously, in the context of Simon's tragedy, our struggles on the road were nothing we wished to complain about.

Rachel, whose pale face was painfully and understandably etched with grief, walked over to us as we stood in the entry. Shaking her head with the most sorrowful look, she reached out and hugged us and thanked us for coming. In a soft, cracked voice, she apologized and excused herself as she went back to the kitchen to resume her conversation with Simon's mother, who was sitting at the oval table and sobbing, with her hand covering her face.

Reuben brought us into the living room to greet his two brothers and their partners. Nathan, Simon's youngest son, who was about thirty, sat there with his much younger girlfriend. Although she had the looks of a model, to me, she looked like a mannequin. Actually, bluntly speaking, both she and Nathan looked a little blank. Danielle and I also said hello at this time to Simon's middle son, David, and his wife Susanna, a very pretty woman with a Hispanic heritage and a very intelligent gaze. In fact, both couples were quite handsome, but Nathan and his girlfriend, whose name I can't recall, looked and dressed as if they belonged in a fashion magazine. David and Susanna were much more casual in their appearance. They had been trying unsuccessfully to have a child. I remembered Simon, with great sadness in his voice, telling me on the phone, just a few months earlier, about Susanna having a miscarriage. Quite clearly, he was yearning for what he would never live to experience—the joy of becoming a grandparent.

David said he wanted to show me something, and the two of us left the others and walked down the hall, which was covered with family photographs. As I stared at the framed images, including some recent ones, I detected hints of fatigue and sorrow on Simon's face that I had never noticed before. Among all the varied photos, there was a near-absence of female faces. Other than a few shots with Rachel, the images were all male—just Dad and his three boys. I remembered Simon longing for a daughter, admitting it to me once as if it were a secret vice. I felt hesitant and anxious as David opened the door of his father's study, and we entered.

After glancing around the shadowy room, whose back wall was covered with shelves of books, Simon's handsome middle son blurted out bitterly: "I hate this fucking room. It's so miserable and dark." He walked toward a bank of windows and opened the drapes. He turned on several lights and shook his head. Because of the dim greyness of the walls and a fixed awning above the windows, however, the room resisted change and remained gloomy and somber.

David motioned for me to join him at Simon's desk. After opening the top drawer on the left, he said, "Take a look at these."

In the opened drawer, there was a small, neat stack of computer-printed poems Simon had written, presumably recently. The poem on top bore an electrifying heading: "Death by Water." I dropped my jaw in amazement. With an absolute minimum of words, my friend had described the ease and tidiness of drowning oneself. "A clean, straight line," the poem's opening image, depicted someone disappearing into water. The shocking title and opening words, of course, foreshadowed Simon's chosen method, the exact exit plan he must have at least been contemplating, before he and Rachel left for Argentina. Aware of the significance of what I had just read, David and I exchanged knowing glances.

I read the other four or five poems in the stack, but nothing was as unforgettable as the one on top. I remember one poem that seemed to be written for David, the son who most intensely shared Simon's profound love for the ocean. The lines that stuck in my mind were: *"Believe in the waves, believe in the sea; Don't, dear son, believe in me."* I imagined Simon wrote these words not long after the terrible scene on Venice beach, not long after his second son had discovered his seamy secret, his stained and hidden world.

While I was reading through Simon's short stack of poems, David walked over to the bookshelves, examining with visible scorn his dad's massive collection. Many of the books were in Hebrew, mostly religious works. Although Simon and I were raised with similarly rigorous religious educations, I had discarded almost all of my Jewish traditions, except for Passover, the celebration of Exodus and freedom which I continue to observe and enjoy. In contrast, Simon had returned to and sought to understand his Hebrew legacy with all the intensity of a devout rabbi. His shelves contained a great number of religious works examining Torah, Talmud, Kabala—with some works written in both Hebrew and English. Among the English language authors in his library, there were many that Simon and I had read and discussed together, books from our university years—Shakespeare, William Blake, Thoreau and Emerson, Herman Hesse, Dostoevsky, Kafka, and Camus. But a disturbingly large portion of Simon's neatly organized collection related to a single subject: the Holocaust.

From a scholarly point of view, Simon's gathering of Holocaust-related books was impressive. In fact, months after Simon's death, Rachel donated them to a local university with a Holocaust Studies department. From a more personal point of view, however, my friend's Holocaust collection baffled the mind. Why would any sane person voluntarily subject himself to reading thousands of pages about the most ghastly and systematic genocide in human history? With dumbfounded awe, I scanned some of the titles: *Why the Germans, Why the Jews?, Nazi Ideology, Christian Foundations of the Holocaust,* and *The Perversity of Complicity.* For his own determined reasons, even while he endured the responsibilities of heading a complex, nationwide company, my hyper-focused friend had chosen to devote a massive amount of time to examining in excruciating detail the horrifying few years in which, in the middle of Europe, the most educated and cultured part of the world, millions of innocent people were deliberately and systematically annihilated.

As the two of us perused his father's Holocaust collection, David grimaced and blurted out, "Enough with all this death and murder shit! I think my dad was a masochist."

I wondered about his comment but kept it to myself. Maybe Simon's choice to absorb himself in studying the Holocaust was an act of heroism, not masochism. I thought of a favorite author of ours, Joseph Campbell, and his famous ideas about the hero's journey. The classic authentic hero had to venture beyond the familiar and safe, exploring dark, unknown, extremely dangerous places in order to make some critical discovery, and then he or she must return home to share that vital new knowledge. To read so much about the Holocaust and to write two books connected to it seemed to me more heroic than masochistic, but perhaps it was both.

From my high school teaching experience, I've understood quite well the common misperceptions about the Holocaust, the convenient myths, that Simon wished to dispel. Students as well as adults tend to be quite fascinated with the horrifying subject, but most fall for a very simplistic explanation: Hitler did it. The systematic murder of millions of innocent men, women, and children supposedly can be adequately explained as the result of one man's obsession, one incredibly insane and verbally gifted man. As I reviewed the rows of volumes with their gruesome titles, I felt a combination of awe and admiration for my friend's heroic effort to correct this dangerously shallow and common misconception of the Nazi genocide.

David motioned for me to join him on the couch. He wanted to let me in on a few more facts about pulling Simon's body from the river, dealing with the Argentine police, and getting Rabbinic permission for his father to be buried in an honorable part of the cemetery.

"It's not been the easiest thing, dealing with all of this," he said with weary sadness.

"I imagine these have been the hardest days of your life," I replied.

"You got that right," he said, shaking his head. "It doesn't get much more fucked-up than this."

"I hope you're not blaming yourself in any way," I said tentatively.

"Why would I do that?" He stared at me with glaring eyes. "Do you mean because I forced my father to own up to what he was doing? He fucking chose to cheat on my mother for seven years! He fucking chose to tie that shit to himself and jump into that river!" As he cried out these words, he fought to hold back his tears.

Looking into his watery eyes, I squeezed his broad, strong shoulders. "Hey man, I know you're not to blame. You did what you thought was the right thing. I imagine your dad, on some level, was probably relieved that you caught him and made him own up to what he was doing. He was probably sick of lying."

"He was sick of something—that's for sure." David wiped his eyes. For several awkward seconds, I stood silent.

"After they pulled his body from the river, and you flew down there to help with your mother and everything...it must have been really hard having to see him like that and identify him for the authorities."

"It wasn't too pretty."

"How bad did he look?" I grimaced in asking the question.

David answered by pointing two fingers at his eyes. "Fish food." We exchanged sorrowful glances, and I realized immediately why there could be no open coffin at Simon's memorial service. I wondered and imagined how much more, beyond his eyeballs, the fish may have devoured of my friend's once handsome, wide and bronzed face.

David explained how the Argentine authorities were able to find Simon's body after only an hour of searching. He described how his parents had fought rather bitterly on Christmas Eve, in the hours leading up to his death. Apparently, Simon had been caught sending an email message to his girlfriend earlier in the evening. Rachel's understandable fury soured the evening at the nightclub. He had downed a lot of strong alcohol, and in an outburst as their taxi returned them to their hotel, he bitterly uttered the critical words: "Well, maybe you'd be happier if I just took a one-way walk to the river and disappeared!" Once the police interviewed Rachel on Christmas morning and she told them what Simon had said, it was relatively easy for divers to find and retrieve his body.

I shuddered and recoiled, pondering what David had just revealed. "Your mother must be going through hell...and you and your brothers as well...Who would think such a gentle man could cause so much pain." The two of us embraced, and my eyes filled with tears.

"And you had no idea he had this death wish in him?" David asked, with raised eyebrows.

"Absolutely not." A wave of shame came over me as I said this. How could my insensitivity, my ignorance, be completely excusable? I asked if there might be anything Danielle and I could do to help out in any way.

He hoped that we could find a way to comfort and simply be there for his mother, who was surely suffering more than anyone. He was glad we were spending the next three nights there in his parents' home. Finally, he made a more specific request: He asked me to read the speech he was writing for Simon's memorial service. I reminded him that Reuben had asked me to give my own talk and that people might get sick of my voice.

"You were his best friend, and I'm afraid of what would probably happen to me if I tried to talk in front of all those people. Will you do that for me? Will you read it?"

"Of course."

"I guess we ought to go back and join the others. Thanks, for being here for us, Ronnie, and for being here for my father."

"It's my honor," I said as we returned to the living room.

Nathan and his girlfriend, as well as Susanna, Reuben and Danielle were all seated on the leather couches and talking when Simon's mother and Rachel came into the room from the kitchen. They were both wearing black dresses, and their tear-stained, swollen faces revealed hints of their incalculable suffering. Everyone else stopped talking. In a soft clear voice, and a distinctly Israeli accent, Rachel asked everyone to come into the dining room for lunch. I was more than ready to enjoy a good meal, but the prospect of what might be discussed at the table made me nervous, the upcoming "family meeting." Might there be new revelations about my friend, more humiliations, to further tarnish his once shining reputation?

Thirteen

"Can freedom become a burden, too heavy for man to bear, something he tries to escape from...Is there not also perhaps, besides an innate desire for freedom, an instinctive wish for submission?"

—Erich Fromm, *Escape from Freedom*

I don't want to say much about lunch that day. Of course, the food itself was great—with fresh bagels, lox, smoked fish, cheeses and Danish—all those fine Jewish delights. But our gathering at the table was a farce. Everybody seated there, except one, Simon's mother, knew the truth about his death. Yet that one person's continued deception demanded that we all play along. Like a child still believing in Santa Claus at a table of grown-ups, Miriam seemed so innocent and pathetic in her ignorance.

"I just can't understand how he could have drowned," she cried out, her Czech roots still quite noticeable in her accent. "He was such a strong swimmer—such a strong man. But what could have made him go swimming all alone in the middle of the night? No one should swim all alone. I always told him that. How could such a thing happen—and to such a wonderful man? To my Simon!"

This outburst made me and probably everyone at the table feel somewhat guilty for our allowing the poor woman to be so painfully bewildered and misled. Witnessing her anguish, however, it seemed quite possible that knowing the actual facts about her "perfect" son's death might have killed the tortured mother. In truth, I don't think she would have wanted to know the awful details about what really happened, images that would have broken her heart.

As we sat at the table and ate, the conversation meandered into details about Simon's memorial and funeral. While I stared at Simon's mother, I drifted into thoughts about my own grandmother, my father's mother, and how I had deceived her for years. With her living three thousand miles away in New York, the mission of deceit was easily accomplished. The point was for her not to know that I had married and fathered two children with a dreaded *shiksa*, a non-Jewish girl.

My orthodox grandma simply could not handle it and therefore should be kept in the dark, my Aunt Millie, the least religious of my New York relatives, advised. Thus, for seven long years, from the time of my first marriage to the time of my grandmother's death, I continued to write seasonal letters, conveniently neglecting to inform her that I had a wife, two daughters and a stepson. Talk about lies of silence and omission! The whole charade burned my conscience, and yet I went along with it. My grandmother's discovery of the truth about my marriage and kids would break her heart, my Aunt Millie assured me, if it didn't actually kill her physically. It would also, in all probability, exclude me from my grandmother's will. My aunt didn't say this explicitly, but I sensed an implied warning. So, for seven deceitful years, I wrote those letters, telling my grandmother a few lively details about my young teaching career and absolutely nothing about my wife and kids. And I lived with the guilt of my blatant fraudulence, my own little scam. But when she died, I got my inheritance, and the sum was large enough to nearly triple the size of our little beach-house in Ventura—a one-story bungalow becoming a three-story home. You could say I was well paid for my lies.

This sad chapter in my life, that deliberate deception of my grandmother, passed through my mind as I looked at the suffering face of Simon's mother. Maybe this is just the way of the world, people deceiving each other, living with major lies of omission because knowing the truth would presumably be too painful or embarrassing. "You can't handle the truth!" Jack Nicholson shouts out in an unforgettable moment in a movie about the mysterious death of a Marine. This human weakness plagues all of us at times. It's even more painful for men to face and admit this about ourselves, since we're supposed to be so tough and strong—so able to endure most anything. Certainly, Simon and I were guilty of this as well, evading the pain of pursuing certain subjects—like my never managing to ask him directly about his relationship with Alan, or his never letting me know anything real about how his love life in the last seven years had moved, intensely and dangerously, beyond his marriage bed.

The conversation at our lunch gathering in Simon's dining room had ceased. Everyone at the table seemed lost in their own thoughts, and the awkward silence only emphasized the sadness pervading the room. Finally, Simon's brother, who had arrived late, broke the quiet spell by speaking up for a minute, which for him was an unusually long speech. Although he had resigned from the parking lot company as its chief accountant, Harvey loosely kept up with the ups and downs of the family business through his brother and nephews, and he was aware of some recent problems that had arisen. Pudgy and pale, the somewhat unkempt younger brother coughed to get everyone's attention.

"Maybe Simon dying is a good thing in a way," he suggested. "At least this way, he doesn't have to deal with all the hassles of the company—including the problem of missing sums of money." Simon's mother gasped, but Harvey continued. "I know my brother was pretty upset about having to explain to the company board members what happened to nearly a million dollars that disappeared kind of strangely. Nearly a million dollars gone and completely unaccounted for! At least Simon doesn't have to deal with that. And I know he was really stressed out about it, even though he pretended not to be."

"Maybe he bought his girlfriend a condo with the money," David suggested.

"Very funny," Reuben retorted. We have no idea what happened to the money or whether our dad had anything to do with it."

"Could we show some respect, please?" Simon's mom shouted. "Please, show some respect!" Her lips trembled as she shook her head in disgust.

Nathan, the youngest son, attempted to defuse the tension between his two older brothers by changing the subject. "I don't think money was on Dad's mind lately as much as becoming a grandpa. He was really sad after you had your miscarriage, Susanna."

"Several of us were really sad," she replied with a pained look. David kissed her on the cheek.

The phone rang and Rachel left to answer it. When she returned to the table, she explained that Jerry and Rebecca would not be joining us for lunch. Jerry had just finished with a surgery which took longer than expected, and the esteemed doctor and his wife would meet up with all of us the next day at Simon's memorial service and the gathering afterward. I looked forward to seeing them because as the couple that Simon and Rachel socialized with most frequently, maybe they could offer some new insight that would help unravel the enigma of our friend's bizarre final decision.

After lunch, Harvey left for the mortuary to make some final funeral arrangements. Thankfully, the ambiguity in the Argentine declaration of "probable suicide" would still allow Simon to be buried in an honorable part of the cemetery, next to his father. Whispering in my ear as Harvey departed, Reuben let me know everything had gone well in his dealings with the cemetery authorities. Again, I wondered whether a discreet cash offer helped seal the deal. When it comes to the privileges money provides, I'm generally suspicious and cynical. I thought of the lines from *King Lear*, the ailing monarch's brilliant epiphany about how inconsistently we determine who must be punished: *"Plate sin with gold and the strong lance of justice hurtless breaks—clothe it in rags, and a pygmy's straw doth pierce it."* Yeah, money talks, and if you've got enough, would-be crimes disappear.

Miriam and Rachel went off to separate bedrooms to rest. A quiet, hard-working Hispanic maid cleaned up everything in the dining room and kitchen. Three couples settled into the soft, black leather couches in the living room: Nathan and his girlfriend, David and Susanna, and Danielle and I. Reuben joined us in a wine-colored chair. Sitting together in the intimate space, with Miriam and Rachel away, we were able to speak more honestly about the tragedy than we could at our dining room lunch. Still, out of caution and discretion, people kept their voices low.

Susanna, who worked professionally as a counselor, analyzed Simon's predicament very logically. A lovely, slender woman with mocha skin, long black hair and warm dark eyes, she asked very pointed questions. "Why couldn't he simply leave Rachel and live as an honest man if he wasn't in love with her anymore? He could live by himself. He could run off with his secretary, his younger, dreamier lover. He could do whatever he wanted. But why did he have to live such a lie? And for seven years!"

Her husband, David, looked at her with great compassion and apparent agreement. Just a few years earlier, Danielle and I had been to their glamorous wedding at a gorgeous hotel in the Palm Springs mountains. As I glanced at his attractive, athletic physique, I hoped fervently that in his marriage, David would not follow in his father's footsteps. Before David met Susanna and before learning of their engagement, I had secretly dreamed he and one of my daughters might fall in love and marry, connecting Simon and me even more intimately. Staring at this handsome, grounded young man, to me it seemed he embodied the best of his father's spirit, without the secret depression or duplicity. No, he would not repeat his father's mistakes. He would not live a lie for seven years, perhaps not even for a day.

The youngest brother, Nathan offered a simple explanation for his father's deceit. He suggested that his dad's double life and dishonesty were simply attempts to preserve his honor and reputation. "He had so many people looking up to him, thinking he was this really great guy—his family, five thousand employees, all his business friends, his synagogue buddies. If so many people think you're Mr. Perfect, who wants to see that image destroyed?" Upon hearing these words, Nathan's girlfriend, the young blank-faced beauty who almost never said a word, visibly squirmed and looked irritated. She whispered something to Nathan, who then declared that they needed to leave.

Reuben excused himself and wanted to head home to the comfort of his Marina Del Rey condo. Clearly, he didn't feel particularly comfortable listening to his younger brothers, or anyone, discussing his father's various sins. His departure seemed a little cold and abrupt, but you could sense why he wanted to leave. He probably felt somewhat judged, especially by David and Susanna, for his years of silently and secretly tolerating Simon's affair. I couldn't blame him for wanting out of there.

Anyway, that left four of us alone to talk more intimately. David brought up a strange encounter he'd had with a rabbi they knew, the same liberal Reform rabbi who, several years earlier, had helped Susanna convert to Judaism. "Completely by accident, I run into Rabbi Silverstein at the market a few months ago, and we get to talking. He tells me about Dad and Heather coming to Sabbath services at his synagogue several times."

He paused and Susanna continued the story. "He also brings up the fact that Heather is taking one of his classes on Judaism that prepares you to convert, the same class I took a few years ago.

So David starts to get suspicious about his dad and his secretary. This is about a month before he actually runs into the two of them walking hand-in-hand like lovers on the Venice beach. But what's he supposed to say to the rabbi? And what's the rabbi supposed to say to him?" Susanna raised her eyebrows to emphasize the dilemma. "A married, respected man, who ordinarily likes to attend a different synagogue, an Orthodox synagogue, shows up for Sabbath services with a 'friend' who is also in the process of converting. Is the rabbi morally obligated to investigate? He's supposed to be a spiritual advisor, not a detective or an interrogator."

David continued where his wife left off. "I don't think Rabbi Silverstein wanted to come across as a suspicious guy who assumes the worst. But obviously, he wasn't completely comfortable running into me at the market. So when I see him there, he asks if everything is okay with my father and my mother. I tell him that as far as I know, everything's okay with them. He asks me if I know that Heather is actually planning on converting to Judaism. I told him I didn't know that and that I'd never really thought about it. And then we paused in our conversation because neither of us wanted to ask any more questions, even though maybe we should have. Don't ask—don't tell—that's where we were. And believe me, it wasn't easy not asking Rabbi Silverstein any more questions, but I just wasn't ready... I guess I'd reached my pain threshold."

Susanna picked up the narration. "But after that encounter with the rabbi, you somehow managed to take more walks on Venice Beach, didn't you, until finally, you discovered what you feared." With large, dark eyes, she looked at her husband, who nodded in agreement. "You found exactly what you feared," she added, as he stared back at her in silence.

After a pause, Danielle threw a difficult question at the young couple: "Do you think Simon was in love with Heather?"

David responded. "I think it started out as mostly a physical, sexual thing, something to give him what he apparently wasn't getting in his marriage. But then it became something bigger. In the family meeting that we called for, our clear-the-air meeting, my father claimed he loved Heather AND my mother—but in different ways."

"If only a man could have two wives," I quipped.

"But then, of course, a woman could have two husbands," Danielle retorted quickly, and Susanna smiled.

"Seriously, we told him—we pleaded with him," Susanna explained, "not at the family meeting, but privately, later on. We told him he ought to move out, get divorced, and try a new life with Heather, since he claimed they were in love. We told him everything could be all right with a little time. He and Rachel successfully raised their kids. The boys are grown men now, and Simon could move on, if that's what he felt he needed to do. He could follow this new love and make a new life. That's what we told him he should do. We talked and talked about it. We tried to get away from all the shame and judgment. There was an honorable way he could move on, but it seemed that no matter how much we insisted and pleaded, he didn't believe us. He didn't really believe that we could accept his getting a divorce and building a new life with a new woman. I think he felt we were hiding our truest feelings—our hate and disgust, if he were to actually make that choice. He was absolutely sure we were deceiving him."

First David and Susanna and then all four of us traded sorrowful glances. Despite the intense, sincere assurances of this articulate couple, their promises to accept his new life with an open-hearted spirit, Simon remained unconvinced. When we judge ourselves harshly enough, we imagine that anyone who lets us off the hook, must be either foolish or pretending.

Fourteen

"We need to be reborn as a human family now, for men and women to be made new; to be washed clean of the past that the world might start again. A soulful love is the psychic womb for a new life, where our kisses have the power to transform us all."

—Marianne Williamson, *Enchanted Love*

That evening, after everyone else had left, Danielle and I had a remarkable and poignant conversation with Rachel. Sitting in the dining area just off the kitchen, each of us in a distinctly different pastel-colored chair, we'd shared a late supper of leftovers from lunch. Uncharacteristically, Rachel enjoyed a second glass of wine. The three of us managed to empty a fine bottle of Zinfandel. With her short-cropped orange-blonde hair turning grey at the roots and deep creases under her eyes, understandably, Rachel looked tormented and exhausted. She was already in her nightgown and robe, ready for bed, but that second glass of Zin kicked in, and rather than retreating to her bedroom, she seemed to finally relax and release some of her turbulent feelings a little. She wanted to share her side of the story. Implicitly, she felt somewhat judged, as maybe most people in her position would. Was she partly to blame for the choices her husband had made?

"You know, I told him he should just move out of our home and move in with his girlfriend," she said in her plaintive, Hebrew-accented voice. "If he did not love me anymore, he should just leave me alone and make himself a new life. I told him that." She stared at me, her immense suffering evident in her washed-out blue eyes and mournful tone.

"He did try separating from you, didn't he?" Danielle mentioned.

"Yes, but that lasted only two weeks. He stayed in a hotel at the beach...At least that's what he told me. Maybe he was staying with his girlfriend. Who knows? I don't know. I don't care anymore. But after two weeks, he comes back. He says he can't leave me, that he doesn't want to live without me. So of course, I take him back. What else could I do?"

"He's the love of your life. He's also the father of your children," Danielle said in a whisper, placing her hand on top of Rachel's trembling palm. "You shared an amazing history together. What else could you do but take him back?"

"You know my mother-in-law, her majesty, Queen Miriam...I think she blames me for what happened to Simon, not for his death because of course, she doesn't even know the truth about that. But she blames me for his affair. She blames me!" She stared at her empty wine glass and then looked plaintively at me.

"Why would she do that?" I asked.

"Because I didn't do what a good wife is supposed to do. She blames me for Simon's cheating because supposedly I had not fulfilled my obligations as a good wife." Rachel looked with pleading eyes at both Danielle and me. "It's true that I wasn't really interested in the sexual thing anymore—I had my own problems...but Simon was having his own issues too with his you-know-what, so the whole thing became sensitive for us, and we settled for just holding each other and kissing each other good night." She dropped her head, shaking it slowly as she groped for the right words and then looked up. "And so dear Miriam, my Simon's beloved mother, believes that it was all my fault...that I pushed her innocent, perfect son to run into the arms of another woman. I can't stand being in the same room with that woman for minutes, let alone hours. I feel her condemnation every time she looks at me." Her eyes searched ours for understanding.

"We're not here to judge you—that's one thing you can trust," Danielle said quickly.

Although I knew my wife's words were simply meant to offer comfort, silently I questioned whether I could prevent myself completely from somewhat judging Rachel. Her blunt admission about the dismal state of her marital intimacy with Simon had shocked me. Certainly, I would not have chosen to use the same words that her mother-in-law used about a wife's duty or obligation, but I could agree with the older woman's main point, that infidelity becomes more likely and understandable if one is not having much of a love-life at home.

What is a wife or husband's moral responsibility, as far as sex goes? If one person loses interest for years in this part of a relationship, must his or her partner do the same? If Simon were alive, he could probably voice the opinion of several rabbis and philosophers on the subject. He enjoyed pointing out that several Biblical patriarchs, including Abraham, the father of the faith, had more than one wife. In indulging in his secret affair while maintaining his marriage, maybe Simon believed he was pursuing the path of least suffering, a compromise congruent at least with ancient, if not present, morality.

One thing was certain: I knew my good friend as a young man had been an extremely sexual person. Countless times, through the thin walls of our Isla Vista apartment, I'd heard him and Allison going at it. I'd seen the scratches from her fingernails, their jagged traces of ecstasy, along his upper back. And one of his strongest, most persistent beliefs was that most people don't change very much. He had this deep-rooted pessimism about our capacity to significantly alter our basic nature. Somehow, he and Rachel had developed opposite attitudes toward sex. Was he so wrong to look elsewhere? Sitting at the kitchen table with Rachel, I admit I found it hard, despite my better intentions, to avoid any latent disapproval of her actions—or inactions. Actually, I felt sorry for both of them, trapped in a painful dilemma with no easy answers.

Rachel told us about their attempt to heal their marriage with the help of a counselor. Like many highly intelligent men, Simon felt no personal need for counseling. His overall hubris, plus his general skepticism of the entire profession made it difficult for Rachel to get him to agree with her to seek professional help. She insisted, however, and he capitulated. At least, he showed up for a few visits. The counselor, a woman Rachel had previously visited privately, recommended travel for the distressed couple. Some of their best experiences together had been their adventures abroad, so it seemed logical enough that travel might be helpful. It would also, of course, prevent Simon, at least for the time being, from falling back into the arms of his Venice Beach mistress. First, the struggling couple tried Vancouver, British Columbia, a gorgeous city they both had visited before and loved. A few weeks later, they flew off to Buenos Aires, a place they had never been.

When they got to the Argentine metropolis, something snapped in Simon's behavior. Besides drinking far more than usual, he made an intriguing decision to change his eating habits. For years, he had avoided foods that were not kosher—ham, pork, shrimp and other seafood. But in Buenos Aires, he dumped his Torah-ordained restrictions and gorged himself on the "unclean" foods that he'd missed out on enjoying. As Rachel described his strange new experiments in eating, I thought to myself that he had chosen a distinct, visceral way of implying that he himself was unclean, that he deserved to end up as a piece of filth at the bottom of an ugly urban river. He had already transgressed God's Holy Commandments by committing adultery and lying about it—why not step over a few more of God's laws?

With agonizing details, Rachel told us about their last night together, their Christmas Eve in Buenos Aires, and a few facts about the night before Christmas Eve as well. They had made love quite passionately that night, with Simon assuring her in many intimate ways that she remained for him a beautiful, desirable woman. The following day, Christmas Eve, however, things were anything but beautiful. For Simon and Rachel, that evening, so sacred and venerated by so many around the world, would become a night of torment.

Just as David had told me when we were alone in his father's study, Rachel did indeed explode into a rage on Christmas Eve, after she discovered, near sunset, that Simon had emailed his girlfriend again. On the very first day of their escape to Buenos Aires, Simon had written an amorous note to his mistress and Rachel had caught him. It had taken days for them to recover from that offence, and then on Christmas Eve, just five days after the first fuck-up, he did it again. What was she supposed to do in reaction to his blatant insult, his thwarting of their attempts to heal their marriage? Did he want to get caught, I wondered, this adulterer whose stomach now was filled with unlawful filth?

She turned very cold on him that night. The fine, live music in the nightclub, his invitations for her to dance—nothing could break through her icy shield. He ended up dancing several dances with a sensuous Argentine woman. Rachel gasped with mild disgust in describing her: "You should have seen the way her breasts, like big melons, flopped right over the top of this tiny dress—and Simon loved it!" While he drank a great deal of alcohol, moving from wine to whiskey, Rachel sipped water and was nearly silent. Was he secretly satisfied with the hatred, anger, and distant iciness he had provoked? Did he already know exactly what he would do in a few hours?

Rachel told us about the ride back to the hotel in the taxi and what he said about maybe taking a one-way walk to the river. Most painfully, she told us about his reaching out to hold her hand as they returned to the hotel and her refusal to touch him. With a crack in her soft voice, she told us of his kissing her goodnight in bed and her not returning the kiss, just rolling over and turning her back toward him.

When she awoke at dawn and saw that his side of the bed was empty, she tensed up immediately, realizing he was gone. Although there was no note, seeing his wallet, ring, and watch left on the dresser set off terrifying alarms in her mind. She remembered with horror Simon's threatening words about that one-way walk to the river. With agonizing fear for the worst, she called the front desk and asked them to contact the police immediately.

After revealing all these heartbreaking details about their last night together, Rachel began to sob. We watched helplessly as she grabbed a tissue and blew her nose. "I can't believe that he's really gone—that he would choose to do something like this! I think he was just sick with depression. It wasn't just about what happened to us. He was depressed about so many things. You know, Ronnie, he was just too sensitive. Every bomb that went off in Israel—he would feel it like an explosion in his own heart. He worried so much about my sisters and their children who still live on the kibbutz. You knew him...he was such a good man, such a beautiful man—to do a thing like what he did. I think he was just sick with depression—sick of the bombs in Israel, sick that his book about Warsaw, that he'd worked so hard on, wasn't attracting any publishers. He was sick with depression for so many reasons—not just all about us. But of course, he would never see a doctor about his sadness, his going more and more to these dark places. I begged him to see a doctor. But my husband didn't believe any doctor could help him, and he wasn't going to take any mood-changing drugs." Aware of my fondness for cannabis, she looked pointedly at me. "He was already pretty upset about taking too many pain pills for his back, so no way was he going to take Prozac or something like that for his moods. And you know this sadness of his and his thoughts about killing himself, they were inside of him a long time before he met me. I'm going to show you something very interesting." Abruptly, she got up and went down the hall to her bedroom.

Danielle and I shared bewildered looks. We both felt helpless and frustrated because of course, neither of us intended to be laying any moral indictment on this poor woman, who somehow yet sensed the need to defend herself. She rejoined us in the kitchen, carrying in her hand a piece of paper.

On the paper was a poem, which Rachel handed to me. It was literally typed, not printed on a modern printer, so I could immediately see it was at least several decades old. Reading it, I realized it was an Elizabethan-styled sonnet that Simon had written long ago. I remembered his showing it to me in our university days. Both of us had been assigned to compose an original sonnet for a class we were taking. Simon's poem sounded a lot like John Donne's classic, "Death, Be Not Proud." Like Donne, Simon had personified Death and tried to stand up to Him. His final couplet was direct and powerful: *"So Death, there is no need to make me grieve, / You do not know the joy with which I leave."*

After Danielle and I read the poem, which seemed to present suicide as a noble way of showing Death who's in charge, Rachel looked up at us with expectant eyes. "So you see, he was thinking about this crazy idea of killing himself years before he ever came to Israel and met me. He had this in his head from a long time ago."

I told her I remembered the poem from a class assignment at UCSB. When he had shown it to me back then, I never considered it to reveal his actual thoughts, his possibly suicidal desires. To me, it was just Simon, trying to sound like John Donne or Shakespeare, and show that he understood the technical requirements of the sonnet form. He'd earned an "A" and a red-inked "Impressive

Achievement" comment from our professor. To Rachel, however, the forty-year-old piece of "evidence" proved that Simon had suicide on his mind, even when he was a young man at university. I said nothing to contradict her somewhat self-exonerating conclusion—but maybe she was right.

Shortly after Rachel showed us the poem, we said we were tired and ready for bed. We hugged and wished each other the gift of a good night's sleep. Danielle and I were emotionally exhausted from the tensions of the day, including listening to Rachel's story. Just hearing the poor woman and her attempt to make sense out of her devastating anguish, made my own suffering seem relatively mild. And yet my heart ached with pain. As Danielle and I lay in the darkness of Rachel and Simon's guest room, I found myself sobbing. For me, that almost never happens.

Danielle noticed and said, "Cheri, talk to me. Tell me what shakes your heart like this."

I didn't know where to begin. Some of my heartache was just beyond words, but my wife, with her acute sensitivity, understood the pathos of the situation, and encapsulated what I was feeling with one sentence: "It's just all such a pity—so much suffering." Yes, indeed it was pitiful. Rachel loved Simon so much, and yet apparently, she had been unable to completely satisfy him or help him fill the void that tormented him. And Simon himself seemed to experience such profound joy in life—in many ways, he came across as the most exuberant and enthusiastic person I've ever known—and yet all the varied pleasures he enjoyed in life couldn't prevent him from choosing death. It was all paradoxical and sorrowful.

There was something else my wife wanted to say. "I know we're both so tired, and tomorrow will be a big day, a very challenging day, but I must tell you one more thing."

"And what is that?"

"You know when David and Susanna said they tried to talk Simon into getting a divorce and starting a new life, but he just refused to believe them and he couldn't really follow their advice?"

"Yes, I remember." I wondered where Danielle was going with this.

"You know why he couldn't do it?"

"No. Why?"

"He couldn't do it because he didn't love this woman, this Heather, in the right way."

"What makes you say that?"

"Because if they loved each other as deeply and completely as two people can, like the way we are with each other—then I don't think he would choose to leave this life, to give up on something so wonderful. What do you think, Cheri?"

Before I could answer her question, Danielle wrapped her long, slender legs around mine under the covers. She slipped her T-shirt off over her head and grinned. There would be no need for more words.

Fifteen

"Tell all the Truth but tell it slant—
Success in Circuit lies...
The Truth must dazzle gradually
Or every man be blind—"

—Emily Dickinson, "1129"

Friday morning, I got up at the first trace of dawn, as I usually do. Simon and I shared a similar scorn for alarm clocks and sleeping late. We both loved that idea, expressed by Thoreau, that one should awake without need of a mechanical device because of one's "infinite expectation of the dawn." On this cold, gray morning, I felt a burden of expectations and hopes as I slipped out of bed, with Danielle still sleeping. In a few hours, to a large crowd of Simon's acquaintances, I was supposed to talk meaningfully about our friendship, while conveniently omitting certain facts about the last years of his life, or how he died. There would also be David's speech about his father for me to read. I felt anxious and somewhat nervous. Understandably, I hoped to speak with enough grace and eloquence to honor my friend, but obviously, the circumstances were unusual and demanding. To ease my nerves somewhat, I headed for the local park with a rolled joint in my pocket. I also carried with me my notebook and pen.

After finding a secluded place in the park under an oak tree, I smoked my joint and let my mind wander over the decades of friendship with Simon. Of course, most of my best memories evoked images of Isla Vista and our years together there. Riding bikes to campus, taking classes together, making music and seeing Simon smile with delight on his harmonica...Catching silky waves together exuberantly, or pondering deep questions on the cliffs...There were so many wonderful times we shared together in those university years by the sea. But there were other images that passed through my mind as well. Our time in Mendocino together or on his kibbutz or our camping in the Sierras or by the Red Sea or more recent memories like when he and Rachel visited Danielle and me in Southern France or when he danced with Danielle's mother at our wedding or when we surprised him on his 60th birthday, driving from Ashland to show up at a winery in the Santa Ynez Valley...There were so many beautiful memories. I looked over my notes for the talk I was to give in a few hours, making a few additions and changes.

When I returned to Simon's house, Danielle and Rachel were both in the kitchen drinking coffee and eating a light breakfast. Rachel's former life as a kibbutznik becomes apparent in the way she prepares breakfast. Along with her coffee and yoghurt, she likes to eat a fresh salad of finely chopped tomatoes and cucumbers with a touch of olive oil and parsley. The three of us enjoyed the colorful, healthy food together.

Anyone hanging out in her kitchen could plainly see that Rachel is a good cook, highly conscious of what's nutritional and wholesome, willing to pay more for an organic, kosher chicken rather than eat one that's been caged up or laced with chemicals. I know Simon appreciated the attention she gave to choosing and preparing exceptionally good food for her family, buying and cooking the sort of things that would keep everyone healthy and lean. Glancing at the beautiful freshly chopped salad, the futility of Rachel's efforts in the kitchen struck me: Despite the fact that Simon, even with some back problems, was unusually physically fit and vital for his age, his relative outer health could do nothing to protect him from the invisible forces that were corroding him from within.

Although the memorial service would not begin until eleven, Simon's family started arriving at his house two hours earlier.

First, David and Susanna arrived. Then Reuben came, bringing Miriam, Simon's mother, who, of course, was to remain completely in the dark about his suicide. Nathan came without his girlfriend, who evidently had fallen ill. Harvey, Simon's withdrawn brother, was the last to arrive, the only one in the family who chose not to dress up for the occasion. He wore jeans, running shoes, a black tee shirt, and a windbreaker with an athletic logo. When Miriam saw her younger son, she scowled at him and chided him for not, in his choice of clothes, showing more respect for his brother. He shrugged his shoulders, seemingly resigned to his mother's criticism.

At 10:15, a limo arrived to take us to the synagogue. Painted on its rear doors, the parking lot company logo hinted at the success of the family firm: All Star Parking. There was enough room in the black-leathered interior for all of us. I've almost never travelled in a limo. The last time I'd been in one was on Simon's surprise sixtieth birthday party, when we had bounced from winery to winery in the Santa Ynez Valley. On the day of Simon's memorial, I could see we had the same driver, and I said hello.

An amiable fellow with a small pot belly and limited English-speaking skills, the driver had known Simon for many years and found him to be "the nicest big boss...a good man, the only boss who ever asked me something about my family."

During the ten-minute drive to the synagogue, Reuben pulled out a folded piece of paper from his jacket pocket and announced that he had something he wanted to read to us. He unfolded the item and proceeded to read Edwin Arlington Robinson's famous poem "Richard Cory," a masterpiece about a man who shared some distinct similarities with Simon. I knew right away Reuben's choice of this poem was extremely daring, perhaps even reckless. The poem's final stanzas could unveil the savage, hidden truth to Miriam about Simon's death:

> *And he was rich—yes, richer than a king—*
> *And admirably schooled in every grace:*
> *In fine, we thought that he was everything*
> *To make us wish that we were in his place.*
> *So on we worked, and waited for the light,*
> *And went without the meat, and cursed the bread;*
> *And Richard Cory, one calm summer night*
> *Went home and put a bullet through his head.*

After Reuben read the poem, there was complete silence in the limo as we all reflected on what we had heard and the profound irony of Simon's tragedy. Yes, what's most important is often quite invisible. Miriam looked bewildered by the poem, apparently having no clue as to why her grandson would choose to read such a piece. She shook her head and stared with uncomprehending eyes, her grief and assumptions about her golden son overwhelming any potential logical inference about suicide. We fail to recognize facts we can't handle, even when they're right in front of us.

I guess you could say the memorial service went well. The Brentwood synagogue was completely filled. It had been chosen for its location and seating capacity, little else. The small Orthodox temple where Simon liked to chant and pray in Hebrew on Saturday mornings would certainly not have worked. The Reform synagogue that Simon attended occasionally with Heather would have been an even worse choice, for obvious and embarrassing reasons. Thus, the Conservative Brentwood synagogue was chosen, despite the fact that Simon and his family never worshipped there, and its chief rabbi, who presided over the service, had never met the man being memorialized. Still, he spoke eloquently about Simon's accomplishments as a businessman, as a solid family man, as a writer, and as a generous supporter of Jewish causes, particularly the Holocaust museum in Washington, D.C.

One of Simon's partners in the parking lot enterprise spoke mainly about Simon's success as CEO of the giant firm. Rotund and rather humorless, the company partner talked admiringly about Simon's uncanny ability to make great business deals, his knack for masking his true feelings and intentions like a masterful poker player. "He'd get people to think he was ready to walk away from a deal," the pudgy man declared with a smile, "like he wasn't really seriously interested in the purchase, and then he'd get the suckers to accept a really low-ball offer." It was painful listening to this business colleague actually praise Simon's capacity for evasion and deception, the same talents that enabled him to reach his self-destructive end.

As for me, first, I gave my own sanitized descriptions about Simon and our friendship, our favorite teachers and passions, giving just enough hints about our juicy past to let people imagine a bit and laugh. Afterward, I read the poignant speech David had written for his dad. It was a beautiful piece filled with intimate images and examples of Simon as a father, vividly described with deepest gratitude by his middle son. Listeners could envision Simon helping David and his brothers with their schoolwork or soccer or learning to swim, ride a bike, catch a wave. My favorite images from David's speech were his kibbutz memories: Simon trotting and dancing outside the dining hall with his delighted son on his shoulders, or the little guy riding along the vineyard paths, sitting proud and tall beside his dad on the green tractor.

When the service was over, a few people walked over to me to offer some personal words. They were people Simon and I had known at Fairfax High School, people who had remained in Los Angeles, faces I hadn't seen in decades. One guy, Mathis Chazinov, whose mother had been my Hebrew teacher when I was a kid, strode up to me with a broad smile. Provoked by the school memories in my speech, he felt compelled to tell me something.

Somehow, rather recently and amazingly, he had run into our favorite English teacher, F.F. Doucette, in some bar, far south in a Mexican beach-town. They had downed margaritas together and talked about old times at Bancroft Junior High. Specifically mentioning Simon, Zack Sklar, and me, the eternally youthful, gallant maestro of language concluded that we had been "the best of the best." Doucette, whose French name and soul are connected to sweetness, left Mathis in the bar with a smile and headed down the beach with a lovely woman half his age on his arm.

The odd story surely made me grin. It's amazing how a compliment from a person you deeply admire can mean so much, even when you've not had any contact for half a century. I remembered with pride Doucette's madly joyous smile and could hear his enthused voice as he pounded my hand with his rubber-stamped name for homework well done: "A virtuous effort, Herr Hertz!" I know Simon also would have thoroughly appreciated the belated tribute uttered from Mexico by our beloved hero, especially the image of him still enjoying the company of a beautiful woman.

I wondered whether there was anyone in the synagogue audience that day who saw beyond what was presented at the service. Outside of his family and a few closest friends, was there anyone there in the packed crowd who knew of Simon's seven-year dalliance with his secretary? Was there anyone who knew enough about his emotional state to suspect that his drowning in Argentina was no accident? Was it possible that his secret lover, his ignominious secretary, was able to slip into the synagogue quietly and stealthily, and sit somewhere in the back in anonymity? Out of some vague sense of fairness, I hoped she was able to be there.

After the service, later that afternoon, about thirty of Simon and Rachel's closest friends and relatives showed up at their Brentwood home for food, drinks and talk. Of course, the discussions had their limitations because of the secrecy involving his affair and the actual details of his drowning. In particular, I remember two conversations from that gathering. They both occurred toward sunset, after people had eaten, and most had downed a few glasses of wine or perhaps a hit or two of Schnapps, a favorite whiskey at Jewish parties.

First of all, I got to meet and talk a little with Dr. Leah Stern, the director of a Holocaust Studies department at a Los Angeles university. She had worked with Simon on the two books he wrote connected to the Nazi genocide. One book was an anthology of short stories set in Poland in the 1930's; the other was a novel, not yet published, set in the Warsaw ghetto during the war years, in which virtually the entire Jewish population was killed. We talked about Simon's two books and his several journeys to Poland to study his subject. A short, attractive woman, probably in her forties, half of her thick curly hair had already turned grey. Simon had mentioned her to me a few times, describing her as "the cute Holocaust scholar," but I'd never met her before. Her light accent sounded Israeli as she spoke with admiration about Simon and his efforts to reveal the truth behind the Holocaust.

"Your friend was a very brave man. Most people in his situation would have been delighted to succeed here in the New World and just completely forget about the whole European nightmare. After all, Simon was born several years after the Holocaust was over. There was no logical reason or ethical obligation for him to devote so much of his time toward trying to understand what is too horrible to comprehend. And it's not as if he didn't have a full-time job to keep him busy, being the head of such a big, coast-to-coast company. And yet he felt compelled to read and read, to listen to survivors and try to fathom what happened. He did all this heart-wrenching research and studying, travelling and interviewing, and he writes these two books."

I asked for her honest opinion of his two works.

"To tell you the truth," she said, sliding her fingers through the grey streaks in her hair, "I think the short stories are much better than the novel. They've got character and depth and complexity. They make you understand some of the major anxieties and ambiguities that affected and perplexed the Jewish people and the *Goyim* in Poland in the thirties, before normal relationships completely disappeared—the world of mutual dependence, prejudices and tensions before the horror. Simon depicted that psychotic period beautifully in his stories. In his novel, however, I don't think he was quite so successful. He wasn't finding any publishers, and as you probably know, he was deeply disappointed. I was trying to help him understand the reasons people were not responding so well to his book. Did you read a draft of his novel about Warsaw?"

From the animation in her face and voice, I could tell that Simon had strongly impressed this scholarly woman, and I wondered at that moment about the two of them. "Yes, I read his novel."

"And what did you think?" Her question placed me in an awkward position.

I admitted that from my perspective, Simon's novel had some serious weaknesses. He had let me read it about a year earlier, just after he finished it. At the same time, I'd asked him to read a play I'd written involving the strange, tragic attacks of September 11th, 2001. Sadly, neither of us was able to be very complimentary about what each of us had written. Simon wisely saw that my play was a clumsy, forced way of conveying my controversial ideas about 9/11. As for Simon's novel, I loved parts of it, but found it too lengthy and, perhaps too contrived, in presenting its Zionist message. We were both too didactic. Understandably, both of us had trouble being completely honest with each other in our critiques, gently sanitizing our harsh opinions of each other's respective literary efforts.

Dr. Stern did offer effusive compliments about Simon's courage, the fearlessness with which he undertook the challenge of writing a novel about the Warsaw catastrophe. "My God," she said, staring at me with sorrowful, dark eyes. "To go to Warsaw and to find a handful of people who managed to survive and to get them to tell their stories...This is not something an ordinary human being would do. Your friend was obviously quite an exceptional man. He didn't deserve to die like that, to drown in a river on the other side of the world—in a place where old Nazis ran to escape. Maybe an old Nazi got to him and pushed him into the river. What do you think?"

I saw a painful searching in her eyes but offered no definite opinion about Simon's death. She pulled out a photograph from her purse and showed it to me. It was a picture of Simon with several thoughtful, scholarly-looking people, including Dr. Stern. They were in Warsaw, posing in a flower-covered patio. Simon was there to receive some award for his short story collection. The image fascinated me. Everyone in the picture looked happy, except for my friend. Standing between an attractive young blonde man and the attractive Dr. Stern, who wore a low-cut blue dress, Simon looked painfully disturbed. Even as he was being honored for his best literary effort, staring out from the center of a group of smiling foreigners, he seemed lost and anxious in his somber leather jacket. Although still handsome, with his imposing stare and curly white hair, he hadn't even feigned a smile.

I mentioned to the Holocaust professor that Simon appeared rather distant and distraught in the photograph. She stared at the photo and then at me, pausing with a pensive expression before she spoke rather enigmatically. "That trip to Poland was really intense for Simon, in a lot of ways—being honored as a writer in the land of Auschwitz." She probed my eyes and then completed her thought. "Actually, it was an intense time for me as well."

Though of course I didn't understand exactly what she meant or implied, I didn't ask any more questions, except in my own mind.

Sixteen

"*Reputation, reputation, reputation—O I have lost my reputation. I have lost the immortal part of myself and what remains is bestial!*"

—William Shakespeare, *Othello*

Telling her I needed to get a little fresh air, I left Dr. Stern in the living room, her last words and that Warsaw photograph whirling provocatively through my brain. On my way toward the back door, I passed through the dining room where a group of men had gathered to sit *Shiva* for Simon. For seven consecutive sunsets, they would meet in that room, sitting and praying in Hebrew, the top of their heads covered with *yarmulkes*, their lips rapidly mumbling in the ancient tongue effusive praises to God's greatness, fawning tributes meant to mitigate the pain of losing a loved one. Regardless of age, these men, mostly in black, seemed antiquated, almost mechanical, as they babbled away so hurriedly their sacred lamentation. But who was I to question the *Kaddish*, a prayer that had apparently soothed souls for centuries?

I stared for a few moments and wondered about my friend's mysterious return to the faith which we had both seemingly moved beyond when we were sixteen. I imagined he returned mostly for scholarly reasons—for love of the Hebrew language and a more profound understanding of the Torah. But somehow, maybe in spite of his intentions, he seemed to get sucked into certain values of that Orthodox world that contradicted the more transcendent and personal, less constrained sense of divinity that we had discovered in the vast stars of the Sierras, in our psychedelic insights on the Isla Vista beaches, and again at the Red Sea, in the midst of those miraculous coral reefs. And included in that sanctified world of tradition to which Simon returned was a good deal of patriarchy.

As the mostly older men mumbled away in Simon's dining room, seemingly with little feeling or attention to the meaning of the words, the *Shiva* made me think of my sister and her departure from the faith of the Chosen People. After our mother had died, we went through the ritual at our parents' home in L.A., and my sister got to discover for herself, quite painfully, the male chauvinism woven into Conservative Judaism. To properly perform the memorial prayers, ten Jewish men are required—ten men—not ten people. For my mother's *Shiva* to be religiously correct, properly kosher, so to speak, someone had to knock on a neighbor's door, a Jewish man who had never known our mother, and then bring that stranger into our home, all so that the requirement for ten adult Jewish males could be met. My sister simply did not count, and the sting of this institutionalized misogyny was powerful. For many years afterward, she refused to enter a synagogue. Staring at the dark-suited men in their prayers and remembering my sister's insulting exclusion, I reflected on the odd fact that despite their differences, most major religions share the same shameful legacy of dogma-driven male supremacy. I sympathized with my sister's exodus from traditional Judaism much more than Simon's return to it.

I wandered off to find Danielle. She had been sitting in the kitchen with Miriam, compassionately listening to the distraught, deceived woman moan about her lost, immaculate son. I managed to ease my wife away from the suffering mother, filled two wine glasses, and the two of us stepped outside to a patio where Jerry and Rebecca were sipping some fine Napa red. Danielle and I had met the handsome doctor and his vivacious wife a few times before at some of Simon's parties, including the surprise 60th birthday gathering at the Santa Ynez wineries. As Simon and Rachel's closest L.A. friends, Jerry and Rebecca might understand more about what was going on with Simon in his last months. Although the two couples had known each other only slightly on the kibbutz, they became close after they all relocated to Los Angeles.

Tall, slender and light-hearted, Jerry is a highly successful surgeon who, like Simon, became an avid cyclist. They spent many Sunday mornings together bent over the handlebars like European racers, riding up and down the Pacific Coast Highway, usually covering between thirty and forty miles. Often, they would end their journeys back at one of their homes, where their wives, and sometimes their sons, would join them for Sunday lunch. Jerry and Rebecca have two grown sons who are now successful professionals, a doctor and an engineer, the Jewish couple's proudest accomplishment. Their boys had grown up with Rachel and Simon's sons, attending the same schools and playing on the same soccer teams. The two couples shared much history from two very different parts of the world.

Rebecca is a very attractive woman. With golden brown skin and dark, intense eyes, she's a nurse whose vibrant smile and shapely legs must have attracted her husband immediately when they met in a Tel Aviv hospital where they both worked. Listening to her talk about Simon, her close connection to our friend was plainly evident. Her voice was plaintive and sympathetic as she discussed his plight. Most importantly, she was the one person we talked to, including even Rachel, who most clearly understood the dangerous depth of Simon's depression.

"I was worried about him," she confided to us on the patio. "I was extremely worried about him. Getting caught with his secretary on the beach, confessing to everything in front of his entire family, moving out of the house, moving back in and trying to reconcile with Rachel, running off to Vancouver, then running off to Argentina—the poor man didn't know what to do. And on top of that—the problems with the business and the missing money, no publisher being interested in his Warsaw book after he bleeds through his soul to write it!"

"Obviously, he needed a good doctor," Jerry quipped, trying to lighten things.

"And what kind of surgery would you have recommended, my good doctor?" his wife shot back. "A brain transplant?"

"He and Rachel did see a professional counselor for a few visits," Danielle reminded everyone.

"A lot of good it did him," Rebecca retorted. "I wish he could have been open to seeing a better therapist," she added, "someone who could help him deal with his dark side...Someone he respected, not just a person Rachel happened to like."

"Getting Simon to see ANY counselor could not have been easy," I mentioned. Surely, they both knew he was not a man who sought professional psychological advice, that he viewed the supposed "crutch" with undisguised scorn.

Rebecca described an amazing recent incident that revealed the intensity of her worry about Simon. It occurred a few weeks earlier, between the Vancouver and Buenos Aires journeys. Simon had gone sailing out of his familiar Marina harbor as he often did. He was a licensed, experienced sailor who preferred the ease and variety of renting sailboats rather than owning one. I'd gone out with him a few times and seen for myself his skills and confidence with the sails, ropes, and rudder. Yet on the day that Rebecca described for us, when Simon was out sailing alone one afternoon, she had become acutely anxious about his safety.

When she realized he had not returned by sundown, she grew alarmed enough to call the Coast Guard. My eyes widened on hearing her unveil this stunning fact. Yes, she obviously sensed the magnitude of his depression. Of course, Simon did eventually return home safely that evening. The Coast Guard had come out to find him, but by the time they located him, he was motoring back into the Marina harbor on his own. Obviously, Rebecca's story fascinated me as I reflected on the level of anxiety, the keen awareness of Simon's precarious emotional condition, that must have provoked this friend to call the Coast Guard.

Clearly, Rebecca and Simon shared a close relationship. I wondered how intimate their relationship might have been. She had the looks and the sort of lively mind that would attract him, but Simon was such good friends with Jerry, his weekly cycling buddy, that it was difficult for me to imagine him having an affair with the friendly doctor's wife. Difficult, but not impossible. Once it becomes evident that a person is capable of extended infidelity, like seven years of it, in Simon's case, the door is wide open to countless other possibilities of cheating. In Simon's situation, it might have even involved men. Who knows? The stark truth was that I had no idea how many other extra-marital affairs Simon may have experienced, and I guess I hadn't wanted to know. Confession opens Pandora's box. Good friends don't ask too many questions, right? Discretion is the better part of valor—or at least, that's what we men have been taught. Don't ask, don't tell, and try not to feel too guilty.

That evening, after everyone but Rachel, Miriam, and Reuben had left Simon's home, Danielle and I went out for a stroll and some ocean air. We drove to Santa Monica and walked to the outdoor promenade along 4th Street, a great place to people-watch, eat ice cream, and catch some lively street music. That's exactly what we did. We entered the pedestrian-packed walkway and passed a tall, ivy-covered dinosaur spouting water. Hearing some lovely singing and acoustic guitars, we approached two thin, long-haired guys, who looked like they might be brothers, performing a fine version of the Eagles' hit, "You Can't Hide Your Lying Eyes." Naturally, while we watched and listened to their harmonies, my thoughts drifted to Simon and all that he had hidden in his eyes, which to me, had always seemed so full of joy.

As we sauntered among the crowds of people on this cool, clear night, we got our ice cream cones and tried to process what we'd been through that day. Between the memorial service and the gathering afterward at Simon's home, the hours had been demanding and intense. We talked about some of the different encounters and conversations we'd shared. We discussed Rebecca's revelations about calling the Coast Guard and the implications of her story. Danielle told me about Miriam sobbing to her that Rachel was responsible for the couple's marital problems and her son's lengthy infidelity because "she didn't know how to be a good wife." I confessed to Danielle the odd feelings I had when Dr. Stern showed me her Warsaw photograph of Simon—how incredibly sad and alienated he looked. Was Simon involved with the professor? Was he involved with Rebecca? We shared our suspicions, knowing that they were not facts, merely suspicions. The discussion made us both feel uncomfortable. Why even speculate about what you would probably never, with certainty, know?

We checked out movie theaters and movie times because, in spite of all the sadness entwined with Simon's tragedy, the following evening, Saturday, would be New Year's Eve. We decided we would return to the Santa Monica promenade the next day to quietly celebrate the New Year with dinner and a movie. Recognizing that there were a lot of good choices for films, with little debate, we decided upon *Ghostwriter*, Roman Polanski's latest effort, which according to several reviews was supposed to be quite good. Simon and I both loved Polanski, especially *Chinatown*. After surviving the

Charles Manson-ordered murder of his wife, the Polish director had lived in Europe for many years, as an escaped refugee from justice, because of his crimes in the U.S. with an underage girl. Yet apparently, the accused sexual offender had come up with another masterpiece. Great men can possess great flaws.

Sandwiched between Simon's Friday memorial and his burial on Sunday, Saturday was going to be an "easy" day for Danielle and me, and easy seemed pretty alluring after the emotional traumas of the last few days. The only thing we wanted to do on Saturday, besides our dinner and movie in the evening, was to check out the Reform synagogue which Simon had attended with Heather. We were curious to meet Rabbi Silverstein for ourselves. It was also quite possible, we thought, that Simon's shunned lover might show up at the temple for Saturday morning services. Would we be able to recognize her? Did we really want to meet her, this unknown woman, who had been so important to Simon these past seven years?

When we returned to Simon's house, everyone but Rachel had left, and she was behind a closed door in her bedroom, hopefully asleep. We crawled into our bed quietly and at least, Danielle had relatively little trouble getting to sleep. Emotional exhaustion has its advantages. Still, my weary, agitated mind wouldn't stop. It scrolled through wild, juicy images of Simon, including visions of him with his secretary on the beach or with Rebecca or the Holocaust professor or even the handsome, blond man in the Warsaw photo.

"Who's to say what's right and what's wrong, when it's all so subjective, so totally dependent on where and when you happen to live?" I could picture Simon asking the provocative question on the Isla Vista cliffs with his eyes gleaming. Yet it didn't feel right for me to be conjuring up all these illicit, salacious suspicions. Okay, forget the negative—focus on the positive.

I struggled to change the pictures in my head, trying to think of things that would relax, not jangle my nerves. I shifted to more pleasing images, envisioning Simon and me on the beach in Isla Vista with two beautiful horses. Breathing more slowly, as I pictured the two of us, I could hear the ocean, the waves swelling and collapsing in their calming rhythm, and I could feel the tension gradually leaving my body. As Simon flashed his huge smile my way, I could see the two of us cantering bareback on the water's edge, on the glistening pastel sand, perfectly joyous, as the sun slowly melted into the rainbow-drenched sea. The image relaxed me enough to help me fall asleep.

Seventeen

"Children of the future Age,
Reading this indignant page:
Know that in a former time,
Love! Sweet Love! was thought a crime."

—William Blake, "A Little Girl Lost"

Saturday, which was supposed to be our "easy" day, did not begin all that easily. Danielle was up at dawn, joining me for coffee in the kitchen, but her thoughts were elsewhere. She was worried about her son who was photographing the potentially volatile demonstration in Marseille that day, the protest against the law prohibiting Muslim girls from wearing their headscarves in French public schools. Knowing his propensity to get right into the center of things and not live as a spectator on the periphery, she feared for his safety. After all, he had taken poignant photographs of the children in his beloved village in Senegal, but he had returned to France with a nasty case of dysentery. Would he be cautious enough amidst the potential chaos of a mass protest-march in Marseille? Maybe it was just her mother's intuition, but her worry intensified as she thought about the possible dangers. Just as she was about to telephone her son, she received a call from her friend in Aix, who definitely had something to say about Albert. In fact, she had him with her in her apartment—her son and a girl he had brought with him.

Mireille assured my wife right away that Albert was all right, yet it was hard for Danielle to avoid gasping with fright as her friend described his relatively minor injuries. He had a cut on his forehead that probably would have benefitted from a few stitches, and his shoulder was covered with red welts. Apparently, a Muslim brother, upset with his sister's participation in the demonstration, expressed his anger at her with a large stick, and Albert stepped between them.

"You're not even religious!" the brother had screamed at his sister. "Why should you care what a true Muslim daughter wears at her school!"

The girl was physically unhurt, yet terrified, and now Albert was involved. He had interfered with what the shouting brother had declared a "private family affair." Although he wasn't hurt badly, my stepson was concerned enough about the girl's safety and his own welfare, that he left the demonstration immediately. He and the girl caught a train from Marseille to Aix, about fifteen miles north, to seek a place of refuge with Mireille. He felt a strong need to protect the girl. No, he and the Muslim girl were not presently in a romantic relationship, at least not yet. And no, Albert did not want to speak to his mother just yet. Perhaps in a day or two.

The phone conversation had lasted about ten minutes, and it was all in French, so I understood only half of it as they were speaking. Danielle explained more afterward. "At least, he's all right," she kept repeating to me, as if saying the words enough times might get her to actually believe in them and calm herself down.

She turned her attention to the Muslim girl. "But why would he choose to get involved with a Muslim girl from Marseille? Of course, I'm not saying it's wrong, but it's asking for trouble these days, with so many of them becoming more religious, covering their heads and faces, and then all the Le Pen people, the great traditionalists, reacting like fascists, crying about the loss of the French culture and wanting to throw the brown foreigners out of the country...Why does my son need to get in the middle of all that?"

Her words surprised me. "My dear reactionary! You should hear yourself. First of all, didn't you just tell me that Mireille said he's not involved with the girl?"

"Yes, but I guess I don't really believe it." She wrinkled her brow.

"And second of all, when you worry about him falling for a Muslim girl—and remember he is half-North African himself, at least in his genes, but don't you sound exactly like your parents?"

"Oh, *mon Dieu*!" She winced and smiled at the same time. "You really know how to stab a progressive woman in the heart. I guess I should not worry about such things before they happen, nor sound so much like my parents at their most foolish moments." On those points, we could both agree.

Rachel showed up in the kitchen soon after my wife's conversation with her friend in Aix. As she put together another kibbutz-style breakfast—with her yoghurt, chopped tomatoes and cucumbers, and more coffee—she empathetically encouraged Danielle to describe what had happened to her son at the Marseille demonstration. Rachel listened closely and understood instinctively the concern for a child's safety that can torment a mother, even when that "child" is thirty. I hoped my relative lack of worry did not imply that I didn't care enough about Albert. To women, we men can seem so hopelessly callous, but we're just not wired the same way. Thousands of years in the merciless Alpha culture toughened our inherited nerves. I care deeply about my wife's son, but quite naturally, I don't worry about him anything like the way she does. I wouldn't have those reactions, even if he were my own son.

Perhaps to help ease the tension of recent days, to take their minds off the grim omnipresence of Simon's tragedy, the two women decided to spend some time together in Rachel's art studio, a converted two-car garage. Both women are avid painters and have shared an interest in each other's artistic efforts. Both enjoy doing portraits, often of people of darker ethnicities. Rachel likes to paint whole bodies, usually nudes, with sharp angles and odd modernistic combinations of bold colors. Some of these paintings were displayed throughout their home. Danielle concentrates on faces, usually with soft pastel shades that seem impressionistic. Just as Simon and I often shared our literary efforts, the two women have enjoyed responding to each other's art.

While they spent an hour together in the studio, I took off for another walk in the park in the cool, foggy-grey air. In a grove of eucalyptus trees, I found myself silently conversing with Simon, conversing and cursing. "How could you do such a thing, you fucking idiot!" I shouted inwardly, as he stared at me, not saying a word, mysterious as a sphinx. The shriek of a large, dark bird on a nearby branch grabbed my attention. He caught my eye and squawked again, as I thought of that hopeless, refrain from an immortal poem: "Never more...never more."

Later that morning, Danielle and I drove to Santa Monica and found our way to the Reform synagogue that Simon and Heather had occasionally attended. We were glad to go there for several reasons. Mostly, we wanted to meet Rabbi Silverstein, this apparently tolerant man David and Susanna had told us about—the liberal rabbi. Besides that, we wondered whether we might get to meet Heather at the synagogue. It seemed likely she might go there for some consolation. In addition, and somewhat curiously, I looked forward to hearing some of the old Sabbath melodies, the chanting of songs in Hebrew, that were a part of my youth for countless Saturday mornings. For years, I had resented my mother forcing me to attend those services, and for decades, I had generally avoided synagogues, yet now, reeling from Simon's tragedy, ironically, I was feeling nostalgic about the old rituals, especially the ancient, familiar melodies that magically connect you with the past.

The synagogue was fairly large, though only half-filled, with maybe 150 people on this particular morning. A skinny, diminutive kid, who reminded me of a young Simon, was celebrating his Bar Mitzvah that morning. Fortunately, he had some musical talent and could sing the requisite prayers and passages from the Torah quite successfully. He didn't do as well in English, however, stumbling a bit through his speech about the meaning of becoming a man. Rabbi Silverstein was probably the ghostwriter, and the insights seemed a little over the head of the speaker. "Manhood" seems rather too much to lay on a kid who's barely five feet tall, hasn't started shaving yet, nor gained much mastery over reading sophisticated sentences. I thought of Simon and his unforgettable message about what a guy really needed to do in order to actually enter manhood, those words uttered with a huge grin as he flashed that *Playboy* centerfold in our junior high hallway.

As the morning service proceeded, Danielle and I discreetly scanned the congregation, looking for anyone who might be Heather. Reuben had told me she was about five-two, olive-skinned, and gifted with long golden-brown hair that was usually folded into a bun. We saw one woman in the back with hair like that, just about the right height, who we imagined might be the grieving lover. She was in the last row of the synagogue and dressed all in black. Closing her eyes and slightly swaying back and forth when she stood in prayer, she seemed lost in her emotions. Stretching the limits of my visual acuity, I searched for evidence of tears, but even thinking I might have seen some glistening drops on her down-turned face proved nothing.

When the Sabbath service ended, everyone moved to an adjacent room of the synagogue for food and celebration. There were small paper cups of sweet, red wine, lots of challah, the braided traditional Sabbath egg-bread, plus assorted cheeses, bagels, lox, tomatoes and Danish. We looked in vain for the woman in black who we thought might be Heather. Rabbi Silverstein, in contrast, was of course, quite easy to find. After he'd led everyone in a Hebrew prayer for the wine and another one for the bread, we approached the smiling, slightly portly man and introduced ourselves. Right away, he effused warmth and kindness, and evidently, he already knew about Simon's death, though apparently not in its cruelest details.

"His death came as a great shock to me—to drown in an Argentine river. What a terrible accident! I'm very sorry for your loss." His voice was soft and sensitive, full of understanding, just like his warm, brown eyes. The rabbi continued: "Your friend was a very exceptional man—quite a scholar of the Torah. I felt flattered when he would come to our little synagogue occasionally and put up with our service when so much of it is in English, and I know he preferred Hebrew. He loved to ask deep questions about the meaning of some passage, like why Moses, with all his heroic feats, had to die in the wilderness instead of the promised land, or why Job, with all his goodness, had to suffer so immensely just to prove some point for God. I remember his pointed questions and the way he would raise his eyebrows and smile when he asked them. If he hadn't been such a successful businessman, he probably could have been a great rabbi."

I smiled at the thought of my friend as a rabbi. "I'm curious whether his personal problems with his marriage might have made him seem like a hypocrite," I blurted out, raising the rabbi's eyebrows a little, and hinting rather directly that we already knew about Simon's relationship with Heather.

"You may or may not be aware of the fact that rabbis don't have to be perfect, and there's certainly no Jewish law forbidding divorce. I myself am in my second marriage. In my opinion, your friend's main problem was his secrecy, not the fact that he had fallen in love with another woman. I feel very bad for her. She was crazy about him." He tapped his heart with one hand and took a sip of wine with the other.

I wanted to know more, but my sense of discretion held me back. How much more did this rabbi know? Did he think Heather was taking a class and converting to Judaism because she expected to marry Simon? And from the rabbi's vantage point, did he believe, seeing them together on numerous Saturday mornings, that Simon was actually in love with her? Did he imagine that in the not-to-distant future he would be marrying the adulterous couple?

I didn't need to ask him how we might contact Heather. Reuben had already given me her Venice address when, at Simon's home, in privacy, I'd asked him a few questions about her. He'd smiled, scribbled something on a slip of paper, and I'd stashed it in my wallet. Was the address on it a condominium my friend had purchased for her in some illicit way? How much did I really want to know?

Danielle and I thanked the friendly rabbi for his kindness and frankness. He and I both agreed that the Bar Mitzvah boy had done an outstanding job, especially his singing.

I was re-evaluating my opinion about Bar Mitzvahs. After decades of teaching high school English and hearing countless students whine about the torturous prospect of speaking to thirty students for five minutes about some book they'd read or some research they'd done, my respect for the ancient Hebrew rite-of-passage ritual has risen dramatically. Singing in Hebrew to a large audience might not make all that much sense to a skinny little kid, but it does make him—or her—jump over a very high hurdle and earn some self-respect and confidence. And the boys still far outnumber the girls in taking on this personal challenge. How sad it is that all Orthodox and many Conservative Jews, even in these feminist times, still prohibit their daughters from this experience and honor, allowing their deference for tradition to overwhelm any notion of equality.

With fondness and appreciation, we said goodbye to the liberal rabbi, this warm-hearted, thin-haired empathetic soul. As we were leaving, he threw in one last comment with a smile. "If you do see Heather, please tell her I'm here for her, any time she wants to see me and talk."

Rabbi Silverstein's compassionate, relaxed acceptance of Simon's relationship with Heather seemed remarkable to me. A more Orthodox rabbi would have never been so tolerant. I thought of my aged Orthodox uncle who lived in New York, dutifully and faithfully following the dictates of tradition. Even though his non-Jewish daughter-in-law had taken a class like the one Heather was taking to convert to Judaism, and even though this woman had actually converted and been a loving wife to his son and a good mother to three children in a successful marriage of over thirty years, according to my traditionalist uncle, her conversion was a Reformist fraud, and the whole fiasco tormented him with endless grief. Inspired by the unassailable conclusions of his Orthodox rabbi, my uncle perceived his son's marriage to this *shiksa* as a horrible, irredeemable tragedy. Nothing could change his mind or lift his grief.

In my opinion, the real tragedy was in my embittered uncle's rigidity, his inability to escape from the "mind-forged manacles" of his orthodoxy. I like that phrase that William Blake came up with, but maybe I'm the one who is mentally handcuffed in my inability or unwillingness to see much of anything good in Fundamentalist religion. There must be something enormously powerful and magnetic that attracts certain people like my uncle and a few billion others toward orthodoxy and dogmatic belief. Maybe it's a simple desire for absolute black-or-white clarity. Good or evil. Heaven or Hell. Kosher or not kosher. And everything concluded with absolute certainty. Convinced most of us would be so much better off if we kept our dogmas on a leash, I wondered again how and why Simon had decided to return to such a strict version of his faith, spending countless Saturday mornings in an Orthodox synagogue.

After our conversation with the rabbi, Danielle and I left the synagogue and headed for the ocean. We wanted to go for a walk along Venice beach, the same place where both of Simon's sons had caught him walking amorously with his girlfriend. As to whether or not we would go knocking on Heather's door, at that point we were undecided. We knew that strolling along the water's edge would feel good on our frayed nerves. After we'd walked beside and listened to the ocean for a while, we could decide whether or not we wanted to meet Simon's grieving lover.

We walked and listened without talking very much. The sun burned through a thin layer of clouds as the greyish sky turned to pale shades of blue. Of course, the mysterious Heather dominated my reflections, and naturally, the allure of meeting her was strong. Maybe she could help unravel the enigma of Simon's depression. How had he seemed to her these last several years, and especially these last months? Had she noticed him becoming sadder or more despondent? What messages did he send her from Buenos Aires— the one at the beginning of his trip and the one just a handful of hours before he died? Danielle, in particular, felt enormous compassion for this forsaken lover who had lost probably the most important person in her life and yet was excluded from publicly mourning him. Even if she had somehow managed to attend the memorial service on Friday, she certainly had to be nearly invisible, a hidden infiltrator. And she would be absolutely unwelcome to come anywhere near the small burial ceremony on Sunday. She was simply a dirty little secret, someone to be ignored. We wondered how she was handling Simon's death, whether she would continue working for Simon's parking lot company. We wondered if she would keep her place in Venice or move far away. We had a hundred questions to ask her, yet our own sense of propriety and our respect for Rachel suggested the time was not right for our visit, not on the day before Simon was to be buried.

"You Americans are such hypocrites!" Danielle exclaimed with frustration. "So many people here have the big affairs like Simon had, but it is all so hidden. It's all a big secret, dirty and ugly and full of shame. Even your President Clinton had his girlfriends, but he gets impeached and treated like a horrid man, worse than a president who lies and makes unnecessary wars, like Monsieur Bush. In France, we do not put so much shame on a person for having a lover. He or she can still be an honorable person, and the person who is loved outside of the marriage—she does not have to be treated like a criminal or a prostitute. You remember when our President Mitterrand died not so very long ago? Right there at his funeral, right on television for everyone to see—there was his wife, and his mistress, and their children! Believe me, I don't wish to have some mistress of yours standing beside me at your funeral—but at least the French people can be more honest about this than the Americans. People may say we have terrible morality, but at least, we don't have quite so much hypocrisy!"

As usual, I found myself agreeing with Danielle's insights. Yes, we Americans are still pretty hung up on sex. During my career as an English teacher, I'd read numerous pages of student writing, rather intimate confessions revealing how, especially in conservative families, teens suffer miserably from their parents' "abstinence only" expectations. Resisting serious birth control, (an act of prevention which would confirm their being guilty of "premeditated sex" rather than the lesser crime of drunken, sperm-of-the-moment sex)—a large number of my students lived in an angst-filled world of secrecy and lies, hoping to avoid accidental pregnancy and the spoiling of their parents' outdated hopes for purity. In our American literature curriculum, we'd read pages about scarlet letters and Puritan ministers condemning their congregations for heinous sins of sexual desire, seemingly archaic crimes of carnal temptations that would guarantee speedy entrance to Hell. But clearly, our culture has not yet escaped from our moralistic, pleasure-denying traditions. As a result, teenagers and even young adults in their twenties and thirties, pretend to their parents that they're virgins, or nearly so. Lovers sneak around in the shadows. They disguise their encounters and delete phone messages. And even older people, like Simon, die with shame, not usually physically, but in their tormented psyches—because they cannot adequately live up to some unbending moral expectation.

Clearly, most Americans are not nearly as free and liberated, or as modern and honest, as we appear to be, and our secretive, sensuous escapades provoke inescapable judgments. Reflecting on the issue more personally, I think of how my father tortured himself into a fatal heart attack because of his duplicity with women, dying just days after his tortuous confession. And as for Simon, I can't imagine that my brilliantly sensitive friend ever felt completely at peace about cheating on Rachel, despite all his inner rationalizations and justifications.

After our walk on the beach and our decision not to visit Heather just yet, Danielle and I returned to Simon's house. Everyone was in the living room relaxing on the sofas and chairs—Simon's three sons, his daughter-in-law, Susanna, and his mother, but Rachel preferred not to sit and stood by the black piano, mostly staring at a photograph of Simon. Not wanting to be rude, Danielle and I joined in the circle of talk for a while, but of course, with Miriam present, we were all cautious and restrained with our words. When the halting, quiet conversation paused, Danielle and I excused ourselves and retreated to our guest room for a nap.

That evening, New Year's Eve, we returned to the Santa Monica outdoor promenade as planned. It felt good to get away from the somber gloom of Simon's home. In contrast, the outdoor mall was hopping with music and strolling couples, including many gay ones, and lots of small groups of one gender or another, people who didn't have intimate dates, but didn't want to be alone on this last night of the year, an evening culturally loaded with romantic expectations. Amidst the cacophony of chattering pedestrians, a lovely soprano caught my ear. We crossed the promenade and walked closer to listen to the enchanting voice of a young woman with long reddish-blonde hair. She looked like a young Rachel as, sitting on a small stool, she strummed on her dulcimer and sang "A Case of You," Joni Mitchell's wistful classic. "*Oh, I could drink a case of you—and still, I'd be on my feet—I would still be on my feet.*"

As I listened to these lyrics, describing an unquenchable addiction to a closest friend, naturally, I thought of Simon. I'd been drinking a very heavy case of him. After dropping a dollar in the sweet-voiced singer's basket, Danielle and I walked on and found a small Italian restaurant where the waiting time wasn't too long. We enjoyed a fine dinner highlighted with red wine, fresh pasta and lots of garlic. With a slight buzz from the wine, we strolled a few blocks to a packed cinema complex where we would see *Ghostwriter*.

Roman Polanski's movie provoked strong responses in both of us. Undeniably, the story evoked many comparisons with Simon's situation and actions. The main character is a highly successful leader with deep, nearly impenetrable secrets. A man mysteriously drowns. There's a long-term affair that becomes more obvious to the cheated-upon wife. And finally, there's a reckless act of seemingly intentional self-destruction at the end. Danielle and I both loved the film and talked about it fervently afterward. I thought of Simon's comments after we'd seen *Midnight Cowboy* with our girlfriends so many years before, his ardent desire to be with a woman who could discuss a great film for more than ten minutes. As I stared at my beautiful wife and listened to her in-depth reflections on *Ghostwriter*, I realized, as I do regularly for so many reasons, what a blessed and fortunate man I am.

The part of the film that grabbed Danielle the most was the ending. "He was so stupid to do what he did in the end. It was as if he were on an unstoppable mission that had to lead to his own destruction. He knew exactly what he was doing, and yet absolutely, he could not stop himself." She might as well have been talking about Simon.

While we were driving back to Simon's Brentwood home, we reached the magic moment of midnight, marking the end of one year and the beginning of a new one, even the start of a new decade. Several drivers around us honked their horns. We did not. A church rang its bells in celebration, but all I could think of was John Donne's mournful line that Hemingway loved: "Ask not for whom the bell tolls—it tolls for thee." The next day, around noon on New Year's Day, we would see our friend get lowered to his final resting place and then begin our long journey home to Oregon.

Eighteen

"One asks for mournful melodies;
Accomplished fingers begin to play.
Their eyes mid many wrinkles, their eyes,
Their ancient, glittering eyes, are gay."

—William Butler Yeats, "Lapis Lazuli"

Rachel, Danielle and I all awoke at dawn on Sunday. The sky was clear and blue for the first time after three mornings of grey fogginess. When the sun rose over the horizon, George Harrison's immortal song came into my head: "Here comes the sun, here comes the sun..." The women and I shared another kibbutz-style breakfast together. Wanting to be alone for a while, Rachel withdrew to her room. Danielle was anxious to call her son, to hear his actual voice and know more confidently that he was indeed all right and had recovered from his injuries. While she called him, I took another walk in the park.

When I returned from my walk, I could see Danielle was relieved and happier. Yes, Albert had actually answered his phone for her call, and their talk had gone well. His cuts and bruises were on the mend. He and the Muslim girl had spent the night at Mireille's. Conveniently, Mireille knew a friend in the neighborhood who had an available room to rent where the girl could stay as long as she wanted. She worked in a clothing shop in Aix, and at least for the time being, she thought it best to avoid Marseille and her angry brother. Insisting that he and the girl were not in a "serious" relationship yet, Albert did admit that they were dating and soundly reprimanded his mother for expressing anxieties that sounded too much like something his grandparents would say. Understandably embarrassed, Danielle vowed to her son that she would not repeat their mistakes.

After the phone conversation with her son, Danielle said she wanted to finish a painting she'd begun the day before. While she disappeared into Rachel's art studio, I spent some time in Simon's study. Rachel had invited me to take whatever I wanted of Simon's clothes and books. I'd already picked out a few items of clothing—some classy sweatpants and a few nice shirts, including my favorite, a dark-green, Western-style corduroy, that Simon enjoyed. In fact, I've been wearing it a lot as I've been writing these words. Even though we wear the same size and he had some nice-looking, expensive ones, I didn't take any of Simon's shoes. I did not want to walk in his shoes.

Alone in Simon's study, I stared at his wall of books, my eyes scanning the titles, my mind wondering which ones I might want to keep. I chose a couple of poetry books—a Yeats and a Robinson Jeffers and a collection of stories by Dostoevsky plus an extra copy of Simon's short story anthology. I also took two volumes from Simon's Holocaust collection, *Why the Germans? Why the Jews?* and *Nazi Ideology*. A few years later, I read those compelling works when my wife and I travelled to Central Europe, a journey that included a visit to Auschwitz.

Among Simon's collection of poetry, I saw my own volume of poems, *Ordinary Miracles*, and pulled it from the shelves. I read my handwritten note to him on one of the inner pages. It said: "To my deepest soulmate, who understands completely the beauty of ordinary miracles. May you enjoy countless ones."

Flipping through the volume, it was interesting to see which poems Simon seemed to like best. Some poems received a handwritten star at the top of the page. Several more noteworthy poems received two or three stars. Entitled "Even Heroes Sometimes

Sink," only one poem earned four stars. With images of a person leaping on a horse bareback and then sailing "untried seas," the poem celebrates overcoming caution and restraint, even though, as the title says, the hero might end up under water. The last lines push one to accept a challenge:

> *so when the moment arrives to attempt or avoid,*
> *leap or retreat, heed perhaps this small warning:*
> *insecurity can be reckless, when on the brink,*
> *caution ridiculous, intimidation needless,*
> *and even heroes sometimes sink...*

How strangely fitting that of all the poems in the book, Simon apparently liked this one best.

I checked the desk drawer where he had left behind his last poems, including the one titled "Death by Water." The poems were gone, but there was a yellow envelope in the drawer with my name on it. I opened it and found a beautiful Mezuzah with a note: "For your new Ashland home—with deepest love—Simon." A Mezuzah is a small, elongated enclosed box, just a few inches long, with the Ten Commandments, handwritten in Hebrew, rolled up inside it. It's meant to be placed above the front door of a home. I wondered when Simon might have bought it or when he had planned to give it to me. A little later, after I showed it to Rachel and expressed my gratitude, she said they had bought it during their visit to Jerusalem the year before. He had planned on giving us the gift when he and Rachel visited us in Oregon. At least that's what he told her. Too bad he never got to see the sacred little present where it presently stands, attached with honor at eyelevel on the right side of our Ashland front door.

Danielle and I packed our bags to prepare for our trip home. After the graveside ceremony, we would be close to the freeway and could conveniently begin our journey back to Oregon. Reuben arrived at his parents' home with Miriam, who, faced with the reality of burying her son, looked even more vacant than usual, lost in a grief beyond words. Reuben would be taking both his mother and grandmother to the cemetery. There would be no company limo this day.

As Danielle and I took our last walk through the house, making sure we had gathered all our belongings, I stared long and hard at some of the family photographs—images from the kibbutz, the boys' Bar Mitzvahs, vacation poses and even a large shot of Simon and Rachel getting married. Undeniably, I perceived more sadness in Simon's eyes in several of the photos, even the large, handsome black-and-white one of him with a half-smile, a close-up image that sits on top of the family's black piano. How had my own eyes missed these evident signs?

There's not much to say about the graveside ceremony. Only the immediate family and Danielle and I attended. Remembering a request from both Reuben and Rachel, I brought along my guitar, a classical one with a soft, sweet sound, and I played a few light chords as people gathered around the gravesite. Beside his father, on a beautiful little hillside, under the shade of a pine tree, Simon was laid to rest that morning. A cemetery rabbi chanted a few prayers in Hebrew. Like Simon's mother, the Holocaust survivor who sobbed non-stop, the rabbi knew nothing about how Simon's life had actually ended. Following the prescribed custom, everyone threw a handful of dirt on the dark wooden coffin, and it was slowly lowered into the ground.

I softly sang a favorite song of Simon's, the Beatles classic "In My Life," by John Lennon. I imagined Simon was right there, hovering like an angel above his grave, listening and smiling in a peaceful way. The achingly beautiful melody and lyrics seemed just right, especially these lines:

Oh, these places have their moments,
With lovers and friends, I still can recall—
Some are dead and some are living—
In my life, I loved them all.

I was exhausted, emotionally overwhelmed, and ready to head home. There were a lot of hugs and a few tears as Danielle and I said goodbye to the family. Harvey, Simon's brother, was more comfortable shaking hands. I was happy to see he was a little better dressed than he had been for his brother's memorial service. He still wore jeans, but his shirt and shoes were nicer, and his mother didn't scold him this time.

After we left Simon's gravesite, Danielle asked whether there was anyone else in the cemetery I wanted to visit. We're talking about Mount Sinai Cemetery, which must be the largest Jewish cemetery in Los Angeles. How odd that even in death, people seem to be more comfortable being surrounded by people of the same faith. You'd think that at least after we die, we wouldn't need to be so parochial and separated. Such wishful thinking!

As my wife knew, there are lots of people I might have visited in Mount Sinai Cemetery. Both of my parents, two extremely dear uncles, a lovely aunt and a sweet friend named Marty Goldstein are all buried there. Marty was a very close friend, a former next-door neighbor, carpenter, and promising writer, who died of a brain tumor at thirty-three after being rejected for treatment at a public hospital because he lacked health insurance. Simon knew him well also, and I still burn, thinking of Marty and our culture's twisted priorities that favor billion-dollar bombers and extravagant missiles over making sure everyone gets adequate basic health care.

Anyway, I had no desire to track down Marty's grave, or any other burial sites at Mount Sinai that day. There was no disrespect in this. I simply had no interest right then in deep reflections on other people

I had loved and lost. I'd had quite enough reflections on death for a while. Maybe if Mount Sinai were smaller and not located right next to an L.A. freeway, visiting the graves of lost loved ones would be more attractive to me. I imagined a little cemetery somewhere among some beautiful trees and hills near Ashland, where I might like to be buried someday in a very thin wooden box. And when the time comes, I'd like my wife to be placed in the ground right beside me. I thought of that great e. e. cummings poem that begins: *"when god lets my body be/ from each brave eye shall sprout a tree/ fruit that dangles therefrom/ the purpled world will dance upon..."* This natural return to and feeding of the earth feels more right to me than cremation, but I wonder whether it's the legacy of my religious traditions pushing me toward that preference. Anyway, I'm glad that at least Simon was able to be buried with honor, even if it did require deceiving some rabbis a little.

Back on the road, this time there were no snowstorms over the Grapevine to delay or intimidate. The drive was easy and fairly uneventful except for one jarring incident. We had listened to the radio for a while, searching for stations with music we liked. Scanning through the choices, however, one inevitably runs into countless religious broadcasts that offer Jesus-praising soft-rock, in addition to passionately righteous sermons. We listened to one guy in a thick Southern drawl, rant and rave about Obama, the supposed secret Muslim from Kenya who wanted to impose socialism on us. With fervent zeal, he screamed his warnings: "Can you not recognize the Anti-Christ, this agent of Satan, when you see the mongrel right before your eyes, demanding that we give up our guns and submit to World Government, the so-called United Nations? When are we going to stand up for Jesus Christ and our nation and take our country back?"

Danielle and I shook our heads and exchanged grimaced smiles, thinking of our fellow citizens and how embarrassingly fearful and gullible some seem to be these days, provoked by silver-tongued charlatans like the quack we'd just heard. Yes, these are strange times.

We turned off the radio, and I suggested that Danielle read us a story or two from Simon's anthology, the stories that take place in Poland during the decade before the Holocaust. She asked which story I'd prefer. We had both read the volume several years ago when it was first published, but neither of us had re-read any of the stories since then. I remembered one tale that had captivated me. It was about two boys fishing together by the river that runs through Warsaw. I asked her to find and read that story, remembering that it was a highly dramatic narrative in which the two young boys, one a Christian and one a Jew, fight over the Jewish boy's watch. Danielle located the story and read it out loud. It was just as good as I had remembered, but its conclusion completely transfixed us.

The Christian boy decided to try to physically grab the Jewish boy's watch, which had been a cherished gift from the boy's father. Rather than allow the bully to steal his beloved watch, the Jewish boy managed to pull his wrist away from the grasping hands of the would-be thief. In a split second, the boy was able to remove the watch and hurled it into the river. The next moments in the story mesmerized Danielle and me. With excruciating personification and detail, Simon described the watch sinking slowly to the bottom of the river and ticking its last few beats before it turned lifeless and still. Essentially, in the amazing conclusion of this story, Simon had revealed a semblance of his own death, writing the prophetic words years before he actually took his own fatal leap.

Evidently, this image of death by water had lurked in his brain for a long time. After she read the riveting words, so vividly capturing the watch's last beats of life, Danielle shook her head sorrowfully. Although Simon had foreshadowed his lethal plan symbolically in plainest detail, no one had deciphered his cryptic hint. Was he playing with us in some perverse way?

Naturally, this short story got us talking about the mystery of our friend's suicide. Just how long ago had he begun seriously contemplating taking his own life? Most painfully, we speculated about what, if anything, might have stopped him. How could his story have had a different ending? We wondered whether we had made the right decision, choosing not to knock on Heather's door. I still had her address folded up in my wallet. Maybe sometime in the future, we'd meet up with her, and maybe she would somehow help us better understand what was going on in Simon's mind and heart, and illuminate, at least partially, the enigma of his death.

We didn't make it all the way back to Ashland that day, but we made it more than halfway, stopping at a town named Williams for a late dinner and a motel. There's a restaurant there called Louis Cairo's that serves wonderful food, especially if you love garlic, as Danielle and I most certainly do. We shared a fish and pasta dish and the cozy establishment's infamously potent garlic potatoes.

After checking into our motel room, first Danielle and then I took long, cleansing showers. I wished I could wash away all the myopia and insensitivity that had blocked me from seeing and understanding the suffering that had trapped and ultimately consumed my dear friend. Would I ever be able to learn from my mistakes and change? These questions wracked my battered consciousness as I struggled to relax and clear my head enough to fall asleep.

Danielle was already asleep and breathing deeply as I rolled over and listened to my own slow mournful breaths. Images of Simon's coffin filled my heart with sorrow. I could see and hear Rachel and Miriam sobbing uncontrollably as he was lowered into the ground. I could picture the watch from Simon's short story slowly sinking toward the river's bottom in its last moments of life. Then I envisioned Simon, eyes bulging, legs bound, also sinking to the muddy river's bottom as he futilely struggled to free himself. Why, in God's name? Why, why, why? Exhausted from the finality of Simon's burial, the long drive, and the anguish of my unending questions, eventually and somewhat tearfully, I finally got to sleep that night, my sadness fittingly mixed with deep gratitude. Eventually, I realized I could smile through my tears. After all, there is some good fortune entwined with such sorrow: We poignantly comprehend that when it comes to losing a cherished one, our grief seems proportionate to our love.

Nineteen

"He comes for conversation
I comfort him sometimes
Comfort and consolation
He knows that's what he'll find"

—Joni Mitchell, *Conversation*

About six months after Simon's burial, a cousin's serious illness drew me back to Southern California. This time I travelled alone. After visiting my cousin in the hospital and wishing him a speedy recovery from his surgery, I decided to proceed with what I had long contemplated: meeting up with Heather, Simon's former secretary and mistress. I had let Reuben's little slip of paper with her address scribbled on it sit patiently untouched in my wallet, but my curiosity was bursting. I needed to know more about this woman who had become such an important part of my lost friend's life. When Reuben gave me her address, I didn't ask him why he hadn't included her phone number, but I remembered his words: "If you really want to better understand my father's situation, you should meet her in person." When he said that, I didn't know whether he meant that seeing her would be more respectful and courteous than calling her, or that I needed to see her in order to appreciate her physical and personal attractiveness.

After driving to Venice and finding a place to park, I easily found her address. Her apartment was on the second floor of a two-story condominium complex with balconies and walls made of mixed tones of brown stucco. A small forest of palm trees surrounded the units. Although I thought I was emotionally prepared for the encounter, when Heather peeked through the opened door after I knocked and stated my name, her undeniable allure and relaxed smile startled me.

"So, you're Ronnie!" she said with great warmth and a slight Southern lilt as she invited me in. "I wondered if you would ever show up. Reuben told me he gave you my address and that he 'forgot' to give you my phone number. Like accidentally on purpose—I'm sure...but I'm so glad you came to see me."

She looked even younger than I expected, probably in her early forties, around twenty years younger than Simon. It was about ten on a clear, sunny Saturday morning, and she was wearing a light blue terrycloth robe that ended just below her knee. A bit of her honey-colored hair drooped out of the twirled towel she wore like a crown. Obviously, she had taken a shower very recently, but even without a trace of make-up, she was unusually pretty—somewhat short, yet trim, olive-skinned and curvaceous, with turquoise eyes, the color of a sparkling sea. Reuben hadn't told me about her eyes. I could imagine Simon's huge inward grin when he first saw her and hired her. I wondered what Rachel must have thought when she first met her husband's radiantly lovely office assistant.

Her apartment was small, but attractive, just a block from the beach. The place was furnished comfortably, yet rather sparsely. As my eyes scanned the room, I felt a little like an intruder, an interloping spy peeking into my friend's secret, forbidden world. Two things caught my attention right away. First, I noticed a large photograph on the living room wall, showing Simon and Heather, arms around each other, smiling widely with what looked like a Hawaiian shoreline behind them. Probably one of Simon's "business trips," I thought to myself cynically. The second item that caught my notice was a book on the coffee table titled, *The Heart and Soul of Being Jewish*. Glancing at the large, illustrated volume, I wondered, of course, whether this woman still planned on converting to the faith, now that her Jewish lover was gone.

Heather certainly effused warmth and friendliness. Apologizing for having no "fresh-baked goodies," she brought us coffee on her sun-soaked balcony and talked relatively comfortably, considering the odd circumstances. I complimented her on her apartment, its uncluttered simplicity and of course, its wonderful proximity to the beach. We could faintly hear the ocean from her deck. Without hesitance or embarrassment, she admitted the apartment had been a gift from Simon long before his death.

"We had already been involved for a few years, and then he found this place for me, for us. We both loved it because it's so right here," she gestured toward the ocean, "right where you want to be. At first, I thought he was just paying my rent. When I realized he was buying this beautiful little haven—for me—I was overwhelmed. I hardly knew what to say. I've never been treated by anyone the way Simon treated me. That man was so kind, so generous. He made me feel like a queen—a cherished, intelligent queen."

Clearly, she didn't know or wasn't worried that her condominium might have been purchased illicitly or connected to missing company funds. To her, the lovely apartment was a rightful gift from a generous man she had loved and revered. I think she understood the value of real estate near the beach in Los Angeles. She grinned when she told me she no longer worked for the parking lot firm. Glad to be free of that downtown office, the difficult commute, and hushed rumors of carrying on with the boss, now she worked part-time as an assistant in a small Santa Monica medical office. In addition to her new job, she was also taking a class in Middle Eastern history at the local community college.

"Simon set me up pretty well," she confessed, while also clarifying that she enjoyed working enough "just to keep busy and feel useful." Evidently, this youthful woman from the Texan heartland wanted to reassure me that her values were rock solid, her motivations uncorrupted. "I was never a gold-digger," she declared with emphasis. "Simon and I just fell in love. It surprised the hell out of both of us."

There was something heartwarming and innocent about her, something simple and genuinely kind. In a way, she reminded me of the beautiful, heartland-raised young woman from Tulsa who picked me up hitchhiking decades ago. I could sense why Simon was drawn to her. She seemed relaxed, sincere, and compassionate. Clearly hoping for a semblance of sympathy, Heather described how awful she felt about the secrecy of her affair with Simon, including the dramatic, unexpected encounters on the beach with his sons. She was remorseful, yet also defensive about the suffering she helped cause.

"I know Rachel. I've met her several times, mostly on business occasions. She's smart and educated, as I'm sure you are aware, and I know she loved Simon. I've felt a lot of pain and compassion for her situation. But Simon and I fell passionately in love—maybe not right away, but over the years...from our time and experiences together...We loved each other more and more. I know he cared deeply for Rachel too. The truth is—and he told me this many times—he loved both of us....in different ways...and it was tearing his heart apart. And knowing how he suffered, even though he mostly tried to keep it to himself, it was tearing me apart too. I still can't believe he did what he did!" Her striking, aquamarine eyes clouded over with tears. Then she looked straight into my eyes and asked plaintively, "Did you ever have any idea, even the slightest suspicion, that he could do such a thing? This wonderful man with so much love and joy inside him!"

I confessed my obliviousness and ignorance. We both just shook our heads and stared at each other in silence. She understood quite well, she said with compassion, Simon's capacity for concealing his emotions. He had masked them from her as well. But he had also shared many stories with her about our escapades, including many during our UCSB days and even earlier times. She even knew the tale about our losing our virginity together.

"I know all about the two of you and Dolly Johnson," she said with a laugh. "I know he really loved you, Ronnie, even though he hid so much from you."

Of course, the most serious part of our conversation involved speculating about Simon. Could we possibly better understand his unfathomable decision? And was his decision inevitable? I offered my ideas about the Holocaust dragging him into a bottomless pit, despite all his noble efforts to make sense of it. She seemed to agree, but then shook her head, offering her own idea for what most might have motivated Simon in the end.

"I think in spite of all his smiles, he became a man who lost his faith. He thought Job, that suffering victim in the Bible, who never stopped believing in God—he thought he was a complete idiot. Simon lost his faith in so many things. I think he even lost faith and hope in Israel. Sure, he would always be a Zionist in his heart, but he could see that all the hatred so many people have for Israel and Jews was like Hitler's dying wish. Even when he tried so hard and wrote those two books, there was still so much hatred for this tiny little country. And then the Israelis pay the Arabs back with walls and more settlements and endless occupation of their lands. Simon knew it was becoming practically like South Africa and that whole Apartheid system. But he couldn't see any end to the mess, and it was driving him crazy."

"I think he ultimately lost faith in himself," I suggested, and asked whether she knew about Simon's unusual eating habits in the days before his death.

She said that in his first email from Buenos Aires, he had written that he was going to eat so much pork and bacon in Argentina, he might start to grow a curly little tail. "He was definitely saying screw-you to all those kosher rules," she said with a sympathizing smile.

I asked if she wouldn't mind sharing what his last email had said, the one written just hours before he died. She paused and then replied that she would rather keep his last words to herself. She said they were very romantic and reassuring words, but they frightened her terribly when she read them.

After this vague allusion to his final message, she paused again, reconsidering with a half-smile, and said, "He told me he loved me 'passionately, profoundly, and irrepressibly for eternity.' Those were his last words to me...I didn't know what to think. I got scared."

After a silence of several seconds, I mentioned the book on her coffee table, and we got around to the Jewish question: Did she still intend to convert? "Yes, I'm still taking my Judaism class with Rabbi Silverstein. I slowed down a little, but I still plan on becoming a Jew. Naturally, I started the whole thing because of Simon, but honestly, compared to where I come from—the good, old Baptist tradition with all its gentle, loving emphasis on burning in Hell because your normal human desires are so sinful and awful... Honestly, compared to that Baptist world, where my father thought I was a cheap slut because I wasn't a virgin, compared to that kind of judgment and shame, I like the Jewish world a lot." She pointed and walked toward her dining room table where two shapely silver candleholders with tall purple candles stood. "Simon gave me those beautiful things. They were made in Jerusalem—and I light the candles and say the Sabbath prayer every Friday night."

As if she felt a need to verify her claim, she sang a few words from the Hebrew blessing as she gracefully waved her hands in the ritualistic way Jewish women are taught to sanctify the Friday evening entry of the Sabbath. "*Baruch Atah Adonai*...See what I've been learning how to do? I love this world Simon introduced me to," she announced with a smile, and then she laughed. "Of course, my mother back in Texas thinks I've gone off the deep end and lost my mind. She tells me my daddy, if he were alive, would have taken out his shotgun if he heard about this. Then she asks me, 'Why would any normal, healthy person choose to become a Jew? That's like choosing to go to Hell and being weird all in one shot.' But I'm doing just that. I'm gonna become a Jew, even if there's no Jewish man who's gonna marry me." Her frank declaration made us both laugh.

Her openness was contagious. Although my next move made me nervous, I thought I might as well ask the question that had puzzled me ever since the day I first heard of my friend's affair and his death. Hoping she would not take offense at my words, I asked, "Did you think Simon was going to marry you?"

She smiled broadly at my bluntness. "I knew if I ever met you, you'd probably ask me that." She paused and turned quite serious, hitting me with those sparkling turquoise eyes. "He never promised me anything. I knew his family and his reputation meant the world to him, and men in his position say they are going to leave many times more than they actually leave. I'm not proud to say this, but I'll tell you, to be honest...Simon was not the first married man I've ever been with—just the best, the very best. And yeah, sure... sometimes we'd talk about getting married. We even fantasized about moving to Maui or the Big Island, maybe getting a few acres where we could have a little farm. We had some beautiful dreams. But they were never promises—they were just beautiful dreams."

As I watched and listened to Simon's soft-voiced lover, I felt a huge wave of empathy and compassion for him and his situation. She and Simon had created their own little world together in this apartment, in the nearby beach with its restaurants and nightclubs, in their brief vacations to Hawaii together, disguised as business trips. I realized that, as different as they are, clearly, Simon's olive-skinned secretary shared some distinct similarities with the wife of her lover. Sure, one woman speaks with an Israeli accent and could be quick at times to criticize her husband; the other, twenty years younger, with her slight Southern lilt in her voice speaks so reverentially about the same man. Both women, however, radiate kindness, honesty, sensitivity, and vulnerability—qualities that would make hurting either one of them extremely difficult. Simon was indeed caught between a rock and a hard place—trapped, cornered, captured in checkmate. Choosing to be with one woman, he would inevitably devastate the other. The legacies of his childhood, his immersion in the Holocaust, and his acute, innate sensitivity and gentleness paralyzed him. He could neither avoid nor endure adding any more suffering to the world—not to Rachel, not to Heather, not to anyone. There was no path he could take that would not create great pain. Yet tragically, the path he chose inflicted the deepest, most widespread, and longest-lasting anguish upon those who knew and loved him. His realization of this truth must have indeed horrified him—even as he tip-toed toward the river in Buenos Aires.

Our balcony conversation lasted about an hour with each of us becoming teary-eyed at different moments. Heather asked me a few questions about Simon's memorial service. She had considered but rejected the idea of sneaking in the back anonymously. Out of curiosity, she had visited his gravesite at Mount Sinai Cemetery, but only once. "I don't feel Simon's presence there, on that hillside beside his father," she explained. "I feel it a thousand times more when I walk along the beach and listen to the waves. You know how much he loved the sea. Maybe he should have been cremated and had his ashes scattered into the ocean...but that would have broken some Jewish law, right?" I nodded, letting her know she was correct in her assumption.

I gave her my Ashland address and phone number and invited her to drop by if she ever took a long trip up north. She gave me her phone number and an invitation to contact her again sometime. I think both of us sensed that our meeting had served its purpose, and we'd probably never see each other again. But I felt good having made this visit, seeing with my own eyes this lovely person who had brought so much love and joy, as well as perplexity and torment, into my dear friend's life.

When I got back home and described the encounter to Danielle, she too felt sorry for Simon's secret lover. Despite what Heather had said about no promises being given, Danielle sensed that consciously or not, Simon must have enticed his mistress with a certain amount of hope, a few tempting but delusional expectations about their future.

"A beautiful young woman like the one you described would be a fool to give up seven prime years of her life if she didn't have a certain amount of hope," she stated confidently. But beyond the physical allure, Danielle intuited the intense emotional attraction Simon must have felt for his lover. "Even though she was his wife and the mother of his children, Rachel was always in a way Simon's teacher—do you not think so? If she didn't correct him on his Hebrew, she might disagree with or modify some opinion he was expressing or point to some important idea he was missing. Maybe she just didn't admire him quite the way he needed or wanted. It seems like his sweet, adoring secretary from Texas gave him that— someone who could revere him, dote on him, and always see him as the wise and wonderful mentor."

Despite their stinging implications, my wife's comments once again seemed pointedly on target. I hope she didn't see me the way she saw Simon, as a man desperately in need of a woman's overwhelming adoration. I want to feel deeply loved and respected by my wife, but certainly not idolized. For various reasons, perhaps some having to do with his enraptured mother, Simon needed to be revered, to be adored and venerated beyond any criticism. And somehow this impressionable younger woman, this cheerfully vibrant, sun-bronzed secretary who became his illicit lover, managed to fill that essential desire, as well as other more carnal ones. Could she have satisfied him in the long run, had he chosen to leave Rachel and be with her? I had my doubts.

Twenty

"...An ordinary mortal, as it were, would be ashamed to wallow in dirt, but a hero was too exalted a person to be entirely covered in dirt, and hence I could wallow in dirt with an easy conscience."

—Fyodor Dostoevsky, *Notes from the Underground*

About one year after Simon's death, mainly on the advice of my wife, I decided to see a counselor in Ashland, hoping he or she might help me work through some of what was still tormenting me about the loss of my dear friend. While I'm not nearly as dismissive about counseling and psychology as Simon was, admittedly, I share some of his skepticism. There's a voice in my head that questions why anyone of good mind should have to pay money and work with a licensed professional to solve one's problems. What about just talking to a good friend, or better yet, shouldn't a person of strong intellect and emotional stability be able to figure out things for himself? Oh yes, there's plenty of Simon's arrogance in me.

Anyway, I decided to follow the advice of my wife, who was sick of my depressive moaning. I would see a counselor, and Ashland is filled with them. You just have to choose the style that suits you best. Do you go for a behaviorist, someone who would concentrate on here-and-now practicalities and positive re-enforcement? How about a Freudian type who would make me probe my earliest memories and dreams to understand my anxieties? Gestalt, Jungian, hypnosis, neurolinguistics, primal scream—Ashland has at least thirty-one flavors of counselors. I decided to try someone recommended by one of my Peace Choir friends. He said she was "keenly perceptive" and not likely to become an easy sucker for my bullshit. He told me this with an understanding smile, not to criticize me, but to acknowledge what we both knew to be true: Sometimes, I just talk too much, and my linguistic deftness could often be detrimental, producing a flood of intellectual chatter that could overwhelm the quieter, more vital message of my heart. Yes, I wanted to see someone who could see through my bullshit. When my choir friend described her, I even liked the sound of her name—Claire Revello.

After making an appointment a week earlier on the telephone, on a wintry, grey morning, I entered her second-story office, a cozy little space near Ashland's railroad tracks. She greeted me with a smile and offered some tea, which I declined. I could sense right away a deep calm she seemed to emanate, and despite my latent skepticism, almost immediately, I felt myself relaxing in her presence. With her long grey hair in a braid, her angled tan cheekbones, her colorful vest, and her turquoise earrings and necklace, she looked like she might be Native American, certainly at least in spirit. I liked the bright photograph on her wall showing a field of orange poppies leading down to a mountain lake. In the bottom corner of the shimmering lake was a Rumi quotation about people meeting in a field somewhere, "in a place beyond all judgment."

I had only one therapy session with Claire Revello, but I think one was enough. It lasted a little more than two-and-a-half hours. She prefers this approach. Expressing a touch of scorn for the counseling style most popular in our culture, she said she favors spending two or three consecutive hours, rather than several months or years, working with someone. With this concentrated approach, she hoped to help one arrive rather swiftly at the critical core of an issue, to assist that person in exploring some positive adjustments, and to move on. I liked the sound of her strategy. It made solving the problem feel more immediately achievable—almost like removing a boil or extracting an infected tooth.

At first, we sat on two leather chairs, facing each other, across from a window which offered a nice view of Ashland's snow-capped mountains. In the second half of the session, she brought out two soft pads, and we lay beside each other on the floor. Her voice is very gentle, almost hypnotic. In the beginning of our meeting, as I began to relax, she got me to talk about why Simon's death was causing me so much continued suffering. I admitted that I fought against even completely accepting the fact that his death was intentional. "Probable suicide" left open other possibilities. Somewhat desperately, I suggested the theory that he was murdered, thrown into the river by a liquor-sodden thief, who was angry and frustrated because Simon didn't have his wallet. Or maybe it was Simon, who was blasted, so zonked from a heavy Christmas Eve of drinking or too many pain pills, or who knows what. So, he jumped or fell into the river, got caught in a strong current, and somehow got his foot entangled in these ropes.

Sensing something doubtful about my speculations, my listener interrupted me and said, "You speak of these vague possibilities, but you don't even believe them yourself, do you?" She paused and stared, and reluctantly, I nodded. "So please, let's not waste our time. Speak to me from your heart, as deep and true as you can."

That was Claire Revello's technique in a nutshell. She would fix her dark brown eyes on me and urge me to get to the center of things. She didn't want to hear my old stories, cogent arguments, or deft analogies. She would cut me off and redirect me to my feelings, and with this focus, she was able to understand in that first hour my profound grief, my shameful guilt, and my intense anger over Simon's death. We explored those painful themes, but I think the greatest gift Claire Revello gave me during our morning together involved developing my empathy. She was convinced my anger, and probably my grief, could subside substantially if only I could see the situation more empathetically. Could I possibly envision things from Simon's point of view? By the time she got me to attempt this feat, we were lying beside each other on the floor. Her soft voice, encouraging and unthreatening, urged me onward, coaxing me to get inside his head and heart, to think and feel and BE Simon in his last minutes of life.

> I try not to look at the clock constantly. I've told myself I'll wait until three fifty-five. That will get me out the door by four, a nice quiet moment to make my departure. There shouldn't be more than one or two stragglers in the hotel lobby. Christmas morning, the perfect day to make my exit. Happy birthday, Jesus. I know just how you must have felt. I'm sick of the cross I've been carrying...
>
> I keep watching the clock...It seems like it's been 3:39 for a long time. I haven't slept one minute...might as well be conscious while I still can...Sixteen more minutes before I go. Rachel is deep asleep and about four feet away. Thank God for king-size beds that make it easy to be separate in the same bed...Rachel will stay asleep, I'm almost positive, and I'm glad. We don't need any more words. This is not about her. She has loved me and given us three sons. She's tried her best to forgive me. The problem is I can't forgive myself, and maybe I'm through with trying...I destroyed this woman's trust long before my thing with Heather...It started back on the kibbutz...just couldn't stop myself sometimes...felt

I had a right to experience everything, to go beyond the usual boundaries…and it was all wonderful…and sensual…and delightful except for the pain it caused my wife….my innocent wife…I don't blame her. We are who we are…Yet we've had an amazing life. We raised three wonderful sons. I stare at this tender, tortured soul…I hope and trust she won't wake up when I leave…But even if she did wake, could she stop me…And how hard would she even bother to try? How many times have I wounded her and yet she's loved me…Thank God your wounds are not visible, my dear, or the blood would cover and saturate these sheets…I hope you won't suffer too much because of what I have to do…It's not because of you…and it's not because of her…

Okay, so the mind wanders and I'm thinking of Heather too…How could I not…Even when I've been staring through the darkness at this pale woman beside me, my thoughts drift to my other woman, the one who has loved me with no hesitation, with no criticism or hang-ups…Sweet Heather, I'll miss her…I wish I could meet her somewhere outside for one last luscious kiss… but God knows we had enough of them…I'm glad I sent her that last email even though I got caught…Is "caught" the right term if you halfway intended it? What do you have to say about that, Jesus? But I will miss that woman…It wasn't just about the passionate sex…I grew to love her in many ways, in unexpected ways…I loved the way she laughed…and her smile…the way her face would light up when she ate a burger as if it were the best burger in the world…And sometimes, I even believed we might make it to Hawaii…and just be away from it all and eat burgers on the beach and I could almost see it...being with that light-hearted woman with her laugh and the easy way she loved me...She'll be okay, I think...I didn't promise her anything...but I know she hoped...I hoped too...but I just couldn't believe in it... not because of any of her shortcomings—we all have them, God knows...Anyway, with time, she's going to be okay...She'll remember the good times...And at least she's got a nice place that's her own now...Probably in a few months, or maybe she'll last a year—she'll be in that apartment I bought for her...She'll be there with a new guy...or maybe they'll be making love at his place... Anyway she'll be with a new guy, and I'll be replaced but she will always love me. Yes, we loved...and I'm grateful, in spite of everything, for all we shared...Dear Heather...I wonder whether you could have ever been accepted by my sons...It's 3:42...thirteen minutes to go...

I keep staring at my wife and thinking about our sons... We made beautiful sons...On that we can both agree... Our sons are going to be okay...Reuben will be angry, hurt, bewildered...but he'll be fine...He's pretty steely just like me...like father, like son...I'm proud of him, really proud of him...And the way he climbed right to the top in the company wasn't just because of me...He worked for it...He's smart and yes, he knew how to keep a secret...He allowed me to hold onto a world I'd kept hidden from everyone...He understood then and he'll understand now...I'm simply making a personal choice... It's not meant to hurt anyone...Reuben will forgive me... much more so than his brother, David...

Will my middle son ever be able to forgive me? I don't think so...Who knows...I know he'll be angry...he's always been the angry one...It tore me up when he saw me on the beach...Heather and I walking together ...I see his face at that moment...and I know I've disgraced him...I sacrificed his innocence, almost as bad as old Abraham sacrificing his son...or being so ready and willing to sacrifice him... But I really did it...I sacrificed his faith in me...and he could never look at me the same way again...David, if you could only feel how much I love you...I see you and Susanna someday soon having children...Have two or three or four...I know you'll be good parents and your children will be lucky... because you and Susanna will shower them with love and beauty...and live by the sea...Think of me sometime when you're by the sea, my son...Yeah, I see us side by side, catching the same sweet wave together...eyeing each other and riding a wave...I hope you'll think of me without all the anger...and just remember our love... Please forgive me, David...Thank God at least you found Susanna, so wise a choice...How I wish Reuben could do that...find his own Susanna...I want all my sons to be happy...happier than I've been...

And Rachel, what will become of our Nathan, our little one, the quiet, forgotten one? Will he find the right woman to light his heart and soul and make him happy? Or maybe it's the parking lots that are blocking his joy, the light in him...I don't know what it is... maybe my own projection...maybe a genetic disposition toward misery and being glum... I just know he doesn't seem quite happy enough...I hope we didn't spoil him...

His tender face was hard to resist...Sweet Nathan...the quiet one...what will you think of me?...You have yet to discover your strength...but I know you will...I see your face as you've learned something new—to ride a bike, to swim, to score a goal...you scored so many goals...You brought us much joy but I brought you shame...I saw your face in the circle, your horrified, open-mouthed astonishment, when all the rot had to be faced in front of everybody...I saw your embarrassment...your disgust... and I know I'm no longer worthy...I've forsaken you and the others with how I've lived...but I hope you'll know I never meant to hurt anyone, not you or either of your brothers or your innocent mother who sleeps right here beside me...her delicate rosy-blond hair lying across her white forehead and cheek...Please forgive me Rachel... and help our beautiful sons to forgive...Everyone will be okay...

But there will be no note, no succinct explanation... What would I say anyway...That I was caught between two women and didn't want to hurt either of them... It's not exactly that situation, though of course that's part of my many problems, my many deep incurable problems...What I've got wrong with me goes beyond all that...I listen to my wife's heavy breathing...I see the aching crevices, the lines my cheating and lying have carved into her face...Yet even when I have betrayed her, too many times to count, she puts up with me and comes with me here to this city on the other side of the world...the underside of the world...this refuge of choice for runaway Nazis...With hope in her heart, my wife came with me to Argentina...but even on this other side of the world, we're still the same people, and we didn't even get to dance the Tango...

I lie here and hear my stomach growling...too much booze, yes...but also moaning from what it's not used to...My belly is filled with pork and shrimp, lobster, ham and bacon, the forbidden fruit I've stuffed myself with all week...I filled myself with delicious filth because I feel like filth...I am filth...Oh, what would the rabbis say? Why would a pious man deliberately choose impiety? What would the rabbis say, what would anyone say, about a man who chooses not to restrain himself, not to refrain from the things he's promised to refrain from...Growl and moan, fucking stomach— maybe you'll wake up Rachel...I growl and moan in my soul...

Oh God, what will be said of me...I fucked it up with those emails...Why did I do that? Did I really wish to get caught? Happy birthday, Jesus. How sure were you that you wanted to get caught? It's Christmas morning...an interesting day to depart...We Jews aren't even supposed to think of you, Jesus, but I've thought about you a lot... What a mess you caused...I would have liked to meet you, Rabbi Yeshua...I think I would have loved you, loved the way you made the stiff old guys shudder... Sometimes you just gotta do what you feel called upon to do. Right?

I've tried to put things in order but I can't control the pain this will cause...We all cause pain in our own way...I think maybe I've seen and felt too much...I don't know why I was drawn to what I was drawn to, but the pull was irresistible...A moth drawn to the darkness...I wanted to understand the darkness, the brutal details... the masses crammed into cattle cars because they spoke a different tongue or talked to God the wrong way... They took showers with gas instead of water, or they were lined up and shot, having dug their own ditches, or they were beaten or starved to death after being closed into a pen...I see them in my fucking mind... Maybe I shouldn't have gone to Poland...Maybe I should have taken Prozac...Would it have numbed or circumvented the pain? But I wanted to keep my mind, my head more "natural"...even if my brain is a natural disaster...

Why do I feel I must complete this vision, this two-block journey to the river...What a strange chosen destiny and yet it feels somehow just right, like this mission I'm completing, this voice I'm hearing...Yeah, like Abraham heard a voice and he followed it...He tied up his only son to kill...he raised his knife and was ready to kill and he was deemed holy...the holy man who listened to the right voice...I'm listening to a voice... I'm hearing a voice...I see what I want to do...I think I know what I want to do...but I'm glad I'm leaving no note, no listing of grievances...the little things that fucking messed up my equilibrium....Yeah, maybe I shouldn't have gone to Poland, to Warsaw...historic Warsaw with its placid river...

There's something about a river...what a fucking way to go...They'll find me soon...I won't be down there very long...at least my body...but where will I be or will I be at all, isn't that the question...I have no idea, I only know I've had enough of this place...Maybe I shouldn't have gone to Poland...got too close to the story...but I wanted to...like a moth drawn to the darkness...I wanted to know how ninety-nine per cent of a million Jews holed up in a Polish cage managed to die...I wanted to tell that story...Maybe it was perverse...but I'm glad I tried...I wrote two books...Some people will read them... who knows how many...Maybe others can tell the story better...I tried and maybe it got to me more than I could control...Warsaw and talking to the living dead, the broken ones who survived...I wanted to hear their stories...and the poor souls opened up to me in their Yiddish, their eyes burning in memories...describing the fucking details...and I listened and agonized and listened some more...Yes, maybe it got to me more than I thought it would...We are such stuff as dreams are made of and nightmares have infected me...I'm surely infected with something and I've chosen my own way of putting an end to my disease...my dis-ease...No I am not very easy about this...It's 3:47...Eight more minutes before I rise from this bed and begin my journey to the end...

I think I can do it but I'm not entirely sure...I've chosen a path and made preparations but is it possible I'll change my mind...Maybe I'm sick. Sick people want to kill themselves, I want to kill myself, therefore, I'm sick....Whether I'm sick or not, this choice feels right... And as far as sickness goes, I'm getting out of it...no old age, no fucking sicknesses and operations...no chemo, no rehab, no open-heart surgeries, radiation, fusion, or

ten drugs to fuck you up...I've had plenty of the drugs...
yeah, maybe too many...My wonderful back...locks up
again and again, and then I take the pills...Yeah, they
warn you but maybe not enough...Too many pain pills...
and then they become the pain...The doctor warned me,
but who's going to take that stuff seriously when your
muscles are so contracted you can barely walk... At least
my back doesn't hurt right now...It's a little tight, but all
that booze helped...and those powerful little pills...

My back felt good and loose in the nightclub...I felt
young and alive...and I liked dancing...yes, with joy
and lightness, I danced...even though it wasn't with
my wife who doesn't like to dance...So I danced with
a pretty Argentine with long dark hair and a slinky,
undulating body, and I felt light and good and I loved
the music...and my fucking back didn't hurt, and yet
even while I danced, I knew what I was going to do
later on...I lie here on my back...I can see my smiling
face of just a few hours ago, bright and pretty drunk,
a live band with lots of brass instruments and a raspy-
voiced lead lady singer in a red satin dress...great
rhythmic music...and I loved dancing with this
dark-haired smiling woman whose husband doesn't
like to dance...and who stays at the table with Rachel...
and so I'm dancing with a beautiful Argentine with
mounds of dark hair that runs right over her half-
exposed breasts and Rachel doesn't like it very much—
but still I danced...even when I could see the sadness
on her face. But after that, the coldness got colder...I'm
not blaming Rachel...I love this woman sleeping next to
me...and I'm hoping she will not awaken...I won't put my

sandals on until I am outside the hotel...There shouldn't be more than a few people in the lobby, not at this hour...

In the tiny glow from the clock I'm trying not to look at, I see Rachel's face, her sensitive, pale, lightly-freckled face, her amazing orange hair, just like her sisters...five sisters with orange hair and four of them still on the kibbutz...I stare at my wife and I think about her sisters...At least I didn't make any moves on them...I do have some limits to my lechery...I wonder how they're doing on the kibbutz...I love my wife's gentle, orange-haired sisters...and all their beautiful children, my nieces and nephews...Rachel's sisters are all like her, not just because of the orange hair, but because they're all honest and idealistic and sensitive... and they'll never leave the kibbutz because they still believe in that dream...I loved and I believed in that dream for a while...and maybe I shouldn't have left...to chase Mammon and live in comfort...Beverly Hills, then Brentwood...a life of luxury...but who could blame me?... Besides, the kibbutz had begun to stifle me...Isn't that how it is with dreams...They begin so bright and then they become stifling...too much toil and strife for not enough happiness and meaning...The numbers don't add up...too much shit for too little pleasure...Oh God, how full of shit I am...I know I've had pleasures, wonderful pleasures...maybe too many... Please forgive me, gentle woman lying like an embryo curled beside me... Though what I'm about to do will make absolutely no sense to you, please, try to understand...You and I made beautiful sons...and they'll have children...and they'll be free, more free than you and me...You and I've been too close to the tragedy...Only with miraculous luck did our parents survive...You were born in the Promised Land...and I in a German displaced persons camp...and yes, maybe I've always felt a little displaced, a little detached...the observer who tries to see and understand everything and maybe I just fucking feel like I've seen and understood enough...Don't need to hang around for any more scenes, any more fucking pain and dying... or waiting around a few pointless years so I can die a decrepit old man with sagging flesh, an aching back, a wilted cock and a decaying brain that's turned me into a moron...I'm getting out while I'm still whole and in control...Anyway, it's my decision, and no one can fucking stop me...

I've got a plan...an exit plan and something to help me execute it...It's just lying in a bush waiting for me... What amazing luck I found it on our first day here, one block from the river, at a construction site...I won't have to resort to rocks in my pocket, my original plan... No, I found a steel bar, half a foot long, its end stuck in a jagged piece of concrete, meshed together with a piece of rope...and best of all...for just the right touch, about a foot of barbed wire...barbed wire...The gift was waiting for me...I found it the first day we arrived...in a pile of demolished concrete, near a bridge...a concrete glob of junk with barbed wire attached. Now it's hidden in a bush...and I can picture things...plenty of rope, plenty of weight...I can see it now...a clean straight line into the darkness, and this will finally be over and done and I will not have to cause, see, or endure any more pain...

I'm not just thinking about my personal agonies...I mean all kinds of pain and I've had enough...I don't want to read another fucking newspaper or see some ass on TV tell me about another explosion in Israel, another synagogue burned in Belgium or France...or...you get the picture... I'm sick of worrying about my people, my dear people of the Torah...especially the ones living in this tiny beautiful land, the land I plowed and loved...I'm worried about that land...the kibbutz with the sisters of my dear wife, this gentle one beside me...I'm terrorized by images of bombs and my poor wife's sisters and their children...I don't need to fucking check the news anymore...The Arabs and the Jews—they aren't getting together anytime soon...I'm so sick of all this hatred and this going around in circles... revenge begetting revenge...and all in the name of God... Dear God...I stare at my wife's soft face and it makes me think of her sisters on the kibbutz and bombs exploding and women screaming and maybe I've just had too many nightmares...

Maybe there is something wrong in me that pulls me to this dark side...instead of thinking about the good things...Oh, my God, am I really going to do this thing... Attach myself to the heavy blob with the barbed wire and rope...Will I tie the knot...The plan is set and I am not lacking in determination...I know what I want to do and I don't feel like I'm crazy, even though that's what others will say...No, this choice makes sense to me...People will say what they'll say...They'll find me and they'll probably say I killed myself or maybe they'll think I was murdered...It doesn't matter...and it doesn't matter where exactly they bury me...in an honored place or not...it doesn't matter...I'm getting out of here...I've had enough... It's 3:51. Four more minutes before I'm on my way...

Of course, I wonder whether I might change my mind, whether I might limp to the edge of the water with the thing tied to my leg...and change my mind...Or maybe just when I'm about to change my mind, someone hidden in the dark will come out and push me in. Yeah...some fucking crazy guy could come out and push me in for no fucking reason...or maybe because he sees my face and rightly guesses I'm Jewish and this crazy guy that's hidden in the dark near the bridge where maybe I'm walking away from the edge, maybe he hates Jews...They've got plenty of those guys here, children of old Nazis that escaped...good old Jew-haters...They're here like they're everywhere, still painting swastikas on synagogues...So this fucking crazy Argentine guy who hates Jews for who knows what crazy reason— because we killed God's Son or make too much money or are somehow too clever for our own good...This crazy guy who's lurking in the darkness, this anti-Semite who makes me confess my identity—yes, I'd like him to be the one to push me in...That would really be the perfect ending...But who needs perfect...mine will be good enough...I've set things up just right...Rachel and I had a fight...I told her I might take a one-way walk to the river...They'll know where to look for me...I won't be under the water that long...and of course, I won't feel anything by then...I'll be free of all things...I'll be with God, as they say, whatever that means...I know it means I'll be free of this pain...and whatever will be, will be...

I look at this frail woman beside me, this pale deep-breathing soul with her wispy orange crown...Somehow she forgave me in her own way and tried to take me back...but I guess I don't want that...My cup hath run over, and I don't need any more of anything...I've had enough wine...enough women...and for sure, enough pain, unusual pain...because of what I've been drawn to... The pain of death camps and displaced persons camps... the pain of Warsaw...the fucking pain in my lower spine and the pain from the fucking pills that relieved the fucking pain in my spine...Oh, listen, to me whine about my pain...Everyone has pain...I've had so much privilege...I got to see half the world...every part of the planet that interested me...every country and city...But maybe I shouldn't have gone to India...It made me sick to see what I saw...That place fucking wounded me... The poor shall always be with us as you said, sweet Jesus...but what the hell did you mean by that...Just how complacent and accepting are we supposed to be? If you were in India and saw the hungry eyes and meagre bellies, what would you say, Jesus, upon whose birthday I choose to make my departure...The poor shall always be with us...but what are we supposed to do about it?

Maybe I should have paid my workers more, the brown ones with their broken English...I gave them jobs and a paycheck and sometimes I listened and learned about their struggles, their trying to make it on what I paid them...I see their pleading faces and hear the desperation in their voices as they strain to be polite, "Mr. Lieberman, it's so hard to get by, the rent is high, my daughter is sick, I could sure use a raise..." Yes, I see them and hear their voices and maybe I should have paid them more...But I also remember the words of my father and his stern voice: "To be good in business, Simon, you must not have too soft of a heart. That's for the mothers. A man must be strong and not have too soft a heart. We have so many workers and they all want more money. Be strong, and take care of your own family." Oh, Father and your lessons about strength and coldness and being a man worthy of respect... I'm so glad you're not alive to have to hear about what happens to me...

It will be hard enough for Mom, beautiful mom...Maybe they won't tell you everything and no one will know for sure what happened...From the beginning, you taught me wonderful things. You loved my sensitivity... You nurtured my awareness and even as I realized how wealthy we were, what privileged lives we lived, you taught me to have an eye out for the poor and suffering...to find ways to give...*Tzedakah*...You told me stories of your suffering, the terrifying ways you managed to survive...You told me those stories...at maybe too early an age...I'm not blaming you, but those stories got in my head...Maybe hearing your mother talk about killings and starvation and torture before one leaves elementary school has some advantage...but it has its dark side too...Even though I was small, I knew more about some things than most grown-ups...That made me feel pretty weird...but so it goes...

I'm not complaining...I've lived an amazing life, but maybe I'm too sensitive...and maybe I knew too much too soon and then I wanted to know more...Maybe I shouldn't have gone to India...shouldn't have gone to Warsaw...but I was drawn to what I was drawn to, like all of us...and I was drawn to a lot of darkness...but God knows I had more joys than most people could dream of...including joy with this woman, this small tender woman lying beside me...She brought me deepest joy and I see her on the day I first met her...my Hebrew teacher with this long mane of orange hair and this bright smile and such love for Hebrew...I started to fall in love with her that first day in class...And oh, how we loved the kibbutz...We loved that dream together and had beautiful children together...this frail, pale woman...I hope and wish that she'll be all right...that she'll not suffer too much and that she'll forgive me...I do feel deep in my heart, that with a little time, she'll think of the good times...our adventures, our Sabbaths, our three beautiful sons...I hope and pray she'll think of the good lives we've lived together and not just the betrayals and disappointments...I hope she knows she is not at all to blame...She's forgiven me as well as she could...but she's been dealing with a pretty hard case...

Maybe I have my own mark of Cain...something you're born with, something that makes you do some fucked-up things...a mark of Cain...inflicting pain on an innocent woman, a gentle soul who's suffered too much from my transgressions, my apparently unstoppable, incurable transgressions...I'm so sick of forcing her to tolerate what's intolerable...What do you do with a husband who cheats...who has a fondness for darkness... How much should anyone try to forgive anyone? I've

had enough fucking forgiveness...There will be no
note, no explanation, nobody or nothing in particular
to blame...because how could I say it all anyway...And
besides, anyone who does what I'm going to do is either
sick or crazy, take your pick, and either one isn't too
good, not the kind of person you could trust...So I offer
no reasons, no explanations...I'm not making a statement
about life that applies to anyone else. God knows
this life is precious and good and rich with joy and
opportunity. But as for myself and the fucking state of
things inside me, all that points in one direction. Some
will forgive, and some will not...I don't think I'll change
my mind... I hope the people I love will understand
and accept my decision, all the ones closest to my heart,
including Ronnie. It's 3:55 now. Time to leave.

Twenty-one

"So the challenge is to take one's woundings and open them to the treasures they contain...so that growth from our wounds can be continuous and powerful, without allowing our minds to be caught in a particular theological or political prism."

—Jean Houston, *A Mythic Life*

Most of the events that I've described occurred in the last days of 2010. It took me nearly six years to feel ready to tell this story, finally beginning it in early October, a few days before Yom Kippur, 2016.

There are lots of reasons I could give to rationalize why I needed to wait so long before I could write about Simon. First of all, I was just too angry for the first few years. Hardly a day went by without my barking out to him, "You fucking asshole!" Usually, these words weren't audible. I especially tended to curse him during the best moments of the day or night. It would be right after making love, or watching the splendor of a sunset, or seeing a great movie, or playing with my grandchildren, or sharing a wonderful meal or music with good friends—right after experiencing these simple, joyous moments—that's when I'd offer my nasty curses, angry and bewildered that he had chosen to miss out on all this.

But even after my therapy session with Claire Revello, even as my anger subsided and my ability to empathize improved, I still needed a few more years and certain clarifying experiences to better understand Simon's mysterious story, including my part in the tragedy—and it is a tragedy. There's a tendency among people haunted by a loved one's suicide to say and believe, "Oh, there's nothing that could have been done to prevent him or her from doing it." That can't be true all of the time, and I don't think it was true in Simon's case.

Simon's oldest son, Reuben, also didn't believe his father's self-destruction was inevitable. Thankfully, Danielle and I still see all three of Simon's sons and Rachel, but we've seen Reuben more than his brothers. He celebrated Passover with us a few years ago at my daughter's house. With her Egyptian husband, Hani, my younger daughter, Elana, is building a small, tight community of friends on a few gorgeous acres in Lagunitas, California. Since they had just moved to the redwood-encircled property, celebrating Passover with them that year was also a sort of housewarming party. I loved having that opportunity to meet up and hang out with Reuben for two days at my daughter's new place. He looked lighter and happier. Finally fed up with the all-consuming family business, he had quit the world of parking lots and was beginning an extended northerly road trip in his silver, electric Chevy Volt.

The emancipated young man had driven north several hundred miles, and we had driven south almost as far to connect with him in Lagunitas. I think Reuben loved the sense of community at Hani and Elana's Passover celebration. Maybe it rekindled some memories of his childhood on the kibbutz. About twenty-five people enjoyed the evening together, sharing lively conversation and spirited singing.

Commemorating the Jews' exodus from Egyptian slavery and somewhat contradicting Simon's pessimism about the near-intransigence of the human condition, the Passover story shows that our lives can be significantly improved, that oppressive forces can be overcome. Our host, my Egyptian son-in-law, smiled with good-natured tolerance as we re-told the ancient narrative, including the "ten plagues," which afflicted his ancestors and challenged the stubborn Pharaoh to let the Jewish people go free. What does it take to change one's mind, to finally let go of what needs to be released?

I was glad to see Reuben's face light up that night, as we ate the ritualistic matza and bitter herbs, and especially as we all sang "One Day," a bouncy, dreamy peace song written by a reggae-loving, formerly Orthodox Jew. "*One day we'll all be free—and proud to be—under the same sun, singing songs of freedom.*" Reuben knew all the lyrics and lubricated with several tradition-required glasses of wine, he sang with unusually liberated delight.

But frankly speaking, Simon's eldest son, the one who chose not to divulge his father's amorous secret, has always seemed a little sad, a little detached. In a way, Reuben's life has resembled the life of his father. Both were uprooted at the age of eight and moved to a foreign country. Simon had spent the first eight years of his life at a displaced person's camp in Germany. Reuben had lived his first eight years on an Israeli kibbutz. Simon almost never mentioned those years in Germany, or the dramatic transition and adjustment demanded when he came to the United States with virtually no English. You could never detect the faintest trace of an accent in his voice, but sadly, I had not reflected enough about how traumatic his childhood and intercontinental move must have been, or how long his sense of feeling like an outsider might have persisted. I should have asked him more questions.

The morning after the big Passover celebration, the Seder, Danielle and I enjoyed some quieter, more private time with Reuben. We walked slowly along a redwood-lined creek, and he talked about his decision to leave the family parking lot company. He didn't like the guy who had taken over Simon's CEO position, the obese, humorless fellow who had spoken at Simon's memorial. But beyond that issue, the eldest son had simply had enough of the parking lot business. He had "other lives to live," as Thoreau would say. With two other guys, Reuben was opening a restaurant in West

Los Angeles, creating their own independent business. And no, he was not in a relationship. He had numerous friends, he assured us, and the way he slightly smiled, suggested some of those friendships might come with "benefits."

Despite all his friendships and the comradery of his circle of buddies, Reuben still seems engulfed in a quiet loneliness. He's always quite thoughtful, tentative and selective with his words, a sharp observer whose feelings are hard to read. After his father's death, he benefitted from some serious therapy with a counselor, who helped him better understand and recover from the trauma triggered by the suicide. Speaking as one who had only recently gained a lot from a counselor's help, Reuben looked directly in my eyes and chose his words with extreme care: "I think my father would be alive today if he had seen a different counselor." As soon as he said that, I couldn't help but wonder to myself, whether he might be alive today if his so-called best friend had been more awake and perceptive.

The power and assuredness of Reuben's statement shocked Danielle and me, and we exchanged similar, disturbed glances. According to his eldest son, Simon's few "therapy" visits with the counselor Rachel had chosen proved to be a futile charade: "If you don't click with your counselor, perhaps don't even respect her, what's the point? And of course, my brilliant father didn't believe he needed any help at all." The stark truth was that Simon didn't really seek or want professional help because he couldn't stomach appearing weak or lacking in self-sufficiency. It was Simon's stubborn state of denial, his intellectual arrogance, his eldest son concluded, that ultimately cost him his life.

Danielle and I were happy to see that at least Reuben appeared to be recovering from the whole trauma. Ironically, his father's tragedy actually seemed to be helping him in a way. We could see he was becoming a warmer, friendlier person, more direct and expressive of his feelings. He seemed to understand himself a bit more as well, and that's what helped him realize that it was time to leave the parking lots behind. Feeling free and unencumbered, he was excited to be heading north in his new car, his silver electric cruiser. He hoped to reach British Columbia, and we urged him to see us in Ashland on his return journey.

A few weeks later, his Volt pulled into our Oregon driveway, and we got to visit again. Reuben was exhilarated from his meandering odyssey through the Northwest. As soon as he arrived, he noticed the beautiful mezuzah above our front door. He smiled on learning it had been a gift from his father. Then, rather cynically, he declared: "My dad sure loved those Ten Commandments—all but one or two."

When the two of us were alone, Reuben asked me if I had ever tried to contact Heather. I told him a little about my visit to her Venice apartment and the warm impression she'd made. I thanked him for giving me her address and mildly encouraging me to see her. With a slight grin, he said he was glad that now I better understood certain aspects of his father's dilemma. Even though Danielle knew of my little visit with Simon's lover, Reuben and I spoke in hushed tones. And no, I hadn't told his mother, at least not yet, about my Venice rendezvous. Another convenient little lie of silence.

Danielle and I enjoy seeing Reuben now and then, usually at his mother's home for an evening meal or Sunday brunch. He appears to be the forever bachelor, but we probe him about what kind of woman he might like to hook-up with eventually. He seems to be a little "old school" in his tastes, preferring submissive types who aren't too "aggressive." Reuben admits he feels more comfortable with females who allow a guy to feel more in control and less criticized. He almost never dates Jewish women or Israelis. It's funny yet understandable, how, although we modern men are supposed to find joy and satisfaction in the new equality between the genders, for many of us, including Simon and his eldest son, something deep in the ancient psyche longs for an easier, more compliant and traditional kind of partner.

Probably the greatest joy that Simon longed for and missed out on, is the delight of becoming a grandparent. Within weeks, maybe just a few days after his death, his beautiful daughter-in-law became pregnant again, and this time, there was no miscarriage. Nine months later, a lovely girl was born and given the middle name "Simone." Two years later, a second grandchild arrived, a boy. There's even a better word than "joy" to express the profound delight and satisfaction that come with being a grandparent. It's a Yiddish word that I used to hear my grandmother, Bubby, utter now and then. *Nachas*—nothing in life is better than *nachas*, she would say. Being a grandpa or grandma gives you *nachas* like nothing else. Simon missed out on that contentment.

His middle son, David, remains angry about his father. Time has eased him toward forgiveness, but he's not there yet. He and his wife, Susanna, are raising their kids in the Malibu hills, in a new home he built overlooking the ocean. David still loves to surf. Gaining more freedom than his father ever knew, he quit the parking lot firm a few months after his older brother and formed his own small construction company. He designs and builds homes, one at a time. He gets to use his creativity, and when it comes to getting good workers and communicating well with them, his Spanish helps a lot. He knows his father, despite all his transgressions, provided him with extraordinary opportunities.

After his dad's death, unlike his older brother, David didn't see a counselor. I guess his innate, pragmatic optimism, and his wise, sensitive wife, helped him move on—plus the needs and delights of raising two young children. He questions whether he'll ever entirely forgive his father—for the way he lived, or the way he chose to die. Yet he seems to be relatively at peace with the whole tragedy.

As for Rachel, she still lives in the same Brentwood house she shared with Simon. Little has changed in the home. Photographs of Simon alone or with the family still cover several walls or sit on polished furniture. She's dated a few men, but she's very cautious and understandably concerned that someone might be tempted to feign great affection or love in order to take advantage of her wealth. Inexplicably, she's lost all contact with Rebecca and Jerry. When she told me of that development, it fed my previous suspicions about Simon and Rebecca's relationship, but I said nothing about any of this to Rachel, and she said nothing further about it. The complete and unexplained loss of what had been a close relationship with a couple as well as their children had clearly caused her great pain. I imagine she has her own suspicions.

Danielle and I manage to see Rachel once or twice a year on our trips to Southern California. The question that burns inside of me that I may or may not ever have the courage to ask Rachel is this: Why didn't she encourage Simon to call me during his torturous last months? Did she not want him to contact me because she sensed I would urge him to leave her, just as I had left my first wife? But why didn't he choose to call me? Did he instinctively know what I would have advised him to do? Maybe my anticipated clear-cut "solution" to his predicament—getting a divorce and moving on—was NOT what he wanted to hear. Maybe if I could have let him know he could openly express his pain and dilemma—if I just could have tried to draw him out more and listen better, and not feel compelled to "fix" the problem—maybe then he would have shared more with me. But then again, why had I not called him? How had I become so complacent and passive about our relationship? The haunting questions still churn and burn.

The most persistent questions, of course, are: Why did Simon decide to choose death, and was his choice truly inevitable? I still can't answer those questions with any certainty. As for Simon's motives, choose your favorites—he had so many.

My understanding of the Holocaust's emotional toll on Simon expanded when my wife and I took a trip to Central Europe in 2015. I thought of him often and in fact, began reading two of his Holocaust-related volumes during our journey. Although we started our trip in sunny Croatia, during late September, traveling the following weeks, the weather changed, and our mood grew more somber. We took buses and trains north as the days grew shorter and colder, knowing that soon we'd reach Krakow and Auschwitz, where four of my grandmother's sisters had been killed a few years before I was born.

Reminding us in an eerie way of the Nazi-inflicted desperation, a contemporary unfolding disaster was catching our attention. We saw dozens and dozens of refugees fleeing the catastrophic war in Syria. They were mostly men in their twenties, but also women and children. Desperately, they were trying to head north and west into Europe, usually carrying only a small backpack or a few blankets. They huddled together in small groups inside and outside the train stations in Croatia and especially in Vienna, and often they were confronted by local police, who demanded identification papers which they would carefully inspect. When we saw these poor, frightened fugitives, Danielle and I counted our obvious blessings. We had wallets with credit cards and passports with privileges, while these fleeing alien outcasts had virtually nothing.

Vienna and Prague are beautiful, fascinating cities, but our short stays there were clouded by the dreary knowledge that in a few days, we'd be visiting the Third Reich's most infamous death camp. Everywhere we walked in those celebrated capitals, we saw gorgeous architecture with elaborate, inspiring carvings, some whose frozen faces stared out at us with silent, unnerving questions. In an ancient church, we heard the symphonic magnificence of Mozart, Beethoven and Bach. Meanwhile, we wrestled with the mind-numbing paradox: How, in this most sophisticated and cultured part of the world, with its glorious music, art, sculpted gardens and cathedrals—how in God's name had this most horrible, genocidal nightmare occurred here?

As I read the books I'd taken from Simon's library, one volume, *Why the Germans? Why the Jews?* particularly captivated me with its economic details. Startling statistics, depicting the enormous gap in wealth between Jews and non-Jews in Germany just before the rise of Nazism, help one understand the intense material envy that fed the madness. One tries to comprehend the horror, but its magnitude and systematic efficiency boggle the mind. The images chill the soul: masses of innocent men, women, and children removing their clothes and marching helplessly into the fatal showers.

Simon immersed himself in those images for years. They were a part of him, entwined with the legacy of his first eight years in that German camp for displaced persons, where his parents, miraculous survivors of the slaughter, had met. For whatever obvious and inscrutable reasons, Simon chose to engross himself in the Holocaust—in his enormous reading, his repeated trips to Poland, his writing of two books. He had embarked upon a heroic journey to confront the core truths of the ghastly nightmare and to tell everyone he could reach about what he had learned. And maybe, like countless soldiers destroyed inwardly from what they've witnessed in war, Simon's descent into the Holocaust gravely and permanently damaged his psyche. He too became a casualty of the madness, a collateral victim of the genocide.

By the time Danielle and I reached the dreaded Auschwitz complex, I had suffered enough through my reading and preconceptions, so that the reality wasn't as horrific as what I had imagined. There are no gas chambers to see, no remnants of the ghastly showers.

The Nazis destroyed the grossest pieces of incriminating evidence. There are, however, shattered remains of the crematoriums and rooms with vast numbers of shoes and toiletries and even a large room full of the victims' hair, shaved after their arrival in the camp, hair that could be usefully converted into cloth for military uniforms—everything displayed behind panes of glass. There is enough to make one sickeningly cognizant of the unspeakable abominations that occurred there.

Our guide told us one vivid detail that characterized the murderous deceit at the heart of the facility. When the trains arrived, besides greeting the disembarking passengers with a small orchestra playing music and an infamous metal banner declaring, "Work Shall Make You Free," those operating the camp made sure all the fireplaces, visible among the rows of rectangular wooden buildings, showed clouds of smoke rising out of their chimneys—an important detail to suggest the warmth and comfort of home. However, once the inmates entered their darkened, claustrophobic quarters, those who were lucky enough not to be directed to the showers and killed immediately, the homey little fires were extinguished, and the dreadful cold became pervasive and torturous. Naturally, walking in the bone-chilling greyness among the long rows of wooden buildings, as I toured this massive, eerie testament to unspeakable human cruelty, I thought of my grandmother's sisters, the four Samuels sisters, who were among the countless thousands murdered here. In a way, I wish everyone could visit Auschwitz.

One unforgettable part of this journey to the most infamous Nazi death-camp involved watching the evening news at our hotel. Donald Trump was on the rise—scapegoating, berating and belittling those who don't belong in the USA, the foreign scum—rapists, murderers and drug-dealers, who speak a different tongue and need to be expelled in order to bring back the true heart and soul of our homeland. How could anyone with any knowledge of history not recognize the nauseating similarities between America's histrionic, blonde demagogue and the infamous, mustached maniac, who paved the road to Auschwitz? Danielle and I cringed with horror and embarrassment as we watched Mr. Trump push his "fascism-lite" on our country.

When I think of Simon's obsession with the Holocaust, I think of my own obsession with 9/11. When you read and read, exploring a dark subject and discovering some very uncomfortable truths, it separates you from a lot of people who might resent what you've discovered. Simon's profound understanding of the Holocaust made him an ardent Zionist, and sometimes, even to me, he seemed far too accepting of Israeli aggressions, even from bullies like Ariel Sharon or Benjamin Netanyahu. Similarly, my research into the attacks of September 11th made Simon uncomfortable. For example, he didn't like my mentioning the five dancing Israelis on a New Jersey balcony who were arrested and interrogated for celebrating and filming the destruction of the Twin Towers. They were thought to be affiliated with Mossad, Israel's CIA. If 9/11 were an inside job, as I believe the empirical evidence proves, Israel was at least peripherally in on it, I assured him. I can still see Simon glaring at me when I shared my conclusion. On some level, our politics became a wedge between us. We loved to argue and debate, but then we could touch extremely sensitive nerves and reach an impasse.

I know Simon felt horribly tormented by what was happening in Israel—the widening hostility faced by the Jewish homeland and the subsequent rise in Israeli nationalism, ardent Jewish voices calling for an expanded nation that permanently annexes the West Bank and Gaza. Some zealots even hope to build another great Jewish temple. It would stand on the sanctified plateau in Jerusalem where the two ancient, massive structures stood, right above the revered Western Wall. Of course, before this monumental holy construction project could be initiated, the intruding Muslim mosque, the sacred, golden-roofed Dome of the Rock, would first have to be demolished. With great sadness, Simon understood the explosive implications of this level of Zionist zealotry.

There was a more peaceful, less aggressive Israel that he had loved. For ten years, he had helped plow its vineyards and raised his young children there. But that Israel was gone, and a new majority with less humane ideals had come to rule the land. They've built walls and settlements and understood how property rights get established by bulldozers and tanks. Those facts greatly depressed Simon, and truthfully, it had become increasingly sad to hear him talk about Israel. How could there be so much hatred for Jews so soon after the slaughter in Europe? Why should a tiny Jewish homeland provoke so much opposition and animosity? If the Jews of Israel were never allowed to feel secure, how would they ever relinquish their need to be aggressive. And if they could not stop being aggressive, how would the hatred ever end? I thought of how white Simon's hair had become, my tender friend who suffered so much because tribal enmities in the Middle East reveal few signs of dissipating soon.

Besides visiting Auschwitz, there was one other thing that had to happen in my life to prepare me for adequately telling Simon's story. I needed to more deeply understand and appreciate friendship itself. In order to better comprehend how I had let my intimacy with Simon slip away, I needed to learn, more consciously and profoundly, how intimate friendships are formed and nourished. What comes to most women more naturally, for men, seems to require more focus and intention.

Living in Ashland, I've had the good fortune of enjoying several circles of friendships, but they've been far from equal as far as encouraging closeness. First of all, there's a group of guys who play tennis together twice a week. We like each other a lot and play with a lot of enthusiasm, but the focus is on tennis, not on developing our friendships. I love playing with the boys, but honestly, we don't know each other very well.

Then there are the friendships formed within our Rogue Valley Peace Choir, which I joined as soon as Danielle and I moved to Ashland. These friendships are a bit more soulful than the relationships among my tennis buddies. Singing beautiful melodies and meaningful lyrics with agreed-upon ideals connects people in a deeper way than playing tennis, I suppose, but still the focus is on singing, not on developing intimacy among the singers. It's taken years to get to know my fellow Peace Choir members, even superficially. Too many people and too little time.

Most of the closest friendships Danielle and I have developed in Ashland spring from a group we refer to as our "Tribe." There are twenty of us, and we've been getting together for several years. The crucial component is that we meet once a week for two hours, and our conscious intention, the group's reason for existence, is to nourish and deepen our friendships. In doing so, we mutually encourage our individual growth. We take on significant topics, trying to be as authentic, transparent, vulnerable, and as true to our hearts as we can. Our group has helped me understand all the ways I failed to adequately nourish my friendship with Simon.

Before my wife and I became tribe members—and no, we don't wear feathers or live communally—I became a participant in the ManKind project, whose initiates are sometimes called "New Warriors." The ManKind Project involves an "Adventure Weekend" for men who aspire to become better men. Without revealing too much about what goes on during the weekend, let's just say that it puts a guy in touch with certain common themes, certain common anxieties that torture our male psyches. The ManKind Project opened my eyes in many ways, as did participating in a small circle of men for a year afterward, a group that met weekly and expanded upon the insights gained during the weekend. I had never been in a men's group before.

I remember telling Simon about MKP and his skeptical reaction to it. It was just about six months before he left for Buenos Aires. He seemed really surprised that I would choose to join a men's group. The idea of becoming more sensitive, more acutely tuned-into emotions, seemed a little too contrived, too much like New Age mush, to my dear friend, who was more trapped in his own old story, his own numbed, isolated and confused state of mind, than he could ever recognize or acknowledge. Maybe the ManKind Project could have been a mind-opening, life-changing experience for Simon, but to him, it probably sounded like counseling—something other people might need, people who were weaker and less self-reliant. In so many ways, my brilliant, liberal-spirited friend remained closed and conservative in his mode of thinking and in his way of dealing with his repressed emotions. I should know—I've been the same way—but at least, I'm trying to change.

I can still picture his face when I told him of the purpose and goals of MKP and my deep enjoyment of being in a men's group. I remember him smiling broadly yet wincing and shaking his head with cynical disbelief as he revived his familiar line, "Ronnie, I just don't believe people are really capable of changing that much."

Tragically, my new-born inward focus, the weekly men's group and all my fine intentions of becoming a better, more keenly sensitive person—all this intensified focus on myself—did nothing to reduce my blindness, my inability to perceive, that something was gravely wrong with my beloved friend. In just a few short months, just as I was sitting in an Oregon living room, meeting with the men's group, discussing our vital personal issues, our shadowy perennial anxieties—my dearest friend, with my complete ignorance, was falling into a vortex of depression that would lead him into the dark waters of the Rio de la Plata.

Twenty-two

"As we discover our own courage to need each other, really need each other, and the awesome power to truly be with each other, men and women face to face, then we will discover how we can give our gifts and meet each other's needs."

—Bill Kauth and Zoe Alowan, *We Need Each Other*

Before putting down this pen, I want to mention two rather hopeful developments connected to my story. The first one has to do with my son-in-law, Albert, and the Muslim girl he rescued in Marseille. The second has to do with Simon's youngest son, Nathan, and a strange, exciting decision he made.

What happened to Albert and "the Muslim girl" is truly heartening. She has a name now—she's not "the Muslim girl" anymore. Her name is Rana, and she and Albert are married. In fact, they have an infant daughter named Leila, who is the joy of my wife's life. No, better yet—she is the *nachas* of her life.

Rana is an exceptionally lovely and wonderful young woman. She and Danielle have become good friends. They're kindred spirits—escaped refugees from strict, fear-inducing religious environments that inundated them with shame and guilt. Rana appreciates and resonates deeply with my wife's conclusion that such rigid, blinding religious indoctrination should be considered a form of child abuse and hopefully someday, when we come to our senses, become a relic of the past.

There was no big wedding for Rana and Albert. They chose a simple ceremony at the city hall in Aix. We visited them there in the beautiful Southern French city last May, a few months after Leila was born. I felt my own deep happiness, seeing my wife cherish her new granddaughter, watching her hold her in her arms, whisper sweet sounds to her, and put her to sleep. Such ordinary miracles... such contentment and joy.

Now that Rana and Albert are married and have a child, her parents have become more accepting of her life choices. They do not want to lose their daughter or grandchild. Even Rana's brother, the one who had attacked her with a stick for marching in a demonstration, has cooled off and actually begun to discover the pleasures of being an uncle and a brother. Maybe Simon was wrong in his cynical conclusions about human intransigence; certainly sometimes people actually can transform themselves in significant ways. The changes in Rana's brother, his opened heart, allowed him to undo years of unconscious prejudice, emancipating him from that "mental slavery" Bob Marley sang about. If only we could all do that.

To anyone with sensitive eyes, Albert and Rana are so obviously in love, so well matched, that it would seem crazy to object to their being together. They're kind of like Romeo and Juliet, without all the tragedy. Albert opened up a small photo shop in Aix where Rana, even with her little baby, is able to help him a bit. There are several photos on the wall showing the tender faces and frightful conditions of Albert's beloved village in Senegal. He hopes to go there with Rana someday. It was heartwarming being with my stepchildren and their beautiful baby when we saw them in France last spring.

On that trip, I also enjoyed getting to know and appreciate Danielle's best friend, Mireille Nicolas, a little more. She's an amazing woman, a former teacher with incredible travels and experiences. Having lived and worked for years in the Caribbean, she's even good friends with Jean-Bertrand Aristide, the legendary former leader of Haiti, whose socialistic popularity angered entrenched interests and forced him into exile two different times. Mireille grew up in Algeria when it was still a French colony fighting for its independence. She knows about empires—and the racism and poverty upon which they feed. She is also a prolific, accomplished writer, and when she listened to me discussing Simon and my unresolved anxieties about his mysterious demise, she fixed her beautiful green eyes directly on me and pronounced with repeated force, speaking in French, that I absolutely needed to write—that I needed to write about my friend. I'm grateful to have received such strong encouragement from this silver-haired, intense woman, who profoundly understands the importance of saying what needs to be said.

The last thing I want to mention is the poignant encounter I had with Nathan, Simon's youngest son, right after Trump's inauguration. A couple of weeks earlier, in the first days of 2017, Nathan had telephoned Danielle and me. He said he had some surprising news he wanted to share with us. I imagined he might be getting married or having a baby with someone. Blurting out his revelations rather quickly, he announced: "I've quit the parking lot company, and I'm enrolled to take classes at UCSB."

The first part of his declaration didn't surprise me nearly as much as the second. I could easily understand his quitting the family company. Like his older brothers, he too would now be happily emancipated from the capitalist frenzy of parking lots, but I was surprised to hear of his university plans.

"You're going to go to UCSB?" I asked, making sure I'd heard him right.

He explained that having long ago graduated from UCLA with a degree in Business Administration, he was enrolled at UCSB as a "limited" student, a student with limited objectives. In other words, he wasn't a part of any graduate program, but he would be free to take almost any undergraduate course he wanted. He planned on taking one class in literature, one in history, and one in either religion or psychology. He wasn't sure about the specific courses yet, but his aim was to follow his own intellectual curiosity and study the subjects that most interested him. That was something he had never done, majoring in Business at UCLA. That education had been all about preparing him to rise in the ranks of the parking lot firm. He had done that, but it was over. Enough was enough. Now he wanted to let his passions determine the future shape of his education. I told him his wide-open goal reminded me of something Simon or I might have said when we were at UCSB.

We didn't talk very long on the phone once I told him I'd be traveling south soon, heading to Ventura in early February. I told him how excited I was about his recent decisions, and we agreed to meet somewhere in Isla Vista when I got there in a few weeks.

A few days into February, just as the winter quarter at UCSB was beginning, I met up with Nathan near Devereaux Point on the north end of Isla Vista, a place where his father and I had loved to surf. It was a warm, sunny Southern California afternoon, and I spotted the curly-haired young man easily, as he arrived on a bike. He was wearing a bright red tee shirt and jeans, and I was wearing, with pride, his dad's dark green corduroy shirt, which Nathan recognized immediately. He looked happier and years younger than when I'd seen him about a year before, when his face had already begun to show the weariness of working too long without much meaning or purpose.

After greeting each other with hugs, we walked north along the path next to the cliffs, and I took him to a favorite spot, a little hillside crevice you could climb down to, hidden from view. It was a comfortable, cozy place where during high tide, you could practically dive into the water. It was high tide. The waves were silky and about five feet high, just the kind of soft diagonal beauties that Simon and I loved to catch for our longest and best rides, in those days before wetsuits and leashes. As we noticed the beautiful swells and watched two guys glide down some nice ones, Nathan informed me he had just bought a surfboard. The sport hadn't worked for him when his father introduced it to him on a Malibu beach when he was twelve. There were too many people, and the waves weren't that easy to catch. But maybe he had quit too quickly. He wanted to give himself another chance. That's why he was at UCSB now—to give himself another chance.

We talked for a while about relationships. He saw himself following the pattern of his oldest brother—choosing women with amazing looks but ordinary minds and getting bored pretty quickly. But he also had observed and begun to envy David and Susanna and the rich life they were developing, based on a relationship of profound love and mutual respect. He finally admitted to himself once and for all, that something like what David and Susanna shared was exactly what he hoped to create for himself. And if he could find that woman, the one he wouldn't get bored with after a few months, he would marry her and have children. I told him about his father's unforgettable line, uttered somewhere nearby along these cliffs, his words about wanting to be with a woman he could discuss a great movie with for more than ten minutes. The memorable comment made Nathan laugh.

The youngest son's career aspirations were at the moment on hold. Though his finances were secure, he said he wouldn't mind working part-time as a waiter or bartender somewhere, maybe a barista at Starbucks, as long as the work environment was fun. He was looking for intellectual stimulation, true love, and simple pleasures—perfect ambitions for a college student, even if he was ten or fifteen years older than most of the other students. He smiled as he specified the three classes he was taking in his first quarter: Existential Modern Literature, Contemporary Crises in the Middle East, and the Psychology of Gender Roles—pretty interesting stuff. Emphatically, I told him how happy I was that in his second chance at university, he would finally get to experience the pleasure of a personally directed liberal arts education, the same huge privilege his father and I had shared.

For a while both of us were quiet, just enjoying the serenity in front of us, the crashing of the waves and their beautiful music. Watching the two surfers catch some long, silky rides, suddenly Nathan came up with a surprising question: "Did you and my dad really help burn down the Bank of America your senior year?"

His unexpected question amused me. "No, we didn't burn down the infamous Bank of America. But we did watch the big sucker glow as it turned into a heap of ashes—and we did set a car on fire."

"You set a car on fire?" He smiled broadly with a look of mild shock.

And so, I explained a little more about how we had the owner's tacit permission, and the car wasn't in running condition anyway. I told him some details about the war-like atmosphere that had overtaken Isla Vista. I described how his father and I had hidden in the bushes from a helicopter and its probing searchlights. I told him about the dump trucks loaded with National Guard, the trash dumpster fires in the streets, the tear gas, the curfews, the mass arrests. I told him about the furor and disgust with the war, the sense of its futility and immorality that were at the heart of all the chaos. And yet his father and I were the lucky ones, the privileged ones. We didn't have to fight the pointless war. We had the luxury, the ability and the desire to learn about the war—and then it became our responsibility to protest against it. I tried to explain all this, with restrained passion, to my friend's youngest son.

Nathan asked me whether I'd ever been to the Vietnam Memorial in Washington, D.C. While Nathan was a young teen, Simon had taken the entire family to see the stark, stunning shrine. Nathan had been quite moved by the tribute to our 58,000 Americans killed in the war, the rows and rows of names etched into black onyx. Yes, I too had visited the starkly tragic, cemetery-like scene, I told him, but I asked him to envision something bigger.

"Imagine," I said, "a memorial for the Vietnamese who were killed in that war—all the people bombed and burned in their villages, just because they wanted to be a free and independent country, the same thing we celebrate every 4th of July. The memorial for the dead Vietnamese would have to have about three million names. It would have to be about fifty times larger than the memorial in Washington. That's a lot of lives, a lot of people killed for no good reason. That's what your dad and I and a lot of people like us were protesting about."

We exchanged ideas about how today's UCSB students might react to the era of Trump, the narcissistic bully who had based his political success on the denigration of so many people and the propagation of so many lies. Would the presidency of such an obvious buffoon, a man who bragged about sexually assaulting women, lead to a new era of campus protests? We offered our different speculations and scenarios. Perhaps the embarrassing grossness and stubborn ignorance of our bombastic new leader would snap more young people out of their apathy. We both wondered whether Bernie running against Trump would have made any difference. And what if the Russians or our own FBI, through Mr. Comey, had not interfered with the election?

We talked about Israel and whether there were any signs of hope for peace there. On this subject, Nathan was not nearly as pessimistic as his father. If we can open ourselves to understanding alternative points of view, we don't have to blindly inherit all of our parents' cultural prejudices. One of his closest friends, he told me with pride, is a Muslim—a Tunisian. Unlike his father, Nathan expressed hope about our capacity to change. His decision to drop out of the parking lot world, rent an apartment in Isla Vista, and go back to college was strong evidence of our hunger for change, he believed. We just have to seize the right opportunities. I'd rather agree with him than with his father. Maybe we just don't change as fast or as fully as we'd like, with most people preferring to endure the suffering they're familiar with, rather than venture into new perspectives and uncertainty. At root, aren't most of us tentative, cautious and somewhat conservative?

It felt really good talking with Nathan, almost as good as talking with his dad. We didn't really try to unravel Simon's mystery together, letting it remain, as perhaps it must, a paradoxical, inscrutable enigma. I told Nathan about my recent efforts to tell his dad's story in writing, at least the story of our friendship. He said he hoped I included a lot of the good times, not just the depressing stuff. Part of the reason he had come to UCSB was due to his father's opinion that the years spent there were the very best of his life, the times that he was most free and open to everything life had to offer. Nathan wanted a little of that for himself. I wished him all the luck in the world, and we agreed to see each other again or talk on the phone soon.

I reached in my back pocket and gave him a handful of pamphlets I'd brought for him. I have a whole carton full of them at home, occasionally passing some around when I happen to be around a college campus. The pamphlets are produced by a group I admire, and support called Architects and Engineers for 9/11 Truth. The cover shows the Twin Towers and has the caption: "What the government isn't telling you about 9/11." When he saw the pamphlets, Nathan took them and laughed, "I know about this. You're really into that conspiracy stuff, right?"

"Some people never change," I confessed. "Check it out for yourself. Massive steel towers turning into powder, into DUST, supposedly because of an hour of fire...Nonsense science leading to endless war. And Building Seven...Ever heard of Building Seven? Check it out for yourself, and then pass the pamphlets around, if you like—or burn them."

Nathan laughed again. "I do know a little about Building Seven, I've seen *Loose Change*, and I admit this is a pretty amazing topic. I'll check out the pamphlets, but I hope you're not letting this dark conspiracy shit take over your life. You and I both know about how a dark, complicated subject can take over a person's life, right?" He looked in my eyes and grinned.

I assured him I knew exactly what he meant and that I had no intention of letting an unsolved 9/11 conspiracy take over my life. Neither the unexposed lies of 9/11 nor the frightening prospect of what President Trump might do—no political bullshit was going to take over my life. And the unsolved mystery of a best friend's death would no longer haunt me. Writing about it has, I hope, freed me from its grasp. There's just too much joy and beauty—too much opportunity for true happiness—for me to stay depressed because of some of the slings and arrows of outrageous fortune.

"Only that day dawns to which we are awake," Thoreau reminds us, and "There is more day to dawn." I believe in that hope and possibility. I felt it strongly as I hugged my dear friend's youngest son and handed him one more item, which I pulled out of my dark green corduroy pocket. I gave him a nice harmonica in the key of C.

"Your dad and I loved making a little music together. We learned how to do that when we lived here." With a broad smile, he accepted my gift, and its implicit invitation. With *nachas* in my heart and bountiful hope for this beautiful young man, I watched him ride away on the brown path, along the haunted, but music-filled cliffs.

I Queried Death
(Simon's UCSB Sonnet)

I queried Death and He once spoke with me.
He terrifies both young and old with threats
And gets them to behave so morally
Because they fear His wrath—in mortal breath.
But there are ways to take our own way out,
No soul can rule what we might like to do—
Our true intentions we don't have to shout,
Yes, freedom can be ours—if we so choose.
With all that one must face while living here,
With all the hate and blood that stains our brains,
Our end is nothing we should have to fear
And we can pick the day we end our pain.
So Death, there is no need to make me grieve,
You do not know the joy with which I leave.

Assignment
(For Mireille)

In Southern France I saw a friend, a lady with the finest mind,
She'd traveled, taught and written books—the deepest, most provocative kind.
She'd sailed across a hundred seas and taught a thousand hungry faces,
Going where the plagues hit deepest: dark, far-away ravaged places.
And yet when we met in café one eve, as usual, she was smiling bright,
Until I told her simple truth: that I'd not taken time to write.
"No, there's no new book of poetry, there's no new play to stage—
All I've got to show for ten years is ten more years of age."
That's when she turned quite serious and raised her glass of wine deep red—
She said something quite memorable that echoed deep inside my head:
"You won't be writing much, dear friend, the day after you're dead—
Why leave what burns inside of you to die in you unsaid?
Wouldn't that be a lie to who you really want to be?"
She fixed her clear green eyes on me and said, "Ecris, Ron, écris!"

Cliffs of Isla Vista
(For Simon)

where these slow silky waves first dazzled our souls
i sit half a year from when you left this world,
trying to understand the meaning of your choice,
confused as my dog here, watching me write words

absurd was one we used a lot—we loved
our Kafka, Sartre, Camus and Hesse—
privileged years to seek philosophy and truth,
while less lucky ones went to Vietnam and death

so many classes, visions, lofty theories
(and alluring ladies) competing in our brains,
so many profundities shared on these cliffs,
(but manfully mute about our own deepest pains)

easier to fathom fates of famous classic heroes
(how could such gifted guys be so stuck in their hubris)
we scrutinized and analyzed humans and their plights
but when it came to us—we were a touch oblivious

and here we saw and heard the best of all sweet music
(Janice and Clapton, Buffalo Springfield, Band and Doors)
now skateboarding kids mostly listen on headphones,
pulsating to rhythms as they glide by nearby shore

*what harsh chords did you hear as you neared fatal leap
(forsaking everything in desperate self-sacrifice)
what solace did you think your decision could provide,
bequeathing others to forever ponder—why*

*i stay a while longer and listen to the sea,
to breathe in deep the waves of our lives—
slow collapsing cries of endless mystery,
serenade of love that never dies*

Gratitude

THERE ARE QUITE A FEW PEOPLE to thank for helping me with this book. Many friends, including several professional writers, offered encouragement and hints for improvement. Zachary Sklar, Nancy Ashmead, and Jeff Golden shared valuable insights and I'm grateful for their eloquent commentary. I thank Fran Leibowitz and Susanne Severeid for their artful suggestions. Besides awakening me to the mysteries of WTC 7, Ed Calaba helped me end a key chapter with added grace and force. Tania Sussman thoughtfully nudged me to include an important missing scene. Ever perceptive, my sister, Madeleine Rose offered some helpful ideas, and I also thank Eric Labowitz for his heart-warming support. My dear friend Zoe Alowan Kauth blessed me with a beautiful painting for the book cover. Harley Patrick of Hellgate Press has been easy and delightful to work with; the same goes for the good folks at Pronto Print in Ashland. Most importantly, I offer my gratitude to Donna, for her immeasurable inspiration and steadfast honesty. As for the dear friend whose loss motivated me to tell this story, I profoundly hope he would be pleased.

Ron Hertz grew up in Los Angeles, graduating from Fairfax High just when the Sixties revolution was beginning to explode. Besides an eye-opening year at the University of Edinburgh, he spent his college years at UC Santa Barbara, where nearly 1000 students were arrested in the spring of 1970 as antiwar passions reached their climax. After university, while commuting from seaside Ventura, he taught enthusiastically for thirty-two years at Newbury Park High School, sometimes feeling like a "subversive in suburbia." That was the title of a poetry/song show Ron performed with his wife, Donna, and friends in Ashland, Oregon. The couple moved to the bucolic, theater-centered town after they both retired from teaching. A proud father and grandfather, Ron is a grateful and animated member of the Rogue Valley Peace Choir, and he is currently working on a new volume of poems to add to his previous collection, *Ordinary Miracles*.

Made in the USA
Middletown, DE
07 June 2022